MUST LOVE
VAMPIRES

Books by Heidi Betts

THE BITE BEFORE CHRISTMAS

MUST LOVE VAMPIRES

Published by Kensington Publishing Corporation

MUST LOVE VAMPIRES

HEIDI BETTS

BRAVA

KENSINGTON PUBLISHING CORP.
www.kensingtonbooks.com

BRAVA BOOKS are published by

Kensington Publishing Corp.
119 West 40th Street
New York, NY 10018

ISBN-13: 978-0-7582-4763-6
ISBN-10: 0-7582-4763-X

First Kensington Trade Paperback Printing: October 2011

10 9 8 7 6 5 4 3 2 1

Printed in the United States of America

For my wonderful new editor at Kensington Books,
John Scognamiglio,
who is not only a joy to work with
but who has given me the chance
to do something I love (funny, sexy vampires—yippee!)
and put down on paper ideas that I've been dying
(ha! pun intended, I guess) to write for a very long time.

Thank you, John, it's been a pleasure.

VAMPNAPPED

Ante Up

Charlotte "Chuck" Lamoreaux stood in the shadows, doing her best to remain invisible. Which wasn't exactly difficult in the main gaming room of a casino like the Inferno.

All around her, buzzers buzzed, bells rang, and tiny lights in various colors either blazed or blinked, depending on how much cash they were trying to leach from their willing victims. But as bright and flashy as some of the machines were, the rest of the casino was muted. Blood-red carpeting beneath her feet, dark maroon paint and paper on the walls, and the only other illumination coming from low-watt sconces circling the room.

It was all designed to lull visitors into a stupor and keep them at the tables and slot machines as long as possible. *The better to part you from your money, my dear.*

And even though ninety percent of the people who walked through the Inferno's doors knew that, knew the cardinal rule of Vegas—*the house always wins*—it didn't deter them one iota from copping a squat and squandering away their paychecks, savings accounts, children's college funds.

Not that Chuck was bitter or anything.

A big, hulking bodyguard made a quarter turn in her direction and she hurriedly spun around, shoving a coin into one of the penny slots she'd been half hiding behind and yanking the one-armed bandit's one arm.

All right, so maybe she was marginally bitter, but the way she saw it, she had the right. Her father had been a brain-dead zombie of the slots . . . and the roulette wheel . . . and the card tables. He'd even occasionally gotten involved in betting on the dogs and ponies, or putting money down on sporting events like boxing matches and football games. The man had never met a wager he didn't like or a dime he could hold on to.

No wonder her mother had finally kicked him out—something that had devastated Chuck and her twin sister, Chloe, at the time, but that they now realized was the smartest decision their mother had ever made.

Their father's gambling was also the reason Chuck made it a policy to spend as little time near the bevy of casinos on The Strip as possible. Chloe, however, had gone in the exact opposite direction, following in their mother's high-kicking footsteps to become a showgirl. She worked right here for the Inferno's very own dance review, Lust.

So even though Chuck hated casinos, she still ended up in this one often enough, just to visit her sister. Most nights, she did her best to skirt the gaming rooms and head straight to Lust's dressing room.

But not tonight. Tonight, she was on a mission, and it very much involved the casino itself.

Or rather, the casino's elusive owner, Sebastian Raines.

Sebastian Raines was tall, dark, and filthy rich. He owned businesses and properties all over the world, but the Inferno seemed to be his pride and joy. At least judging by the amount of time he spent in Las Vegas, living on the top floor of the hotel in a penthouse suite that apparently took up the *entire* floor. It was also rumored that the place was beyond plush, beyond state of the art . . . it was supposed to be *incredible*.

Of course, that might only be wishful thinking on the part of the local gossip mill, since no one had ever actually seen Sebastian Raines's private living quarters. No one who'd lived to tell about it, at any rate.

Chuck was determined to be the first.

Raines, dressed to the nines in a dark designer suit and his trademark dark glasses, started moving again. He was making the rounds of some of the tables, something he did sporadically on his way to press the flesh with the high rollers and *really* high rollers in the private rooms at the rear of the main floor.

As usual when he made a public appearance, he was surrounded by an army of black-suited bodyguards who looked as though they downed steroid Big Gulps for breakfast, lunch, and dinner. They were tall and wide and bulging with Hulk-like muscles. But even so, Sebastian Raines stood out above them all by at least three inches.

He might not be as broad in the shoulders or spend quite as much time bench pressing armored vehicles as the members of his entourage did, but he was definitely taller. And handsomer. And more imposing.

Abandoning the penny slot machine she'd been pretending to play for the past several minutes, she followed behind, doing her best to look like just another bunco babe wandering around in her natural habitat.

When Raines—and his trained goons—paused again, she quickly did the same, diving at yet another machine waiting to spin its row of pineapples and coconuts. Quarter slots this time, and she dug into her pocket for the proper change.

She was probably the only person in the place hoping *not* to strike it rich. But even though a nice, fat jackpot would do wonders for her bank account—as well as eliminating her reason for skulking around in the first place—the last thing she needed was bells and whistles and alarms going off, drawing all kinds of unwanted attention when she was trying her best to blend in and go completely unnoticed.

She'd poked around and followed people before on research trips, but never to this extent. Never for a story quite like this one.

Normally, her investigations consisted of interviewing loonies who swore they'd seen Bigfoot, or standing beside a stretch of scorched desert, pretending she believed some lonely Trekkie's account of being abducted by aliens. It was her job to believe it all . . . and then add even more embellishment in the stories she wrote for the *Sin City Tattler*.

She was actually quite good at it. A childhood spent sitting backstage while her mother did three shows a night had apparently paid off. While her sister had watched the dancers with wide-eyed fascination, Chuck had always had a book with her, as well as notebooks that she'd filled with her own creative ideas.

Writing for the *Tattler* wasn't exactly her dream job, but it paid the bills. It was also kind of fun. She wasn't a UFO-chaser or conspiracy theorist herself, but some of the stories she covered—or, yes, invented out of thin air—were highly amusing.

The one she planned to do on Sebastian Raines, though, was her very best idea yet. It was front page material, and if she played her cards right—no pun intended, she thought with a short mental snort as she scampered past a blackjack table to the next bank of slot machines—it might even land her a position at a larger, more prestigious, and *definitely* more respected paper.

Provided she could pull this off.

The first order of business was to follow him, watch his every movement.

The second was to somehow get into his penthouse and see if she could find evidence to support her theory that he was not who—or more to the point, *what*—he claimed to be.

The third was to not get caught . . . which should maybe actually be at the top of the list, since it would probably mean jail time and a nice, fat restraining order, if she did.

And fourth and finally was to prove—*prove* without a shadow of a doubt—that billionaire businessman and casino mogul Sebastian Raines was exactly what she'd begun to suspect months ago.

A vampire.

Shuffle

One week later...

"Thanks for letting me do this," Chuck said somewhat breathlessly to her twin sister, Chloe.

"Oh, sweetie, you're the one doing me the favor," Chloe replied. "Aidan and I have been trying to get some alone time all week. But you better hope nobody catches on, or we're both in trouble."

Chuck wiggled her hips and jiggled her bazooms, feeling for all the world like a marlin on the business end of some deep-sea fisherman's hook while the two of them struggled to get her into Chloe's skimpy costume. It was more than skintight. It was the first layer of dermis; the drywall beneath three layers of paint, two layers of wallpaper, and a couple more layers of paint.

It also didn't help that, even though they were identical twins, Charlotte was just a little bigger on top. Which meant that by the time they managed to squeeze her into the red-and-orange sequined ensemble, designed to look like the fires of Hell, she was ready to pop right back out again.

"Nobody will catch on," she insisted, sucking in a breath and praying the twins—the *other* twins—would stay put long enough for her to get through the night.

"If they do, we'll both get fired. You're sure you know the routine? All of it?"

"Backward, forward, and inside out," Chuck assured her sister. "We practice together almost every day. You know darn well I could do this in my sleep."

Chuck was no showgirl, nor did she want to be. But their mother had signed them both up for dance classes almost before they could walk. Ballet, tap, ballroom . . . Charlotte and Chloe had tipped their toes and twisted their hips to just about every type of music in existence. They'd also gone the whole *Toddlers and Tiaras*/teen beauty queen/college scholarship by way of pageant route, but that wasn't something Chuck liked to talk—or think—about.

But even though you could take the girl out of the dance class, you couldn't always take the dance out of the girl. Chloe had followed in their mother's footsteps—quite literally—by becoming a showgirl, shaking her stuff onstage six nights a week at Lust, and doing her part to keep Vegas's tourism boom booming. The male faction of it, at any rate.

Chuck, however, only worked through Chloe's routines with her because it was a great workout. If she didn't, she would probably never exercise, and her penchant for junk food already made her the bustier, hippier twin. She didn't need to become the "morbidly obese one" while her sister remained the perpetually "pretty one."

"If you mess up," Chloe continued to fret, "tell them you aren't feeling well. Tell them you have an inner ear infection that's throwing your balance off."

"You've been saving that one, haven't you?"

Chloe didn't blush—they'd been too close all their lives and had gone through too much together to be embarrassed by much of anything. Instead, she cocked her head and flashed a wide grin.

"Yeah, but you can use it if you need to."

"I won't need to," Chuck assured her. "You can still use it to beg off for some hot date."

Chloe fiddled a bit more with Chuck's makeup, fluffed the long, orange feathers hanging off her butt and making her look—in Chuck's opinion, anyway—like a giant rooster, and then reached for the humongous headdress that was the one piece of the costume that gave Chuck pause. The thing weighed a ton, and visions of her neck snapping in half, her skull hanging at a perfect ninety-degree angle, kept flashing through her head.

This entire scheme had been her idea, but that didn't mean she wanted to spend the rest of her life as a quadriplegic. Not for a story. Not even this story. It was a good one; a make-or-break, career-building story. She just wasn't sure it was worth sipping Thanksgiving dinner through a straw.

"With any luck," Chloe said, oblivious to the squeak of wheelchairs rolling through her sister's mind, "I won't have any more hot dates to call in sick for. I think Aidan might be the one."

"The One?" Chuck asked as Chloe lifted the feathered, sequined, five-thousand-pound medieval torture device onto her head. "Capital T, capital O?"

"Uh-huh."

She winced as hairpins were driven into her scalp to keep it in place. "Aren't you moving kind of fast?"

"You know my policy—the faster the better. And this one is on the hook."

Speaking of hooks . . . Chuck wiggled around, trying to get comfortable in the costume her sister wore every night. Or some variation of it, anyway.

Black fishnet hose and five-inch, rhinestone-studded heels. Faux onyx and ruby chandelier earrings and choker necklace so heavy they were becoming embedded in her flesh. Feathers and sequins everywhere. She couldn't decide if she'd be better off walking The Strip thumbing for johns, acting as a stand-in for one of the Gabor sisters (Zsa Zsa, for sure), or running for her life from Colonel Sanders.

How did Chloe do this on a regular basis without either breaking her neck or slowly losing every ounce of her self-respect?

Of course, Chloe would never willingly switch roles with Chuck, either. The most creative storytelling her sister had ever done was when she'd tried to convince herself the stick hadn't turned blue.

"Just be careful, okay?"

Chloe's penchant for serial dating made Chuck nervous. This was Las Vegas, for God's sake. And even though they'd both grown up here, both been raised by a former showgirl who'd taught them street smarts before she'd taught them to use the big girl potty, that did not mean they couldn't still be hurt.

They called it Sin City for a reason, and there were all sorts of unsavory elements crawling around, just waiting for an eager, vulnerable woman to cross their paths. Or even a reluctant, self-sufficient one who wasn't paying close enough attention to her surroundings.

Then again, perhaps Chuck didn't have room to talk. She hadn't had a date since *MacGyver* was still on the air. Nuns got more action than she did, and lately, she'd even begun to wonder if her virginity might be growing back.

Medical experts would probably say that was impossible, but stranger things had happened. And she should know— she was the Queen of Strange and Bizarre Occurrences.

"I will. You, too. This is kind of dangerous, you know," Chloe reminded her, as though they hadn't had this discussion a million times since Chuck had concocted her plan just one short week ago after trailing Sebastian Raines through his casino for several hours and turning up nothing. Now she intended to snoop around his home turf—preferably without getting caught. "If anyone finds out what you're doing and why . . ."

"They won't." She hoped. "We're identical"—give or take a few Little Debbie Snack Cakes—"remember? We used to do this all the time in school. I can pretend to be you almost as well as I pretend to be me."

Chloe chuckled at that just as a shout from the dressing room on the other side of the minuscule bathroom door made them both jump. Their eyes met, and even though Chuck had run through this a thousand times in her head, her heart was still pounding, and tension bounced between them.

"Showtime," Chloe said, and she meant it in more ways than one. She gave Chuck a final once-over, checking her long, fake, glittery lashes, the lines going up the back of her stockings, the fluff of her feathers.

"All right," she said, pressing a slim plastic card into Chuck's hand. "Here's my employee key card. It will get you into all the areas we're allowed to go, but guests aren't." She blew out a nervous breath. "Break a leg."

Chuck winced. She knew her sister meant it in the best possible way, but Chuck didn't want to hear about breaking anything when she was very afraid she might end up doing just that.

"You go out first, and I'll hide here until the coast is clear."

That, too, was part of The Plan. Chuck nodded, and when Chloe leaned in for a quick hug, she hugged her sister back—really, really tight.

This wasn't the first time she'd done something slightly wacky or gone above and beyond for a story, but it *was* the first time she'd come up with something quite this over the top. Or dragged her sister into one of her wild and crazy schemes. Which meant that if it went wrong, it could go terribly wrong for both of them.

Sebastian Raines stood in the backstage shadows of Lust, watching the end of the evening's final performance. No one saw him; or if they did, their brains didn't register his presence.

He was one of the richest men in Nevada, possibly the entire United States or even the world. He'd built the Inferno from the ground up, making it the single most popular casino in Sin City. But that didn't mean he spent a lot of time observing the everyday goings-on of the place or the activities of the countless humans who kept his business ventures flush with greenbacks.

He made his rounds, popped in on some of the big spenders, and let himself be seen out in public just enough for people to know he was the boss and he *was* in charge of everything that went on under his roof.

But after the last hour, he could understand why Lust—the Inferno's version of an entertainment venue-slash-gentleman's club—was so very popular.

The dancers onstage were fully dressed and doing nothing more than shaking their perfectly synchronized bon-bons, but their costumes were sexy enough—and suggestive enough—to convince the hundreds of men in the audience that they might have a chance at something more at the end of the night.

There would be no lap dances at Lust, though, and no dollar bills being stuffed into g-strings, either. Not as long as Sebastian's men did the job they'd been hired to do.

All of the dancers onstage were walking wet dreams, beautiful and shapely, and flashing just enough skin to tease the audience, working them into a fine lather before trotting off to the safety of their group dressing room.

But only one interested Sebastian.

The one who had been following him on and off for the past few weeks. The one who was soon to be engaged to his brother, unless Sebastian could find a way to stop her.

This wasn't the first time Aidan had fallen head over heels for a pretty face—or a tight body. It wasn't even the first time he'd seemed determined to shackle himself to one of them.

When it came to other people's motives, Sebastian's little brother had a tendency to be slightly naïve. He'd been that way before they'd been turned, and hadn't changed much in the last few centuries.

Which was why Sebastian once again found himself in the unenviable position of having to play . . . well, big brother. But in a manner he didn't particularly like, and that he was sure Aidan wouldn't approve of if he knew what Sebastian was up to.

There had been many times in the past when he'd had to run off eager lasses intent on landing themselves a wealthy

husband in Aidan. More recently, he'd been able to run simple background checks, and then a hefty check of a different
sort—along with a well-worded, but solemn threat—was
usually enough to send them packing.

This time was different, though. Something about this particular woman was different.

According to Aidan, Chloe Lamoreaux was nothing more
than a showgirl in his (Sebastian's) own casino. And that was
something Sebastian would normally believe . . . Aidan always went for the showgirl types. But that didn't explain
why someone who was supposed to be a simple dancer, with
no ulterior motives for dating his brother, had been following
him.

Even in a casino full of people . . . full of cigarette smoke and
the mingling of a zillion different perfumes and colognes . . .
he'd sensed her almost immediately. Smelled something sweet
on the air that had never been there before.

He hadn't been able to place it; still couldn't. But it had
caught his attention and caused him to roll his gaze in a slow
sweep of the area until he'd spotted her standing on the far
end of the room, doing her best to blend in with the small
crowd surrounding a blackjack table.

She hadn't done a very good job. Not only did she not
look terribly interested in the card game, but she'd worn
sunglasses indoors—something only he had a habit of doing—
and cast furtive glances over her shoulder every few seconds . . .
very pointedly in his direction.

So what did a woman involved with his brother want with
him?

Was it simply a money thing? Sidle up to one brother, but
keep her options open in case the older sibling—who happened to be the power behind the monetary success of Raines
Enterprises—might be a better bet?

Or was there something else going on?

The only thing Sebastian felt certain of was that Chloe
Lamoreaux was not to be trusted. The first he'd heard of her
was when Aidan had announced that he planned to pop the

question to a woman he'd been dating less than a month, then rush her off to the nearest all-night chapel for a quickie wedding.

Which was *so* not going to happen. Not if Sebastian had anything to say about it. (Which he most certainly did.)

Aidan might be content to fly headlong into yet another disastrous relationship; to take a woman at face value and simply assume she was exactly what she said she was. But Sebastian wasn't nearly as trusting. There was much more to learn about this Lamoreaux chick before he would be willing to welcome her into the family.

Like what she was up to. And what she *really* wanted with Aidan . . . and with him.

Deal

By the time Chuck followed the other dancers offstage, she was sweating like a pig and breathing like a cow in labor. She felt like a cow in labor, too.

She might go through Chloe's dance routine with her almost every night for the sheer calorie burn, but knowing the moves and actually doing them onstage with a dozen other girls . . . under blazing-hot lights . . . in full battle regalia . . . were two totally, *totally* different things.

Never again would she scoff at her sister's choice of occupation or play into any of the stereotypical beliefs that showgirls were nothing more than high-priced strippers. And never again would she concoct any ridiculous plans that even remotely had her stepping into her sister's rhinestone-dotted, five-inch heels.

She was lucky to be alive! Lucky to have made it through Chloe's three-in-a-row performances without either passing out or fracturing something vital. There had been some close calls, too, and she was sure Chloe's fellow dancers were wondering what the hell was wrong with her tonight. She just kept smiling, pretending to be her sister, and was ready to pull out the "inner ear infection" excuse, if she needed to.

Still huffing, Chuck fell back to the end of the chorus line as they *tick-tick-tack*ed their way across the stage and down the short flight of stairs. She needed to get out of this getup and into street clothes, but knew from Chloe and her own after-show visits to Lust's dressing room that it tended to be a bustle of sequins and feathers and loud, boisterous girl talk for about an hour after a show.

Not something she was opposed to normally, even if her life wasn't nearly as exciting as some of the dancers'. She might investigate Elvis sightings—which in this town, Elvis Impersonator Central, was a job and a half—and hang out in trailer parks where seven-hundred-pound women grew *around* their living room furniture, but that was a snoozefest compared to some of the things Chloe's fellow dancers had experienced. Being propositioned by honest-to-goodness mobsters . . . dancing—and more—in Amsterdam, Tokyo, Hong Kong. One of Chloe's friends had even done a tour with the Hell's Angels.

Tonight, though, she had things to do, and sharing war stories—of which she had very few—wasn't one of them.

She minced her way down the steps leading offstage, being very, *very* careful not to twist her ankle (or worse) only to draw up short when a long, imposing shadow fell across her path. Jerking her head and twenty pounds of headdress up, she found herself staring into a pair of dark, mesmerizing eyes . . . set into the face of the very man she'd been following for weeks now. The very man whose apartment she'd been planning to somehow break, slip, or finagle her way into later tonight.

Eep.

Had he found out about her sloppy attempts at stalking him? Somehow learned that she'd been digging into his past? Or maybe he'd figured out that she wasn't who she was pretending to be tonight.

If any of those turned out to be true, this could be very bad for her. Very, very bad.

Getting on the wrong side of the richest man in Las Vegas—a man who likely owned the ground you were standing on at any given moment, if you were standing within the city limits—was never a good thing. Getting on the wrong side of the richest man in Las Vegas who just happened to *also* possibly be a bloodsucking creature of the night . . .

She was a writer, and even she didn't have the words to describe what a cluster fuck that could turn out to be.

She swallowed hard, mind racing as she tried to come up with an excuse for why she'd been following him, checking him out, why she'd switched places with her sister. Nothing came to mind, which made her sweat even more than the past three hours of hoofing it under the thousand-watt stage lights.

"Um . . . hello," she squeaked when he showed no signs of moving out of her way.

How would an employee of the Inferno greet its rich and powerful owner? Would there be obeisance? Groveling? As a showgirl, would she bat her overly glittered lashes and cock an inviting hip?

She shifted around awkwardly, raising a hand to the back of her head, thrust her breasts forward, and fluttered her lashes until one of them got stuck, rendering her blind in her right eye.

When she reached up to pry them apart, she lost her balance and flailed wildly on her platform ice-pick heels, frantically attempting to stay upright.

Sebastian . . . Raines . . . Dracula reached out and grasped her upper arms just as she began to topple, effectively stopping her from falling on her keister.

Well, how embarrassing to be rescued from certain doom by the very person she intended to "out" as a bloodsucking fiend. But doubly embarrassing was the fact that when he touched her, a zip of electricity ran all the way down her spine and into her girly places from where his fingers gripped her bare arms. *That* hadn't happened since cell phones were the size of lunch boxes.

And what the heck was her body doing getting all turned on by a vampire, anyway? Didn't it know that was a sure-fire way to become a human Slurpee? To be turned into a slobbering, brain-dead minion of the damned?

She didn't want to become a bug-eating Renfro or a mindless Mina. . . . Not even if, as a Mina, she would get to experience life-altering orgasms at the hands—and other body parts—of this tall, dark, handsome, sexy, powerful, mesmerizing . . .

Oh, God, it was happening already! He was hypnotizing her into finding him attractive. Into wondering what it would feel like to have him nibble at her neck (literally) while he banged her into oblivion.

Get ahold of yourself, Charlotte! she ordered silently. And as usual, the use of her given name caught her attention and snapped her back to reality.

Then Mr. Tall, Dark, and Most Likely Fanged had to go and confuse her all over again.

"Chloe," he murmured in a low, mesmerizing voice.

Had she mentioned how freaking mesmerizing he was?

She blinked, caught off-guard at having him address her by her sister's name . . . even though it meant her ruse was working.

"Chloe, look at me."

She was looking at him—who could stop?—but his demand had her looking more closely, and directly into his eyes.

They were beautiful eyes . . . stormy gray around dark black pupils. She could see her reflection there, even in the lousy lighting of the shadowy backstage area, and so much more. They were like the ocean after a storm . . . like storm clouds drifting overhead . . . like swirls of smoke floating heavenward.

She was concentrating so fully on holding his gaze that her own vision began to blur. She didn't notice his hand coming up until it was directly in front of her face.

Holding up two fingers, he placed them lightly over each of her heavily made-up eyelids. Glitter, apparently, was a lousy vampire repellant.

Drawing them slowly down . . . which wasn't difficult, since she felt half-asleep already . . . he whispered, "Sleep."

And she did.

* * *

Chuck awoke several seconds before she opened her eyes. It was as though she were waking from a long night's sleep . . . and yet she couldn't remember going to bed. She couldn't even remember going home.

The last thing she did remember was surviving her ill-planned spin in her sister's shoes—if the Godawful things could even be termed something so innocuous—and then tip-toeing her way offstage.

Oh! And she'd run into someone. Not another dancer. Someone tall. Imposing. She remembered being intimidated enough that her mouth had gone dry.

But who had it been? Eyes still closed, her brows drew together in confusion. Why couldn't she remember?

Lashes fluttering, she pushed those questions aside for the time being and fought past the haze of grogginess that seemed to be fogging her brain to finally open her eyes.

Okay, she definitely hadn't made it home last night. Unless home had miraculously become the most spacious, modern, *gorgeous* apartment on the face of the planet.

Even just looking up at the high ceiling and what she could see in her peripheral vision let her know that wherever it was, it was far beyond her pay grade at the *Sin City Tattler*. A cross between *House Beautiful—Vegas Style* and *Interior Design for the Modern Bachelor*, every surface was clean and crisp and sparkling, in chrome and glass and varying shades of ocean blues.

Chuck started to sit up . . . or tried to . . . but couldn't seem to move. Oh, God, had she broken her neck, after all? Had she gotten all the way through the show only to trip and fall and paralyze herself on the way back to the dressing room? Was that why she couldn't remember much of anything after stepping offstage?

Heart pounding in her chest, she told herself not to panic. First, she should check her extremities. If she could wiggle her fingers and toes, then she probably wasn't paralyzed. Maybe she was just super-sore from contorting herself into angles that no human being without pretzel DNA should ever even attempt.

Slanting a glance down the line of her body, she noticed that she was, indeed, still in Chloe's "Flames of Hell" costume, complete with fishnet stockings and sprigs of feathers showing here and there. She told her brain to tell her hands to wiggle her fingers . . . and exhaled a relieved breath when they did just that. Her feet were still in their black, rhinestone-studded torture devices, but when she told her brain to tell her ankles to move them up and down, they did.

Whoo-hoo! She wasn't a doctor, but she was pretty sure being able to move her hands and feet meant she wasn't paralyzed from the neck down. Maybe just from the neck up, since her head seemed to be what she was having trouble with.

Getting really adventurous, she raised her arms to the top of her head and found her skull still encased in the nine-thousand-pound headdress she'd worn onstage. A second relieved sigh filled the silence. She hadn't tripped and half-killed herself, she was just lying flat on her back, still pinned and stapled into her sister's Chicken Little helmet. And because it weighed a ton and a half, it was keeping her from sitting up.

Working the dozen or so pins free that were holding the piece of costuming in place, she lifted it carefully away from her head and ran her fingers through the tangle of her hair. Just being free of the thing made her feel ten years younger and a hundred pounds lighter.

She sat up—finally, and much more easily than her first attempt—and took a better look at her surroundings.

Holy crap, she was in the belly of the beast. She'd been imagining this place so much the past couple of months, it was as though her intense desire to see the opulent penthouse for herself had made it materialize right in front of her.

Granted, crossing the barrier into Sebastian Raines's private quarters at the top of the Inferno had been her chief, number one goal. The main objective of her Master Plan. But part of her Master Plan had also been to change into street clothes first and to have a clue as to how she'd gotten there.

And that was the Big Question, wasn't it? *How the heck had she gotten here?*

Okay, she'd traded places with her twin sister.

Check.

She'd gotten through the night's performance at Lust without twisting her ankle, breaking her neck, or being found out.

Check.

And that's where things got hazy.

Uncheck.

So had she tripped and fallen, after all, and perhaps been rescued by the mysterious casino owner himself? Chuck's heart stuttered in her chest at the thought.

Holy alien autopsy, Batman! Was that who'd greeted her at the bottom of the stage steps?

She squinted her eyes, concentrating on the fuzzy vision filling her head, trying to zero in on the person's facial features as they floated around the outskirts of her memory. It had definitely been a man; no woman would have been that tall, that broad, that . . . menacing? Had he been menacing, or just overwhelming?

He'd also been wearing a really nice suit . . . designer and silk would be her guess . . . which added to the unlikelihood that it had been a woman.

She also remembered silver eyes, a wide, sumptuous mouth, hair as dark as midnight. . . .

So . . . yes, it very well could have been Sebastian Raines standing at the base of those stairs, waiting for her. The question was: *Why?*

Had she screwed up onstage—either the dance steps themselves, so that he felt he needed to reprimand her, or her role of pretending to be her sister, so that he was prepared to call her out?

And why did she feel as though she'd thought all of these

thoughts before? It was like that movie *Groundhog Day*, where Bill Murray had gotten stuck living the same day over and over and over. Chuck felt more like a hamster, though, running and running on its little wheel, but getting absolutely nowhere.

Regardless of Raines's reason for meeting her as she came offstage—if he truly had been there—it wouldn't have required a trip to his penthouse, would it? Unless she'd done something truly humiliating like swooning at his feet.

If that was the case, she was *so* going to claim dehydration, exhaustion, and overexertion. Because admitting that the stress of her very own ruse to switch places with her sister for a night had caused her to faint was just *too* freaking humiliating.

Since no one seemed to be around to answer the myriad questions swirling around in her brain, she shifted slightly on the long, midnight blue sofa where she'd been . . . passed out? sleeping? drugged into oblivion? . . . and tried to decide what to do and how to handle her current situation.

Adjacent to the sofa was a matching armchair, and she realized suddenly that she *wasn't* alone in the giant penthouse. A beautiful, regal black cat sat there, blinking bright yellow, slitted eyes at her.

If there was one thing Chuck couldn't resist, it was a furry, adorable little animal. Cats, dogs, birds, rats, ferrets, hamsters . . . she was just a total sucker for critters of nearly every kind.

"Hello, sweetie," she said in a soft voice, immediately going down on her knees in front of the chair and reaching a hand out to stroke the cat's sleek fur. "What's your name?"

Of course, it didn't answer, but at least she felt like she had one friend in the otherwise near-empty room.

"I don't suppose you know what I'm doing here," she went on, half to the cat and half to herself. "Or how I can get myself out."

No response. Not even a low rumble, which was sort of surprising, since animals tended to love her as much as she loved them. Cats usually began to purr the minute she touched them, and just got louder as she continued to give them adoring, undivided attention.

"Well, even if I don't know how it happened, I wanted to get into Sebastian Raines's penthouse, and here I am. So maybe I shouldn't look a gift-swoon in the face."

Climbing back to her feet, she put her hands on her still-sequined hips and glanced around, wondering where to start in her search for evidence of Raines's vampirism.

"I sure could use a change of clothes, though," she muttered. "This outfit is starting to get a little breezy."

High Card

The first thing Chuck did was get out of the bear trap shoes that were well on their way to cutting off her circulation and sending out an engraved invitation to gangrenous amputation. It took some major unbuckling, and then major prying that would have gone faster if she'd had a shoehorn. Or a crowbar.

Once she had them off, she began to pace along the length of the low, chrome-and-glass table in front of the plush, L-shaped sofa. Thankfully, she'd ensured that all of her toes still wiggled and possessed feeling, which made pacing easier.

So where should she start? If she were a true investigative reporter instead of one who simply wrote up the details of stories that someone else handed her—or that she pulled out of her more-than-vivid imagination—what would she do? Where would she start her search for proof that Sebastian Raines was sporting a pair of razor-sharp fangs?

Her gaze swept the room. Well, since she was here . . . She hurried over to the bookshelves and cocked her head to peruse the spines. It was an odd collection of well-worn paperbacks and older, leather-bound editions.

Interesting. The Inferno's intrepid leader apparently appreciated the classics, as well as more modern mainstream fiction. But there was nothing incriminating here. No *Guy's Guide to Being a Modern-Day Bloodsucker* or *Embracing Your Inner Immortality*.

The few DVDs neatly arranged near the giant plasma television were no more illuminating. They were, however, *boring*! No *Hancock* or *Die Hard* or even the *X-Men* quartet, just documentaries on everything from the two World Wars to the Wright Brothers' invention of the very first flying machine.

The rest of the room was nothing but expensive paintings, vases (pronounced *vah-zez*, she was sure), and even a couple of small sculptures displayed on their own Grecian—possibly left over from his days in actual Ancient Greece—pedestals. One of them probably cost more than she made at the *Tattler* in a year.

But it wasn't the pricey bric-a-brac that bothered her, it was the fact that none of it seemed like *vampire* bric-a-brac. Weren't the undead supposed to live in crypts, sleep in coffins, and decorate with things like chains and swords and suits of armor? Not to mention spider webs and wax-covered candelabras.

Then again, Sebastian Raines was a modern-day vampire—if he truly was a vampire at all—so maybe he'd adapted. Maybe he kept all of his booty, acquired over the thousands of years of his life, somewhere else. A storage facility, maybe. Or a mausoleum at the local cemetery.

She should have checked for something like that while she was trying to dig up dirt on him, she realized belatedly, wishing she still had Chloe's torture shoes on so she could kick herself in the butt.

But even here, in this amazing apartment where Sebastian probably hosted dozens of fancy parties and upscale soirees with all of his wealthy and influential human friends—human, most likely, but maybe a few fellow vamps, too—there had to be some sign of his bloodsucking tendencies. A pint of blood in the refrigerator . . . a box of soil from his homeland . . . a complete and total lack of mirrors.

Well, there were no mirrors in this room, that was for sure. Just a lot of very highly polished reflective surfaces. Did that count?

She wanted to check the rest of the penthouse, but once she got into the other rooms, she was afraid she would get distracted and forget to come back to the kitchen. So first she headed there.

The cat, who'd been watching her curiously this whole time, hopped down from the armchair and followed.

Wow, if the living room had been impressive, the kitchen was a foodie's wet dream. Top-of-the-line appliances, gleaming silver in the overhead light. Obsidian marble countertops and central island. And two racks hanging from the ceiling at opposite ends of the large space—one holding a variety of wine and cocktail glasses, the other a variety of cookware.

Chuck's idea of a gourmet meal was Hamburger Helper, so most of what she was looking at was lost on her. But on behalf of culinary students everywhere, she could certainly appreciate Raines's taste and attention to detail.

She wondered if he actually used this part of the penthouse, of if it was just for show. Or maybe he had a personal chef. Or a stable of women who stayed the night and then cooked breakfast for him in the morning.

Wait. With a shake of her head, she asked herself what the heck she was doing thinking semi-jealous thoughts. That wasn't like her *at all*. She'd never even met Sebastian Raines—unless she had, indeed, fainted at his feet. But even that couldn't be considered meeting-meeting him.

She'd been following him, sure, but in a purely investigative capacity. Like a scientist observing gorillas in their natural habitat. The fact that she found him moderately attractive was beside the point.

And wait times two. What was she doing wondering about his eating habits, when her whole hypothesis was that he was a vampire, and therefore didn't *eat* regular food? Or didn't need to, at any rate. She wasn't entirely clear on the whole do they?/don't they? thing when it came to the food issue.

Her research had uncovered differing opinions on the topic. Some claimed vampires became deathly ill if they consumed anything but fresh (meaning straight from the source) human blood. Others said they could eat and drink anything they liked, but it didn't nourish them the way blood did. Which meant that they could take human food or leave it, but they couldn't forgo true feeding (i.e. blood—*gack!*).

So the kitchen—as outstanding as it was—could be just for show, too. To which she offered a hearty *Bravo, Mr. Raines!*

Noticing that the cat was once again staring at her from its perch on one corner of the marble counter, she cleared her throat and dragged her mind back to the matter at hand. She wasn't here to get orgasmic over Raines's plush, multimillion-dollar digs.

But, oh, it would be *so* easy.

Before her knees went any weaker, she began a thorough search of the kitchen. Cupboards and drawers, refrigerator, oven, dishwasher.

"Okay," she muttered to herself, "this is not helpful. The cupboards and refrigerator are all full, and he even has three kinds of garlic on hand." Garlic! What kind of vampire was he, dammit?

She slammed a jar of the stuff down on the counter, making the cat jump.

"Sorry," she apologized with a wince. "But this flies in the face of everything we've been told, little black kitty cat. Either I'm wrong, or hundreds of years of myths and legends are."

Stepping back, she looked around, trying to decide where to dig around next. "But I'm not wrong. I can't be. I *need* this story, and I'm *going* to find my proof."

Her gaze snagged on the glass-fronted, floor-to-ceiling wine cabinet beside the fridge. "Ah-ha! I'll bet this is it," she continued talking to herself—or, if anyone ever asked, Raines's cat.

Yanking open the narrow door, she started pulling out one bottle after another, lining them up on the counter. There had to be three dozen, at least. And judging by the labels, some of them were old.

Old enough to have been brought over from the "old

country"? (Wherever that was.) Old enough to have been bottled by Sebastian himself, if he'd been some seventeenth-century vintner?

Or maybe he'd simply been carrying some of these around with him since he'd been turned. That was certainly one way to get your hands on a bottle of uber-valuable wine without falling victim to its equally staggering price tag.

She studied them each for several long seconds. If she were a vampire stocking her kitchen with human food for appearances' sake, the perfect hiding place for her supply of blood would be in with the wine. The question was: Which bottles were blood and which were actually grape by-products?

Sebastian would know, of course. He probably had them marked, or had a system for arranging them so he wouldn't grab the wrong one when humans were around. But she was going to have to find his secret stash by trial and error.

Picking up a bottle at random, she turned it from side to side, struggling to see through the dark glass to the liquid inside. She was *not* looking forward to this, but it was the only way to discover Sebastian's private source of nourishment and get one step closer to proving that he truly was one of the walking dead. Undead. Whatever.

Retrieving a corkscrew from one of the drawers she'd ransacked earlier, she went to work on the bottle in her hand. No sooner did she get it open with a small *pop* than the cat—who had been sitting quite peacefully at the end of the counter—jumped up on all fours. He moved so quickly, he actually startled her for a second.

If that's how the poor thing reacted to a simple bottle of wine being opened, she wondered how he'd deal with the even louder sound of a champagne cork being popped.

"It's all right, kitty. I just need to check some of these to make sure they're actually wine."

She reached for a glass from the rack hanging over her head and poured a small sample from the open bottle. It was red, but only wine red, not human-blood-leeched-from-anunwilling-victim red. And it swished like wine. (Blood, she assumed, would be thicker.) And smelled like wine.

Her nose crinkled at the thought of what she had to do next. Not only was she taking the chance of ingesting actual, *gack*-tual blood—yuck!—but even if it wasn't, she didn't particularly like wine to begin with.

Sigh. The things she was willing to do for a story.

She might be in one of the most luxurious penthouses in all of Las Vegas instead of a dark, dank, drippy cave that smelled like guano, but she still couldn't say yet that this little research trip was much better than the night she'd spent camped out in hopes of catching a glimpse of Bat Boy.

Taking a deep breath, she brought the glass to her lips, squeezed her eyes closed, and tossed back the mouthful of liquid.

Huh. Her chin came down as she swallowed. Wine. It was just wine. Pretty darn good wine, if she did say so herself, but still just smashed and fermented grapes, not strangled and fresh-squeezed vagrant.

Re-corking the first bottle, she moved to the next. Poured an inch and went through the whole swirl, sniff, swallow thing again.

More wine.

Bottle number three. (*Swirl, sniff, swallow.*)

Bottle number four.

Raines's cat moved closer, up on all fours now, back arched. Its long, black whiskers twitched as it raised its lips and hissed, baring tiny little white teeth. Well, except for those two long canines at the sides—those looked kind of big. And sharp. As sharp as any vampire's fangs could be.

"What's wrong?" she asked the obviously upset feline.

Chuck glanced over her shoulder, checked the suite's front door and the portion of hallway that she could see from the kitchen. Nothing.

With a shrug, she went back to her systematic re-corking of bottle number four and testing with bottle number five. (*Swirl, sniff, swallow.*)

Bottle number six. Seven. Eight.

The cat hissed again, and again, growling low in its throat between bouts of trying to spit her to death. She didn't know what the heck its problem was; *she* was the one having to slug down gulp after gulp of stinky alcohol. Although, come to think of it, it wasn't really *that* bad. The first few sips had been a little hard to get down, but things were moving much more smoothly now. She was even beginning to enjoy this, though it was disappointing not to have found her quarry's stash of fresh blood yet.

But she wasn't a quitter. She'd uncork and taste every one of these bottles, if she had to. And, hey, she only had about four to go, anyway, so she might as well.

While she worked to open yet another of the unopened bottles, the cat jumped down from the counter and sprinted past her as it raced out of the kitchen. As small as the animal was, the impact of it brushing past her in her current state— yeah, yeah, so she suspected she was well on her way to being tipsy—sent her teetering slightly, even in bare feet.

She reached out, catching herself against the edge of the counter with her free hand while she carefully balanced the glass of wine in the other. It might only have an inch and a half of crimson liquid floating around at the bottom, but she wasn't going to risk spilling a drop.

"Kitty," she called out, wondering what had gotten into the unfriendly feline.

Still clasping her glass, she tiptoed around the corner and into the long hallway leading to the rear of the apartment. She knew she should finish up—and probably clean up—in the kitchen before she went snooping around elsewhere, but the idea of following the cat was too tempting.

Cats were notoriously sneaky and stealthy. They knew all kinds of dark, secret places where they could hide or nap . . . and where their vampiric guardians could hide all kinds of evidence of their blood-sipping, sun-avoiding tendencies.

Her bare toes dug into the plush, ocean-blue carpeting as she hustled past a couple of closed doorways, one on either side of the hall, and toward the one that was slightly ajar at the far end of the wide corridor.

"Here, kitty, kitty," she crooned just above a whisper. "Where did you go, sweetheart?"

She didn't know why she was suddenly so concerned about being overheard. She'd just spent thirty minutes, maybe an hour, popping the corks of every bottle of wine in Sebastian Raines's kitchen stash. At any point during that little exercise in futility, someone could have walked in and caught her in the act. Sebastian himself, or one of his giant, no-neck bodyguards.

So either the penthouse was empty and she truly was completely alone—not counting the only cat in the world who apparently *didn't* think she bathed in tuna juice on a daily basis—or her captor(s) were hiding away, leaving her to her own devices until they were ready to jump out and start giving her the old rubber hose treatment.

She was sure rubber hoses hurt . . . along with all of the other five hundred methods of torture she could think of off the top of her head. And the ten thousand more that got added to the list if she started thinking about vampires torturing humans.

Gads, she'd read too many horrific novels and watched too many shows about appalling myths and legends while researching this story. She had fangs and bloodletting and torn jugulars on the brain.

The door at the end of this particular hall was open a couple of inches . . . just enough for an eight-pound laze-about cat to slip through. Bending at the waist, she put her fingers on the knob and pushed lightly, taking baby steps inside in the slow, hunched-over position she thought would be most nonthreatening to Mr. Hissy-Pants.

"Come on now, kitty," she continued to cajole. "There's nothing to be scared of, and I need you to show me where your master's bodies are buried. Not literally," she added with a shiver, mumbling the aside to herself more than the still-missing feline.

She seriously hoped there were no *actual* bodies piled up around here. That would be just . . . gross.

Of course, for all she knew, the billionaire Raines could have a harem of blood slaves chained up in one of these back bedrooms. Or willing ones lazing about on silk sheets all day, simply awaiting the moment he would return to drain them nearly dry—with an accompanying orgasm brought on by sudden blood loss. Or so she'd read about somewhere along the way.

Must be nice. Even she might be willing to let a vampire bite her if it included a free Big O for every pint she donated. Lord knew she wasn't getting the Os—big or otherwise—from anyone else.

She scanned the dark room, but saw nothing more than darkness and the vague outlines of really nice furniture.

The good news: She was pretty sure she'd just found the Big Kahuna's bedroom. His secret lair within his secret lair.

It surprised her a little that the room didn't seem to be decorated in Transylvania chic. There were no flickering candelabras. No long strips of sheer white linen draped from the ceiling and over the windows, fluttering in a faux dramatic breeze. And no large, black lacquer coffin—or better yet, one of those ancient pine-box types that was wider at the shoulder end than at the ankle end—where the ghoulish undead took his respite during daylight hours.

It looked to her as though there was just a bed—a really big, "just right" Goldilocks bed, wider than any king-size she'd ever seen—and a bureau, and average Martha Stewart drapes open at the windows.

The view was spectacular, no doubt about it. Just like in the living room, Sebastian Raines's penthouse offered probably one of the best vantage points in the city. Every floor-to-ceiling window—of which there were many—overlooked some portion of Las Vegas, with its bustling streets, sparkling lights, and bright neon signs. During the day, she knew she would be able to make out mountains and people and the rippling desert heat reflecting off of the surrounding rooftops.

So what did Sebastian do during the day? Vampires couldn't tolerate sunlight, that was a given. She'd read conflicting reports about their reactions to garlic or reflective surfaces (i.e. mirrors), but all of the "experts" definitely agreed that sunlight was a giant no-no for the descendants of Count Dracula. Or Vlad the Impaler, depending on which bloodsucking origin you wanted to believe.

Which made her wonder why he insisted on occupying the Inferno's penthouse suite to begin with. He could have just as easily built his empire with a nice, cozy living space far underground in the sub-sub-basement. That's where *she* would live, if she were mortally "allergic" to the sun.

But she was sure he had a system. Maybe he made it a point to be tucked safely inside his closet every day before dawn. Or maybe the entire penthouse was just for show and he really *did* live in the sub-sub-basement. There might even be an express elevator somewhere that connected the two—penthouse to crypt—that he used to zip from one to the other just before the sun began its red-gold climb into the morning sky.

Oh, yeah, she was cookin' now. She'd have to remember that line for her story; it sounded very deep and impressive and drew a great picture of the rich but reclusive hero (that would be Sebastian) dashing off to his secret, underground lair where he slept alone and lonely, hidden away from the rays of light that could so easily claim his life.

Uh-huh. That was front page stuff, right there.

If she didn't find anything of consequence up here, in his "nighttime residence," she would start poking around downstairs—*waaaaaay* downstairs—next. Provided she ever made it out of this place alive, since she still wasn't sure how she'd gotten up here to begin with.

On top of that, the bad news was that her only companion seemed to have disappeared. The room was dark, which made it hard to make out anything of consequence, but she still didn't see any black, roundish lumps that could be a cowering (or attack-ready) kitty. She also didn't hear any purring or hissing that might give her a hint of the cat's hiding place.

But since she had been the one to run him off, it seemed only right for her to try to find him again. Lure him out and make nice.

If that included snooping around in the closet, under the bed, and inside a few dresser drawers . . . well, it was her duty as an animal lover and, um, "guest" of the casino's owner, really, to be thorough.

Her wineglass clinked when she set it down on the edge of the bureau nearest a door she suspected led to a closet. Knowing Raines, and having seen parts of the rest of his amazing living space, she had no doubt it was huge and luxurious.

She turned the handle, opening the door slowly, just in case it wasn't a closet, but a hidden torture chamber. Or maybe the room where those brainwashed concubines lazed around until Sebastian came to drink them dry.

Slipping an arm around the jamb, she felt along the wall until she found the light switch and flipped it on. She'd been right, it was a closet, but "walk-in" didn't even begin to cover it. Her entire *apartment* could fit inside and probably never ruffle a seam on one of the six million designer suits hanging from its long silver rods.

"Holy Beau Brummell, Batman," she mumbled to herself. She had never seen so many suit jackets, slacks, shoes, and ties all in one place—not even lined up on racks at the department store.

The tiny squeak of a floorboard sounded behind her, and she turned, expecting to find Fraidy Cat finally coming around again. Instead, a giant shadow towered over her, broad and menacing and *looming*. And when it opened its mouth, the low, ominous voice sent every bit of courage she'd ever possessed skittering off to parts unknown.

"Looking for something?"

Pair

In retrospect, perhaps he should have turned on a light in the bedroom before moving up behind her. Because she screamed. Like a banshee.

Not a tiny yip of surprise or even a shriek, but a long, high-pitched scream that threatened to shatter his eardrums— as well as those of every dog, bat, and coyote within the city limits.

Reaching out, he clapped a hand over her mouth. He *had* to stop that ungodly racket before his head exploded.

At his sudden movement and what he was sure she likely saw as a physical assault, she flailed her arms . . . and knocked her glass of wine off the dresser.

His thirty-thousand-dollar-a-bottle Chateau Mouton-Rothschild.

Dammit. What more was this woman going to do to ruin his life and personal possessions?

She was after his brother, and possibly the Raines family fortune. She was a threat to their biggest secret. She'd opened every one of the bottles of precious, nearly priceless wine he kept in the penthouse out of pride and for appearances only. *Not* to be opened on a whim. And now she'd ruined his carpeting.

Did she have any idea how much the stuff cost? So much, they didn't charge by the square foot, but by the square inch.

He was *really* beginning to regret abducting her.

With a mental flick, he flipped on every light in the room so that he no longer stood in shadow and no longer looked like the monster-slash-demented rapist she apparently took him for. When she finally got a clear look at him, the screaming stopped . . . but the open mouth and fear in her eyes didn't.

Her nostrils flared above his hand, and her chest—her ample, nearly bare, sequin-studded chest—heaved with her rapid breathing.

But it was her pulse that caught Sebastian's attention. The pounding of her blood in her veins, the staccato beat of her heart *ka-thump, ka-thump, ka-thump*ing behind her rib cage.

And she smelled good. Better than good—delicious. Of flowers; a type he couldn't quite place . . . maybe lilies or tulips, something unusual and not often found in women's perfumes and body lotions. And beneath that, the underlying scent of citrus. Not from an outward fragrance, but deeper, from within. Something in her blood itself.

He inhaled deeply, feeling his pupils dilate and his gums throb as his fangs descended. Not to mention what was happening below the buckle of his belt.

Attraction to this woman was unacceptable. He might not want her tricking Aidan into a quickie marriage that would give her access to his numerous bank accounts, but that didn't mean it was all right for Sebastian to ogle her the way he was doing. If his brother was interested in Chloe Lamoreaux—as undesirable a match as she might be—then she was off limits to him. Protecting his brother (even from his own stupidity) was one thing; stealing his brother's girl (even an unworthy one) was another. And entirely unacceptable.

But that didn't keep his cock from hardening behind his zipper, or her unique scent from seeping into his pores. It didn't keep him from envisioning the two of them together. On the extra-wide, custom-made bed only a few feet behind them, with its navy blue, merino wool and thousand-count Egyptian cotton sheets. Naked and writhing with lust.

He imagined peeling her out of her Flames of Hell costume, with its red and orange sequins and the waterfall of even oranger feathers fluttering at her rear. Revealing the rest of her lightly golden skin inch by inch. Laying her down and putting his mouth to her breasts, her smooth stomach, the insides of her quivering thighs.

As though the outfit she wore to dance at Lust didn't showcase enough of her mouthwatering figure, he'd seen her onstage. He knew that she had a tight, athletic body, with curves in all the right places and ankles that reached her ears when she was adequately motivated.

He pictured her that way, with his body nestled tightly against her, pounding them both into oblivion . . . and a jolt not unlike that of a nine-thousand-volt cattle prod caused his dick to leap, shaking him from head to toe.

Fangs fully engaged now, he slammed the curtain down on such erotic thoughts. This situation was bad enough as it was. The last thing he needed was for her to notice that he was sporting either a giant erection *or* a set of razor-sharp, non-FX incisors.

And he might have had a shot at getting himself under control in both departments if he didn't suddenly scent *her* arousal. There was still a hint of fear—of him and of the situation she suddenly found herself in—but her blood was heating with something more, almost as though his visions of fucking her senseless had permeated her mind, as well.

Which was possible. His kind had the power to instill thoughts in humans; to make them believe they'd seen things differently than they had, or to wipe their minds completely. It was how they survived, how they managed to feed without leaving traumatized victims in their wake.

Just because he'd never successfully transferred his own thoughts or desires to someone before didn't mean it wasn't possible. He supposed.

Or perhaps she was equally attracted to him, all on her own. No vampire mojo involved.

He arched a brow. Now, there was an interesting thought.

His gaze skittered down to her chest, wanting to see if her nipples were peaked, but the materials of her costume were too thick to tell. He did, however, notice the tremble of her legs and how she clenched them slightly when she noticed where his attention had wandered.

Because she was frightened . . . or because she was turned on?

Knowing he shouldn't be toying with her like this—sexually or otherwise—he straightened and chastened himself to focus on the matter at hand.

"I'm going to remove my hand from your mouth now," he told her in a low voice, "but I need your promise that you won't scream."

True, his men had orders to stay well away from the penthouse this evening, and it was unlikely anyone else would hear, no matter what kind of commotion she made, but better to be safe than sorry. Plus, given his excellent vampire hearing and the fact that she'd already burst his eardrums once tonight, he'd prefer not to have to gag her the entire rest of his time with her.

"Do we understand each other?"

Slowly, heavily made-up eyes still wide, she moved her head up and down.

He nodded in return, then just as slowly slid his hand from her mouth, ready to slap it back, if necessary.

But she didn't scream. She did let her tongue dart out to lick her dry lips, though, an action that sent a flicker of heat straight to his groin.

He bit back a groan—barely—before taking a single step away from her and bending at the waist to retrieve the toppled wineglass. Setting it on the bureau from where it had fallen, he perused her briefly, trying to decide where to begin.

His initial goal has been merely to keep her from running off with Aidan, giving the couple a chance to rethink their desire to tie the knot so quickly. But after discovering that she'd been following him, and her rather odd behavior in his kitchen with his—*whimper*—once-prized wine collection, he now realized he needed to do more than simply keep her locked up, away from Aidan. He needed to figure out who she was and what she was up to.

Before he could say anything, however, she beat him to the punch.

"I'm sorry," she said. "I didn't mean to snoop, I was just looking for your cat."

Which was both the truth and a lie. Yes, she'd been looking for him—or rather, his feline form—after he'd raced from the kitchen in order to shift out of eyeshot.

But she'd also been snooping, from the moment she awoke on his sofa. And when she'd thought the only witness to her nosiness was a silent, disinterested house cat.

But what had she been looking for? Proof of something, obviously—but what?

He winged one brow upward, letting her know he didn't believe her. At least not entirely.

She licked her lips again, nervously this time, but that didn't keep another stab of lust from grabbing him by the balls.

"I would have called for him, but I didn't know his name," she added, pausing to let him fill in the blank. He didn't. "What is his name?" she finally asked flat-out.

"Sebastian," he answered blithely, amused when her eyes widened in surprise.

"You named your cat after yourself?"

"Something like that," he murmured.

Then, before she could pelt him with more questions, he grasped her elbow and steered her away from the closet, toward the bedroom door. Once they were far enough down the hall that she wouldn't notice, he mentally extinguished the lights behind them.

Without a word, he dragged her to the kitchen and situated her in front of the countertop that was littered with hundreds of thousands of dollars' worth of wasted wine. The very thought of how much he'd paid for some of the bottles and how long he'd been saving others made his blood pressure soar. His only saving grace, he supposed, was that he kept the *most* valuable bottles in his collection tucked safely away in a commercial storage facility on the other side of town.

"Would you like to explain this?" he asked, feeling like a father taking a child to task for coloring on the walls.

She had the grace to look chagrined, blood rushing to the apples of her cheeks to turn them an attractive shade of pink. Reaching behind her, she tugged at the feathered tail sprouting out of her ass, drawing his attention to the firm, round, sequin-covered twin globes. His blood pressure continued to climb, but this time for an entirely different reason.

"I, um . . . was really thirsty."

He raised a brow, letting her know he didn't believe that for a Las Vegas minute.

"A glass of water would have quenched your thirst," he told her flatly. "This is . . ." Overkill. A travesty. A grape-flavored nightmare. "Something else. And you were looking for something. What?"

Her eyes widened at that, and she immediately began shaking her head. "I wasn't looking for anything," she declared in a high, nearly falsetto voice that belayed the truth of her words.

"You were. You said as much while you were violating my wine collection."

If possible, her eyes flew even wider and the splashes of color at her cheeks drained away, leaving her pale with shock. "How do you know that? I thought I was alone," she added in a low murmur, almost as though she didn't think he would hear.

But of course, he did hear. He could hear her heart beating in her chest and the breaths sloughing in and out of her lungs.

He couldn't very well tell her that he'd heard her ongoing monologue because he'd been perched on the counter the entire time, though. That sort of thing tended to go over badly with humans. Let her believe the entire penthouse was wired, and that he'd been both watching and listening to her every move since she'd awakened.

"What are you looking for?" he asked in a low voice.

"Nothing," she denied quickly with a sharp, negative move of her head. "I wasn't looking for anything."

Sebastian's eyes narrowed, darkened. He didn't make a habit of using his powers on defenseless humans. To wipe their memories of having seen him in certain situations, yes, but not to delve around in their brains and search for information. That sort of thing wasn't usually necessary in this day and age, and he preferred to conduct business fairly, knowing that at the end of the day, any profits he made or lost were due to his entrepreneurial skills and *not* the cloak of preternatural hypnosis.

But there were times, such as this one, when a little otherworldly woo-woo was necessary. And considering his brother's eagerness to rush this woman down the aisle, as well as the fact that he'd kidnapped her and wasn't sure how long he could keep her here before she started putting up a fuss or he started cruising toward a felony he couldn't talk his way out of, the sooner he found out what she was truly up to, the better.

Wrapping his hands over her shoulders, he ignored the spark of awareness that sizzled at the touch of bare flesh to bare flesh. He caught her gaze and held it, staring deeply into her eyes. *Deeply.*

"Chloe," he murmured softly, "tell me what you're looking for."

Her brow wrinkled slightly, even as her violet eyes began to dilate, grow foggy. "Chloe?" she said in a strange, faraway tone. "But I'm not . . ."

And then she blinked, her expression went blank, and she sagged in his arms.

Two Pair

Either Chloe Lamoreaux was extremely suggestible or . . . Or he didn't know what else. He'd never had someone pass out on him just from a small bit of mental pressure pushed in their direction.

With the unconscious showgirl in his arms, Sebastian stalked down the hall, *back* to his bedroom, and draped her across the bed, atop the thick navy coverlet. Stepping back, he stared down at her, considering.

Perhaps his powers had grown over the years without frequent use and without his realizing it. Which didn't explain why the random women he fed from on a regular basis reacted exactly as they should from his gentle nudges to allow him to take their necks and the mental erasings that followed to remove their memories of ever having met him.

Or perhaps he'd pushed too hard. If she was tired, ill, maybe even worn out from his first blast of power when he'd knocked her out to get her upstairs . . . Any of these things could be a factor in her current response, he supposed.

None of them kept him from admiring her half-naked body, though. Still encased in fishnet stockings and the high-shine, overly-sequined costume he was beginning to realize was a little over the top, even for Lust.

The problem was, he wouldn't mind seeing her out of it. He couldn't imagine that the skintight outfit, made out of those materials (if they could even be called "materials" instead of "hardware") was comfortable.

Crossing to the closet she'd been about to snoop through when he returned to human form and caught her off guard, he flicked on the light and studied his options. Despite the number of women he had in and out of the penthouse on a regular basis, few of them left personal items behind. He made sure of it.

He wasn't exactly a T-shirt and jeans type of guy, so his "casual" options were limited. Deciding on a plain white undershirt and pair of dark maroon pajama bottoms, he stalked back to the bed. He knew they would likely swamp her, but the more coverage he could offer, the better. Frankly, she was lucky he didn't dig out his ski-wear and dress her head to toe in a thick down snowsuit.

Bending close, he started to strip her. Not the finest idea he'd ever had, considering the singe to his fingertips every time they touched. If he were smart, he'd wait until she woke—or wake her intentionally—and let her dress herself.

But he suspected that if he offered her that option, she would turn it down, preferring to remain in the ridiculous—and no doubt binding—costume rather than climb into something from his personal wardrobe. So he would take that particular decision away from her and just get the job done. But not without extreme personal distress.

The one-piece outfit fit her like a second skin, which meant that in order to peel it from her unconscious body, he had to dig his fingers in between the bodice and the full globes of her breasts. His nostrils flared at the feel of that soft, silken skin against his knuckles. If only the damn thing had a zipper. But it didn't—he'd checked.

Feeling his blood heat, pooling uninvited in the vee of his legs and the gums around his aching, fully distended fangs, he turned his head, doing his best to avoid the full blast of her lushly naked form. Perhaps doing this by feel wasn't the best idea, either, but it beat the alternative all to hell.

Watching what he was doing, seeing her pale skin and voluptuous curves come into view inch by agonizing inch, would most certainly send him over the edge. And then he would have guilt to deal with, and apologies to make, to both this woman and his younger brother.

Like a Band-Aid, he tugged the costume down in one great yank, making sure to snag the waistband of the drool-inducing fishnets along the way. When he had her completely stripped—at least he hoped she was completely stripped—he quickly shook out the clean and pressed pajama bottoms and worked them over her feet. All by feel and with his eyes tightly closed.

Oh, if his brother could see him now. Well, no, that probably wouldn't be very bright. The last thing he wanted was for his brother to see him with his *naked* girlfriend draped across his bed. But in another time and place, with some other woman naked and passed out in his bed, Aidan would find this highly entertaining.

Aidan thought Sebastian rigid and uptight; never a smile, a chuckle, or the tiniest hint of a sense of humor. Never a thread or hair out of place. He was all business all the time. Hundreds of years of being the eldest sibling—not to mention an immortal who needed to keep that small fact a complete and total secret—had made him that way, and he refused to apologize for it.

Which was why this particular situation was so unlike him . . . and why Aidan would probably laugh himself stupid over it, if he knew.

Even Sebastian could see a modicum of amusement in the picture he surely made, undressing one of his showgirls with his eyes squeezed tightly shut. This was far from how he normally performed when he had a beautiful woman in his bed.

Letting the elastic band snap at her waist, he turned away to find the undershirt, then did the same Blind Man's Grab to get it over her head and down to cover the rise of that sumptuous chest. Even though his eyes were closed (and he didn't peek, really he didn't), that didn't stop him from imagining every detail of what he was working so hard to cover. Especially as his fingers slid down her arms, along her waist, and pointedly avoided getting too close to those breasts that even now had his muscles tensing and his mind going straight for the triple-X section of the pay-per-view menu.

Just as he had the hem of the undershirt pulled down around her hips, and thought it was probably safe to stand back and check his work, she groaned. His eyes popped open at the same moment hers did. Surprisingly, she didn't look nearly as shocked to find him towering over her as he felt.

"What happened?" she asked in a sandy, sleepy voice.

Sebastian's first instinct was to tell her—to explain why she was in his bed and how she'd gotten into his clothes before he ended up with a screaming, shrieking female on his hands. Again.

Then he remembered his initial goal in "coaxing" her to open up. He'd meant for her to go cross-eyed and spill the beans, not faint at his feet, but now that she was once again conscious, but still groggy . . . There was no time like the present.

With slow movements, he approached the bed, rearranging the pillows at her back and helping to prop her into a better sitting position before lowering his hip to the mattress beside her.

"Chloe," he murmured, "listen to me."

She blinked, but held his gaze. Unable to resist, he lifted a hand and brushed it down the side of her face, through the soft waves of her chestnut hair.

"I need you to answer some questions for me. All right?"

Her eyes were just the right shade of violet—wide, black pupils with a ring of bright color around the outside. And while there was still knowledge there, intelligence, awareness, she was mesmerized, as well. Just enough. With no signs of being ready to slip back off into oblivion.

Good.

"Chloe," he said softly.

She shook her head, making his mouth turn down in a

frown. "Not Chloe. Charlotte." Then her nose wrinkled. "Hate that name. Call me Chuck."

It was Sebastian's turn to blink in confusion. Not Chloe? How could that possibly be? And yet this explanation was something she'd uttered a million times before, he could tell. She was obviously used to telling people she hated her given name and would prefer to be called by the shorter, more masculine "Chuck."

Reorganizing the order of the questions swimming around in his head, he decided to start with the easy stuff—*scoff* . . . there was the understatement of the century—and build from there.

"Who's Chloe?" he asked simply.

In an almost mechanical tone, she said, "Sister."

"Older or younger?"

"Younger by two minutes."

Twins! he thought as comprehension dawned. Followed by, *Son of a bitch.*

He'd grabbed the wrong sister. How the hell had he grabbed the wrong flipping sister?

Sebastian played back over everything he knew about *Chloe* Lamoreaux, mostly supplied by what little Aidan had shared about his latest lady love. Brown hair, nice body, showgirl for Lust, the dance revue club in his very own casino.

His gaze traveled the length of the feminine form stretched out along his bedclothes. Brown hair, rockin'—er—*nice* body (if *nice* was equivalent to the sexiest, hottest, most nubile thing he'd ever seen), and she had to be a showgirl.

He'd watched her onstage. Caught her as she'd walked *offstage*. Found her wearing one of Lust's trademark red-and-orange "Flames of Hell" costumes, complete with feathers and sequins and stockings and platform neck-breaker heels. If that wasn't clear confirmation that she was a dancer, he'd go downstairs, walk up to the nearest roulette table, and put his entire vast, vast, vaaaaaast fortune on black.

And yet this wasn't the sister he'd been after. He didn't think. Either he had it wrong . . . or Aidan did.

His brows knit in consternation. "What does your sister do?" he asked. And then, for clarification, added, "As her job. What's her occupation?"

"Showgirl," Chuck answered automatically, still glassy-eyed. "Dances at Lust inside the Inferno. Doesn't want to forever, though. Kicks are hard on the knees. Guys' pinches are hard on the ass." She chuckled at that, as though it was a long-standing joke between the two sisters.

Well, at least he and Aidan were right about that much.

"And what do you do?"

If he was expecting a similar explanation, he should have remembered that where this woman was concerned, it was just one surprise after another.

"Reporter. For the *Sin City Tattler*." Her nose wrinkled at that. "Good at it, but no respect. Tired of making up shit about flying saucers and Bigfoot sightings. Need a good story. One really good, true story." Her lips tilted upward, flashing her pearly whites.

That grin—which he'd seen a time or two on cats that had just swallowed beloved goldfish—told him she already had a story in mind. He wasn't sure he should care or even needed to know, but curiosity won out, and he found himself asking, "What story is that?"

She was still staring off into space, not really seeing him, and yet she sat up straighter, as though getting ready to impart some grave secret. "Sebastian Raines," she whispered.

His eyes rolled back in his head. Christ on a cracker, was there no reprieve from the roller-coaster ride this woman had him on? It was one sharp climb and sudden drop after another.

Pressing two fingers to the arch of his nose, he tried to push back the headache throbbing there. A bloody headache, when he'd never suffered one before in his life.

Vampires didn't get headaches, or if they did, it was tantamount to a gnat buzzing at the hide of a rhino—so insignificant as to go completely unnoticed.

But here he was with the mother of them all.

Or maybe it was an aneurism. An aneurism brought on by stress was entirely possible. It would certainly explain the intense pain banging against the inside of his skull like a jai alai ball.

At this point, he could only hope for death. It wouldn't last, of course, but it might be a nice reprieve.

Lowering his hand from his face, taking a deep breath to shore himself up for whatever answer she might give to his next question, he asked, "What about Sebastian Raines? What story are you working on about him?"

She leaned in even closer, until their noses nearly touched. He smelled that scent again—flowers touched by citrus—as her gaze drilled into his.

There was something there this time. Not recognition, but an intensity. *Feeling* behind what she was about to say.

"He's a vampire," she told him in the merest wisp of breath. "And I'm going to prove it."

Three of a Kind

Chuck came to herself in a blink. Literally.

It was the oddest thing. One minute she was asleep—she thought—and the next she was wide awake, sitting straight up in bed.

Not her bed, though. She glanced around, realizing she was not just in the bedroom of Sebastian Raines's phenomenal penthouse, but taking up space on his personal mattress.

She did not remember that. Going through his wine rack and beginning to snoop in his closet, yes. But climbing into his bed . . . Who was she, Goldilocks?

No, she definitely didn't remember getting into—or on to, as the case may be—his bed.

Or his clothes.

Looking down, she noticed she had somehow gotten out of Chloe's "Flames of Hell" costume and into . . . Oh, no. They couldn't be . . . Sebastian Raines's pajamas? Half of them, anyway—the bottom half—and a plain white undershirt.

Didn't a woman usually get undressed, have (hopefully) mind-blowing sex, *then* jump into a man's clothes? She had no recollection of any of those things. And if she'd been lucky enough to *have* mind-blowing, twisty stix pretzel sex, she really wanted to remember it.

In her peripheral vision, she noticed a form and turned her head to discover that she wasn't alone in the room. A man—

Sebastian Raines himself, she assumed—was standing with his back to her, staring out the window at the bright city lights playing against the still-dark night sky.

His black hair and the midnight blue of his tailored suit melded with the shadows hanging all around him, making him nearly invisible. It was only the paler hue of his hands clasped behind his back and his face in profile that had caught her attention at all.

She must have made a noise . . . or perhaps he heard the slight inhalation of her surprised breath when she noticed him standing there . . . because his arms fell to his sides and he turned in her direction.

The oxygen she'd sucked into her lungs just a moment before got stuck there at the sharp lines of his features and the intensity in his silver-gray eyes. She honestly couldn't tell if he was angry, or if the stony expression was normal for him, but she was pretty sure she would never want to cross him, just in case.

His lashes fluttered slightly as he closed his eyes for the briefest second before opening them again and fixing her with a steady, determined gaze.

"What makes you think I'm a vampire?" he asked in a low, graveled voice. Without warning, without preamble.

Chuck gasped, more shocked than if he'd thrown a bucket of ice water over her head. How did he know she thought that? How had he found out?

Was that why she was here, in his apartment? Had he somehow discovered she was following him and dragged her up here to torture her for information, to find out how much she knew, and then either drain her dry before killing her outright or turn her into one of the walking undead?

In her best imitation of a crab, she scurried backwards on the mattress until she hit pillows and the immovable bulk of the bed's headboard. As though moving ten inches farther away and curling herself into a ball was going to keep Nosferatu from eating her for dinner.

"I . . ." The single short word came out as little more than

a squeak. She paused to clear her throat, then tried again.
"I . . ." Breathy this time, with only a hint of squeakiness at
the end. "Don't . . . know . . ." Her mouth went dry and she
could barely force out the rest. "Wh-what you're . . . talking
about."

He raised a brow—an evil, menacing brow?—and she
shivered.

"Yes, you do." He stated it matter-of-factly, but remained
exactly where he was. No going all Bela Lugosi on her or
swooping in like a vampire (*snork*) bat, fangs bared. "You
talk in your sleep."

Okay, she *totally* didn't think that was true. Of course,
since she'd been sleeping alone much longer than she cared to
admit, she couldn't exactly call any witnesses to the contrary.

But while they were on the subject, how the heck had she
gotten *to sleep* in the first place? She didn't remember lying
down, feeling drowsy, deciding to take a nice, restoring nap
in a complete stranger's—not to mention her unsuspecting
(or maybe very suspecting, given the circumstances she currently found herself in) quarry's—penthouse.

Much like when she'd first woken up in the living room
earlier—and how much earlier, she had no clue—her memory
was horribly sketchy. Unless it was some strange dream, she
thought she remembered standing in the doorway of his
closet, then having him come up behind her, scaring her half
to death. There had been some screaming, and his hand over
her mouth . . . and then a small confrontation in the kitchen
over all of the opened, half-drunk bottles of wine she'd left
there.

Maybe. And nothing after that.

It was completely bizarre for her to suddenly be having
these horrible gaps in her memory. Now she knew how Swiss
cheese felt.

A sudden thought popped into her head, making her gasp
in alarm. And not because she was about to be nibbled on by
some demon of lore, either.

Oh, God! This was how brain tumors were diagnosed.

Loss of memory. Gaps of missing time. Blackouts followed by awakenings in odd places without viable explanation. She didn't smell toast, but that symptom could be next.

"If you were a vampire," she suddenly blurted, "and someone was dying of an incurable disease, could you change them?"

It was his turn to be caught off guard, she guessed, judging by the lift of one dark brow.

Folding his arms across his broad chest, he rolled back on his heels, studying her. "Why do you ask?"

She struggled not to choke on her own emotions, not to let the tears pricking behind her eyes spill over. "Because I think I'm dying. I think I've got a brain tumor, and it's getting bad fast. I can't remember anything. I don't know how I got here or how long I've been here or how I got into these clothes."

She plucked at the white cotton shirt that hung off one shoulder and billowed around her like a toga sheet. Oh! And it clearly showed her dark areolas and stiff nipples.

Gack, how embarrassing! She quickly folded her arms over her breasts, hiding them as best she could. But there was no doubt Sebastian had already seen them. How could he not, even without super-duper vampire vision?

He rolled his eyes at her, but not before she noticed his gaze flicking over her barely hidden upper assets.

"You don't have a brain tumor," he told her in a near-scoff.

She gave him a cross look before snapping, "How do you know? Are you a doctor, as well as a wealthy casino owner and clandestine bloodsucker?"

"I'm not a doctor, no," he said slowly.

Chuck waited for him to elaborate, but he didn't. And even though she could feel the tumor growing exponentially inside her head with every second that ticked by, some of her brain cells were still in tip-top shape.

"Oh, my God," she murmured. "You're telling me . . . You're telling me that you're not a doctor, but you *are* a wealthy casino owner . . . and a vampire."

When he didn't respond to that accusation, either, simply continued to stand there, staring at her with those strangely eerie shadow-gray eyes, she knew she was right.

"I knew it!" she crowed, hopping up on her knees and bouncing like a schoolgirl at a sleepover. "I knew it. I was right."

And then sensibility returned, and she realized where she was . . . and what her sudden knowledge could mean to her dubious future.

Falling back on her heels, she went still. "Are you going to kill me now that I know?" she asked in a low voice. It didn't waver, which was nice, even though inside she had begun to shake.

One corner of his mouth lifted in momentary amusement. "No, I'm not going to kill you."

He stepped toward her, his face once again a flat, unreadable mask. To her credit, she stayed where she was instead of doing the first-girl-to-trip-and-die horror movie shriek and scuttling to the other side of the bed.

But she watched him. Watched his sleek, muscular frame flow like water beneath the immaculate cut of his silken, almost metallic suit. His dark hair was perfectly styled, and his skin was light, but not too light. It was clear he didn't spend much time out in the hot Las Vegas sun, but he wasn't as pale as parchment paper, either.

Stopping just beside the bed, he let his long fingers trail along the edge of the navy spread, his attention focused with odd intent on the pattern of stitching he found there.

"First, I'd like to know why you suspect me of being a vampire," he said, "and then I'm going to do something I've never done before."

At that, he lifted his head, meeting her gaze head-on. Her stomach lurched and butterflies took flight. But not because she was nervous or he scared her. She was very much afraid the sensations swamping her were due to . . . sexual attraction.

No surprise there, not really. Even if Sebastian was a member of the blood-chugging elite, he also happened to be extremely *hawt*. Tall, Dark, and Handsome with a capital T, D, and H.

She licked her lips, doing her best to stifle the unexpected and long-absent yearning prickling beneath her skin. "What's that?" she asked, although she was almost afraid to know.

"I'm going to tell you everything."

Sebastian had spent the entire time he'd waited for Charlotte—Chuck—to swim back to consciousness trying to decide what to do with her.

He knew what he *should* do: Take her home, wipe her mind of any recollection of her interactions with him, and go after the Lamoreaux sister he'd meant to grab in the first place.

But it had been so long since any human had even thought to imagine what he truly was. So long since he'd had someone to talk to, really talk to.

He couldn't explain the strange urge bearing down on his soul, pushing him to confide in this woman he barely knew. Scratch that—didn't know at all.

He'd stumbled upon her, mistaken her for someone else, and now wanted to sit down and tell her his life story? Obviously, he was losing his mind. Or maybe her brain tumor theory was contagious.

But the need was so strong. She was beautiful, and already suspicious of his true identity, which meant she would be a rapt audience for his tale. And he wouldn't mind spending a few more hours with her . . . being open with her, honest with her, having a genuine conversation in which he didn't need to lie or resort to subterfuge to conceal his true nature.

He would have to remove any traces of their interaction later, of course. He might be feeling momentarily vulnerable and more affable than ever before in his existence, but he wasn't stupid. And before he would allow her to walk away with her head full of true knowledge about him and his race—or worse yet, allow her to go home and write about him for her tabloid rag—he *would* turn into the monster humans thought vampires to be and do something dire, if necessary.

Tilting his head in the direction of the bedroom door, he said, "Come with me," and then started in that direction, knowing that she would be too curious not to follow.

While she was still several paces behind him, he passed through the kitchen, grabbing two long-stemmed glasses and one of the bottles of wine she'd opened earlier. No sense letting it go to waste.

A small smile curved his mouth as she padded across the tile after him while he circled through and headed for the living room. Setting the bottle and glasses on the low glass table fronting the wide sofa, he took a seat before pouring them each a drink. Holding one out to her, he patted the cushion beside him.

She might be wearing layers of his clothes, with very little of her own figure visible beneath, but damned if her own innate femininity didn't shine right through. He could make out the line of her breasts *and* the pebbled thrust of her nipples, which had his fangs pricking against his tongue. When she sat, she crossed one leg beneath her, revealing the shape and long musculature that had gotten her through three consecutive shows onstage, even though she apparently didn't belong there.

He filed that away as something else to ask her about. Perhaps down the road. But first, he wanted an answer to his original question . . . and then he knew she would want answers to hers.

Taking a sip of the nearly black Chateau Margaux, he studied her, just as she was studying him. Like a bug under a microscope. Or maybe more like the slide of a deadly bacteria under a microscope—warily, but with a good dose of curiosity thrown in, as well.

"Now," he said, "tell me why it is you believe I'm a vampire."

He was careful not to flash his fangs as he spoke, other-wise her theory would be proven, and she'd have no reason to answer. He also didn't want to scare her—and for some odd reason, humans tended to react badly to a man who re-vealed two long, razor-sharp incisors when he smiled. Maybe that's why he didn't do it very often. Go figure.

She swallowed hard. Her fingers clutched the glass in her hand so tightly, her knuckles turned white, but she didn't bother tasting the blackberry wine inside.

"Well . . ." She paused, cleared her throat, and began again. "Powers of deduction, I guess. You're very elusive. Even though you're one of the wealthiest businessmen in Las Vegas—possibly the entire United States—you're rarely seen out and about. And if you do go out in public, it's always at night." Her eyes narrowed as she met his gaze squarely, in-tent. "Always. To my knowledge, you've *never* been seen in daylight."

She waited a beat, apparently expecting him to comment, but he remained silent, waiting just as long for her to con-tinue.

"Well, you have to admit, that's weird, considering that most ribbon cuttings and press conferences and everything else take place between nine a.m. and five p.m., not the other way around. And the number-one known trait of vampires *is* aversion to sunlight," she pointed out, as though he might not be aware. Right.

With a tip of his head that might have been taken as a nod, he prompted, "What else?"

"You're handsome and wealthy and could have a dozen beautiful women hanging on you, if you wanted, but you're never seen out on a date. You're not involved, not married, no children . . ."

He raised a brow, wondering if she realized she wasn't de-scribing the life of a solitary vampire only. "So you think I'm gay, too?"

Her eyes flashed wide and she sat back, startled. "No," she

responded quickly. "The thought never crossed my mind, actually."

Since he didn't particularly care what anyone thought about his sexuality, he shouldn't be relieved by her admission, but oddly, he was. Supremely relieved.

And that relief grew even stronger when her brows knit and she downed her entire glass of wine in a single swallow before asking, "You aren't, are you?"

"No, I'm not." He raised his own brow, inquiring lightly, "But why do you care?"

"I don't," she responded much too fast and with a shake of her head that was just a bit too . . . energetic to be believed. "I don't care. It's none of my business."

"But whether I am or am not a vampire—an evil, vile, murderous creature of legend—is?"

It was more statement than question, but she answered just the same.

"I'm a reporter. It's my job to sniff out leads and investigate stories."

"Like alien abductions and Bigfoot sightings," he murmured, recalling her earlier admission.

She looked at him askance, and he realized that she'd told him about writing for the *Sin City Tattler* while under his spell.

Well, shit, he thought with a cringe.

"More talking in my sleep, I suppose," she said deadpan, and he knew she suspected something hinky was going on.

"Something like that."

With a shrug, she leaned forward and poured herself a couple more inches of wine. "It's true, writing for the *Tattler* gives me a chance to stretch my imagination and make up all sorts of weird stuff. In case you were wondering, though, some of it *is* at least loosely based on fact," she added, as though she was used to defending her occupation.

"I'm sure," he replied in the same flat, serious tone. "Why, just last week, I had the ghosts of Elvis, Marilyn, and James

Dean over for dinner, and all three of them mentioned hoping no one would find out or they'd end up on the cover of the *Tattler*."

"Ha-ha, very funny," she said with a twist of her mouth that told him she was definitely *not* amused. "Look, all I'm saying is that I've seen grilled cheese sandwiches with burn marks that *do* bear a remarkable resemblance to Jesus. And I definitely believe Bat Boy exists."

"Bat Boy?" he repeated, although he was almost afraid to ask.

She nodded enthusiastically. "I *totally* think I saw him in a mall once. Seriously, this kid had pointed ears and giant bug eyes."

"Maybe he was part elf."

He expected her to scoff at his *obvious* joke—it had been obvious, hadn't it?—but instead she leaned toward him, an intent expression spreading across her features.

"Do elves really exist?" she asked in a low, inquisitive tone.

"How the hell should I know?" he snapped, lurching back in surprise.

She shrugged her shoulder. The one left bare by the sagging neckline of his undershirt.

The sight shouldn't have aroused him quite so much, but it did. His gums *and* his dick throbbed, and he found himself toying with the sharp edge of one fang with the tip of his tongue. Worse, he was picturing *her* tonguing his fangs, and later his cock . . . and that was *not* good.

Though he knew better than to think she could read his thoughts, her gaze went unerringly to his mouth and he both saw and felt the hitch in her breath.

Dammit, how did she do that? *Why* did she do that? It was as though every time he had an erotic thought about the woman sitting next to him, she had it, too. Which was impossible, of course.

When she seemed to have her breath back, she lifted her

face to meet his eyes rather than staring almost wantonly at his lips and teeth.

Her words, when they came, were airy and unfocused. "I just thought that since you're a vampire . . . *if* you're a vampire," she added in case that wasn't entirely a given, "you might know about other preternatural beings, like werewolves or fairies or—"

"Elves?"

She inclined her head.

"Sorry," he said softly. "I don't have an Encyclopedia of Paranormal Creatures."

Her brow lifted, and a small smile played across her lips. "I do. Of course, as far as I know, it's complete fiction."

And then she fell serious, those violet eyes darkening as they drilled into his. "But you aren't, are you? Fiction, I mean." Her attention flicked back to his mouth and the overly long incisor she'd spotted there earlier. "You really are a vampire."

Straight

Chuck couldn't believe it. She was sitting on the sofa beside an honest-to-goodness vampire. A vampire!

She was almost giddy with excitement. Sure, there was a fair amount of trepidation roiling in her belly, too, but mostly she was just too darn pleased with herself.

Even if Sebastian went all feral and ate her for his supper, she figured she'd die happy in the knowledge that she'd been *right*! She wasn't crazy, and she hadn't let the wild imaginings of her previous stories for the *Tattler* get her all whipped up over nothing. Sebastian Raines was definitely something.

Whoo-howdy, was he ever. Was it wrong to be sitting here, drinking his wine, silently writing up bullet points for her article, *and* lusting after him like a sailor on shore leave? Well, like the female version of one, anyway, whatever that might be.

"I want to interview you," she blurted out suddenly, bouncing up on her knees on the soft sofa cushions.

It had never occurred to her before—probably because she'd never intended to actually come face to face with him. Follow him around his own casino, dig into his past and present, and sneak through his penthouse looking for clues to his otherworldliness, sure. But actually sit down with him and ask him questions directly? It was an underpaid tabloid reporter's dream come true.

Careful not to spill her wine in all her sit-up-and-shake puppy dog excitement, she asked, "Would you let me?"

His dark lashes fluttered over his even darker eyes. "I've never been interviewed," he replied slowly. "Get more requests each week than you can imagine, but I've never granted a single one."

"I know."

And she did; she'd scoured the Internet, old newspapers and magazines, even microfiche, for God's sake, for any hint of something personal about Sebastian Raines in Sebastian Raines's own words. She'd found nothing. Oh, there had been plenty of articles written *about* him—about his properties, his multimillion dollar corporations, even a few with a where-did-this-guy-come-from? tone—but always from an outsider's perspective.

With a small inclination of his head, he said, "I told you I'd tell you everything, so I will. But my frankness comes with a price."

Chuck's heart leapt. Whatever it was, she would pay.

Did he want actual cash? Probably not, since he had about nine thousand, sixteen trillion more dollars in his bank account than she did, but she was still willing to offer.

If he was more in the market for a live-in maid, or even a live-in mistress . . . well, she was up for that, too. She'd already been drooling over him from afar, so putting herself out there like that (*ha*—putting out) for the story of a lifetime wouldn't exactly be a hardship.

As for the other . . . well, she could scrub a toilet as well as anyone, she supposed.

"You won't remember anything once I finish."

She blinked, slamming on her brain's brakes and laying rubber until she could pull a mental U-ie. Wait. What?

"What?" she repeated aloud, knowing she was blinking like a camel in a sandstorm.

"That's the deal, Char— Sorry. Chuck."

He said her name as though he didn't particularly like it,

and definitely wasn't used to calling a woman by a man's name. She got that a lot.

"What does that mean?" she asked carefully.

Was he telling her that he wouldn't *allow* her to use anything he told her when they were finished? An off-the-record-type interview. Or was he telling her she wouldn't remember the interview when they were done in a Mafia boss, you'll-sleep-with-the-fishes sort of way?

She honestly didn't know which made her feel more sick to her stomach. Swimming with the fishes would be bad, but not being able to use the most coveted interview on the planet would be devastating. Heartbreaking. Even if he didn't put her in cement shoes and drop her to the bottom of Lake Tahoe, she would probably take a voluntary dive off the Hoover Dam, anyway.

"It means that I can answer your questions. I can tell you everything you've ever wanted to know. But when we're done, your memory of this evening will be completely erased and you'll remember nothing."

"How . . ." When her voice squeaked on the word, she paused, collected herself, and tried again. "How exactly will that happen?"

One corner of his mouth quirked up in a self-deprecating grin. "Come now. Do you think all vampires do is drink blood from unsuspecting victims?"

Inside her chest, Chuck's heart was *ka-thump-ka-thump-ka-thump*ing to beat the band. Holy hell on a hamburger bun. That was as good as an admission that he was, indeed, a vampire.

Granted, he hadn't come right out and said, "Why, yes, ma'am, I am a bloodsucking fiend of the night. Wanna see my fangs?"

But she'd *seen* the fangs, hadn't she? No full-on, double-fang action, but there for a second, just a minute or two ago, she'd definitely seen . . . more tooth where most people had less tooth.

And though she hadn't asked him directly whether or not he was a vampire, she'd certainly made it clear that's what she was after, and nothing he'd said so far led her to believe his answer would be no.

The glass in her hand trembled, and her lips started to go numb. Was she having a heart attack? Was this what one felt like? Or maybe she was simply on the verge of a panic attack.

Either way, this was IT. Big I, big T, nothing was ever going to top this in her entire life. If she one day gave birth to a litter of porcupines and got into the *Guinness Book of World Records*, she would still look back at the night she'd sat across from an honest-to-goodness vampire and gotten the story from his very own bloodstained mouth, and consider it the most exciting thing that had ever happened to her.

But could she go through the most exciting event of her life, get all of her nagging questions answered, *know* she'd finally proven that vampires really did exist . . . and then consent to having it all wiped away as though it never happened?

She thought about it for all of about a millisecond. The time it took for her fingers to flex more tightly around her wineglass and her gaze to once again zero in on Sebastian's impressive, almost Romanesque profile as he reached for the bottle to refill his own glass.

Yes. Yes, she could. She *had* to know. Wanted it more than her next breath or her daily, top-secret Snickers bar.

It killed her, absolutely *killed* her to think that when she woke up the next morning, she might not remember a single thing about tonight, but it was a risk she was willing to take. Who knew, maybe his vampire mojo or whatever it was wouldn't work. Maybe she would wake up not only remembering the events of this evening, but as far back as having her ass slapped by the doctor when she'd been born.

A frown crossed her face as one last thought occurred to her. "This whole . . . erasing my memory thing," she murmured, nibbling at one side of her bottom lip. "It doesn't involve any sort of electro-shock or frontal lobotomy-type stuff, does it?"

He chuckled. "No, I assure you it's entirely noninvasive. Except for the loss of recent memories, of course."

Of course.

Taking a deep breath, she nodded, and forced the words past a throat closed tight with anxiety. "All right. As long as you promise not to leave me a drooling vegetable staring at *Phineas and Ferb* all day, I'm in."

"Who?"

She waved off his question with a flip of her wrist. "It's a cartoon. For kids." Something she knew only because she spent way too many hours awake when she should be asleep, with only the Disney Channel for company.

"No, I will not leave you drooling over this *Phillius on Verb*, or anything else. You'll be perfectly fine, except for a few missing hours of your life you'll probably wonder about. After a while, you'll even forget that they ever went missing."

"Then I want to know," she told him, making her voice strong and sure in hopes of convincing herself, as well.

He inclined his head. "Where would you like to start?"

Well, shoot, she wasn't expecting that. Her brows crossed. Where did she want to start?

She already knew he was a vampire. At this point, that was a given. He'd never come right out and admitted as much, but . . . yeah, it was a given.

And she assumed he drank blood, couldn't go out in sunlight, and had been around since the invention of the wheel or soon thereafter. The whole nine undead yards.

She wanted to know more than just the everyday minutia of an immortal's existence. Although, yes, she was sure that was all fascinating. She'd come back to it later. But for now, she wanted to dig deeper, learn something a little more substantial than whether or not he slept in a coffin or had to carry dirt from his native land in his pants pocket twenty-four/seven.

When she thought about it, what she wanted to know most was really pretty simple. And probably what had driven her to go after Sebastian like a pitbull with this "there's a vampire living in Las Vegas" theory in the first place.

Licking her lips and meeting his steel-gray gaze, she asked, "How does it feel to know you're going to live forever?"

It wasn't the first question Sebastian had expected from her. Frankly, it wasn't even in the top ten.

What does blood taste like? Do you sleep in a coffin? (And can I see it?) How many people have you killed in order to feed? (And how do you hide the bodies?) Those were the kinds of questions he'd thought someone enamored of vampire legends would be most eager to ask once they found out the legends were true. Well, parts of them.

But he watched Chuck's eyes, intensity written across her heart-shaped face, and he knew it wasn't just idle curiosity that had her asking that question first. There was something else, something deeper. Something personal, maybe?

"I don't know that," he responded truthfully.

She cocked her head, clearly not understanding.

"Vampire immortality is a fallacy. We can die, just not easily."

"But you don't age, do you? You don't get sick and die like we mere mortals."

"No, but mortals also don't burst into flame when direct sunlight hits them. You can move about the world completely undeterred. Get on a plane in L.A. at noon one day and step off in Australia at noon the next. Visit Disney World every year and take a spin in the teacups with the two-point-three tots in tow."

"But *you're* never going to die. At least not unless you forget to use your SPF 3000 or trip into a wooden stake. You're never going to catch cancer and make your wife a widow almost before she was a bride."

Ah. "What was his name?" Sebastian asked quietly.

The room filled with eerie, absolute silence for the space of a single heartbeat—or in Chuck's case, a dozen, since he could hear her heart racing a mile a minute beneath her breast. Her mouth wobbled and her eyes turned glossy, tears pooling along her lower lashes.

"Matthew," she said, the single name sounding ripped from her lips with soul-deep emotion.

"What happened?"

Expression bleak, she murmured simply, "He died."

Sebastian didn't respond. He knew there was more to the story, and suspected she wanted to share, but wasn't about to press. He might be a vampire—impervious to human aches and ills, according to her—but he knew about the pain of loss. Probably more than she could ever imagine. If she wanted to talk about it, she would. And if not, they would move on to another, less personal subject.

A moment later, she began to speak again, her voice a soft quaver. "We were high school sweethearts. Grew up together, did the whole hand-holding, note-passing, prom night loss of virginity deal. And then we got married. Too young, really, but we were in love."

Lifting her head a fraction, she gave a ghost of a smile. "Head over heels, stupid in love. And we paid for it. Neither of us attended college. We just got mediocre, minimum wage jobs to put food on the table. But we were happy."

The smile that had begun to build on her face fell. "And then Matthew got sick. We didn't know what was wrong at first, but then he was diagnosed with cancer, and a year later, he was gone."

"I'm sorry."

Sebastian could hear the absolute devastation in her words, feel the grief radiating from her in waves. And yet here she was, sitting beside him, strong and whole and highly inquisitive.

She'd tracked him down, hadn't she? Become suspicious of his lifestyle and figured out what he was when no one else seemed to give it a second thought.

He wondered if she realized exactly why proving the existence of immortality had become such a driving force in her life. But then, a lot of vampires *became* vampires for much the same reason—personal loss and a desperation to do something about the unbearable hurt it brought with it.

"So you're looking for a man who can't get sick and isn't going to die on you," he ventured. Perhaps not the wisest or most empathetic comment he could have made, but she seemed like the type who appreciated getting right to the point.

Her eyes went wide. "No. I—" She blinked, her mouth falling open for a second before she snapped it shut. With a sigh, she said, "I never really thought of it that way, but maybe I am. It would be nice not to have to be *afraid* anymore."

"Afraid of what?"

"Afraid of getting involved. Afraid of meeting someone, falling madly in love, and then having my heart ripped out when I lose him."

"Who's to say you'd lose him?"

"Who's to say I wouldn't?" she countered.

"Just because one man died on you doesn't mean another would," he offered in a low, cautious tone.

"And it doesn't mean he wouldn't," she replied matter-of-factly. "I'm just not sure I'm willing to take the chance."

A niggle of curiosity played at the back of his mind. "How long ago did Matthew pass away?"

"Eight years."

"Is that how long it's been since you've been with someone? Dated, been involved with . . . been intimate with?"

He wasn't sure he could believe that. She was a beautiful, vibrant woman. He would think that, even if she weren't sitting here with glitter still caking her eyelashes, and he hadn't seen her high-kicking across Lust's stage just hours ago.

There was no way she could go nearly ten years without male attention. He pictured a bevy of horny, salivating men lining up at her door every night of the week.

Her gaze skittered away, a delightful blush of color staining her cheeks as she gave a baleful nod.

"Seriously?" he asked, more than a little astonished. "It's been that long?"

The color on her cheeks brightened, but she didn't hang her head. Instead, her chin went up a notch.

"Yes, okay? It's been a really long time." And then under her breath, she grumbled, "Which probably explains the fantasies I've been having lately."

He lifted a brow, his temperature kicking up a notch with piqued interest. "What kind of fantasies?" he asked in a surprisingly even tone given that his throat felt as though it was stuffed with feathers from the headdress of her costume, which was lying on the floor near her feet.

Her mouth twisted and she gave him a look he took to mean, *What kind do you think?*

"The usual kind," she said aloud. "And, oddly, they all seem to be about you."

Flush

Okay, Chuck thought, she probably shouldn't have said that. There were a lot of things she probably shouldn't have said since waking up in Sebastian's bed.

What the heck was wrong with her? She'd had this guy in her sights for months now, but with a strict "observe and report" policy. Getting into his apartment was one thing; sitting on his sofa, telling him he was the star of her very own X-rated Chippendales daydreams was something else altogether.

And how the heck had that happened, anyway? The man was hot, no doubt about it. No red-blooded American woman could look at him and *not* have all of her girlie parts throb with lustful longing.

But while she'd *admired* his dark good looks—and knowing he was eminently bankable didn't hurt, either—she hadn't pictured him naked, stripping him bare with her teeth, or imagined him lying on top of her, filling her, bringing her to orgasm again and again and again.

Until tonight.

The images filled her head like snapshots, or a slide show, big and bold and larger than life. And it surprised her to realize how much she wanted that. All of it.

Which maybe wasn't so surprising, given her eight year dry spell. But in that eight years, she hadn't even been attracted to anyone of the opposite sex. Never.

It was as though she'd gone through the last decade with blinders on, not seeing men as men, but simply genderless human beings.

Now suddenly, she saw a man. A tall, dark, handsome man. A sexy, amazing man who oozed masculinity and sexuality and mystery and danger.

He was a vampire, for God's sake. Who could be attracted to a vampire?

Well, okay, Mina for one. Ninety percent of the female population, for the other—at least if the depiction of the bloodsucking undead in films and literature was anything to go by.

Twilight, Dracula, Moonlight, The Black Dagger Brotherhood . . . Her research had forced her—oh, yeah, big sacrifice; she'd only balked for about the first three pages of J.R. Ward's *Dark Lover*—to read and watch *everything* she could find that was even remotely related to vampires. Movies, television series, classics, romance novels . . . Her living room now looked like the underground lair of some sad, depressed, black-clad Goth teenager.

So maybe she wasn't crazy. Maybe her hormones, which had been lying dormant (not dead, apparently—thank goodness) all this time, had simply picked this moment to wake up and start doing the Macarena.

She wasn't even sure she should try to tame them. It had been so long since her sexuality had made itself known, she almost felt as though she should revel in its sudden awakening. Throw them a little party, a la Mardi Gras or Hormones Gone Wild.

She gave Sebastian another once-over, liking more than ever what she saw. He really was a tall drink of holy water.

Provided he was even interested in getting horizontal with her—or vertical, or at a ninety-degree angle; she certainly wasn't going to be picky—why shouldn't she throw caution to the wind and go for it?

Sure, he was a vampire, but everyone had their quirks.

Matthew had been Lutheran. For a few years back in the late nineties, she'd been a vegetarian.

And he'd already informed her in no uncertain terms that he was going to Etch-a-Sketch her memory when they were finished so she'd have zero recollection of their evening together. Which meant she would have no regrets. She could hang by her ankles from the ceiling or dance naked on one of the blackjack tables downstairs, and she'd never know the difference.

Of course, she was the good twin. Or maybe more accurately, the less uninhibited twin. While Chloe had been on the cheerleading team in high school, Chuck had kept busy with the school newspaper. While Chloe had spent every weekend out with friends—and boyfriends—Chuck had stayed home to read.

And while Chloe went through boys—and later men—like Skittles, Chuck's idea of a hot date was a night at the library with *Jane Eyre* or *Wuthering Heights*. It had taken her forever to realize Matthew was interested in her in *that way*, and once she had, that was it; he'd been her one and only boyfriend, her one and only lover, her one and only husband.

So she didn't exactly have a lot of experience in the "hot sex" department. Not that she was a bowl of Kibble and Bits. She owned a mirror and knew she had it going on, as far as her looks were concerned. Junk food addiction notwithstanding, she had nice boobs, a nice butt, and fit into Chloe's "Flames of Hell" costume without too much overflow.

Face-wise . . . well, Chloe was gorgeous, and since they were identical twins . . . Just because she didn't spend as much time primping and reapplying her lipstick didn't mean she was Bride of Frankenstein material.

So Sebastian shouldn't be too turned off, right?

But was he turned on? Even a little bit?

Lifting her wineglass to her lips, she used it to camouflage the direction of her gaze. She hoped.

How did one tell if a man was turned on? she wondered.

Other than the obvious, of course. That's what she was looking for, but damn the muted lighting and the folds of his
black slacks. She couldn't see anything of importance.

"Looking for something?"

Sebastian's low voice caused her to jump guiltily. The wine
sloshed, and she jerked her head—and her gaze—back up to
his face.

Busted, she thought, like a first-class fool, noting the quirk
of his lips and knowing gleam in his eyes. And not for the
first time tonight, either. Her entire face flushed hot with hu-
miliation.

How did Chloe do this all the time, with guy after guy,
without bursting into flames of embarrassment?

And the sex! Flirting and trying to gauge a man's interest
was hard enough; Chuck could barely imagine stripping
naked and having actual sex with a bunch of them, too. Well,
not a bunch as in "all at once," just consecutively over a span
of time. Her sister might be outgoing, but she wasn't a slut.

With a mental head slap, she realized that somewhere during the last ten years, she'd apparently turned into a Puritan.

But she really wasn't! Or at least, she never had been before.

She used to like sex just as much as the next person. And
though she and Matthew hadn't made a habit of doing anything in bed that would make the fine citizens of Las Vegas
raise a brow—it was *Vegas*, after all; people could buy used
panties out of vending machines, if they wanted (*blurg*)—
they'd been adventurous in their own way.

"No," she answered quickly.

A total lie, and she was sure he could tell by the way her
voice squeaked when she said it. *Oh, no, I wasn't looking for
anything. My eyes weren't glued to your crotch like a croco-
dile scoping out the weakest zebra at the watering hole.*

"Really?" He raised a brow like the upper curve of a question mark.

It was a damn sexy eyebrow . . . as was its mate and the

rest of his handsome, chiseled face. But she was sort of beginning to hate that expression. The one that told her his curiosity was piqued, or he wanted her to elaborate on something she was trying to keep to herself.

"Because it looked as though you were staring at my—"

"*No!*" she screeched, cutting him off before he could finish *that* thought. Shaking her head like a rag doll, she said, "No, definitely not. I was not staring at your . . . anything."

"Funny," he murmured in a low voice, "I could have sworn you were."

If she blushed any more in this man's presence, she swore she was going to burst into flames brighter and hotter than the ones on the outfit she'd been wearing earlier.

Come on, Chuck, she told herself, mentally straightening her shoulders and sliding her spine back into place. *Pull yourself together and act like the strong, independent woman you pride yourself on being.*

"What do you care if I was?" she countered with a cocky eyebrow lift of her own. Ha! Let him get a taste of his own medicine.

"Oh, I would care," he replied. "In fact, I would be quite intrigued."

That caught her off guard. She blinked a moment, trying to find her thoughts and her voice. "Why?" she finally worked up the saliva to ask.

"Because you're not the only one having fantasies."

Chuck's heart thumped as though someone had punched her in the chest. So hard, it stole her breath.

But it also quickened her pulse. Heated her blood. Made juices flow to areas that had been as dry as the Mojave Desert for longer than she could remember.

"What kind of fantasies?" she managed in a wisp of sound.

"The usual kind," he said, tossing her earlier words back at her.

In one smooth, almost practiced move, he set his glass

aside and slid toward her on the sofa. Crowding her, corner-
ing her, pinning her between the overstuffed cushions at her
back and his wide, silk-covered chest.

"What are you doing?" she asked breathlessly, feeling the
heat of his body radiating toward hers, and the laser-sharp
intensity of his gaze tracking her like prey.

"Getting ready to seduce you . . . and make some of those
fantasies come true."

She opened her mouth to protest—mostly because she
thought she should, not because she didn't want the seduction or any hot and sweaty fantasies he felt compelled to ful-
fill. But before she could get a word—or even a squeak—out,
Sebastian covered her mouth with his own.

The minute their lips touched, she was a goner. He felt like
warm velvet, and tasted of thick blackberry wine and dark,
secretive vampire.

Not that she had a clue what vampires tasted like, other
than the one she was slurping at right now. She would have
thought he'd taste like blood—that was what they thrived
on, right? So she'd expected a metallic, coppery flavor.

Instead, she got warm and spicy and just . . . male.

Her fingers kneaded his shoulders, and she pushed up,
wanting to get closer, wanting more. A low mewling filled the
air, and it took her a moment to realize the sound was coming from her.

She never mewled. Or moaned or groaned or panted or
begged. At least she hadn't in a very long time.

But he had her doing just that. She was making noises in
the back of her throat—desperate, sexual noises. And in her
head, she was doing even more. Panting, begging, all of the
above.

His hands found the hem of his own oversize undershirt
and delved beneath, stroking the smooth skin of her waist.
They were so big and warm, even against her rapidly rising
temperature.

When they found her breasts, she gasped, letting her head
fall back and struggling for breath while his thumbs ruth-

lessly teased her stiffening nipples. She let the sensations wash over her, long-denied feelings of lust and longing coming alive and battling like a couple of prizefighters to get out.

"Wait," she gasped when she could finally catch her breath. And it took a couple of tries, as well as a lot of licking of her dry, parched lips.

His hands continued to squeeze and torture, his mouth joining the fray to suckle a line up the length of her throat.

"Wait," she said again, using her hands at his shoulders to push him back just a smidge.

He made an unhappy sound deep in his throat, but finally lifted his head and met her eyes. His glittered, dark and dangerous, and behind his slightly parted lips, she was sure she saw the glint of long, sharp canines. Longer and sharper than normal. Longer and sharper than they had been even earlier.

"You're not going to bite me, are you? Suck me dry?" she asked.

"Oh, I'm going to suck you. And probably bite a little, too."

His erotic threat made her stomach clench. Along with muscles that fell much lower and wanted nothing more than to wrap around him and squeeze.

"You know what I mean. Real biting, the kind that breaks the skin and makes you anemic. You're a vampire and I'm a human, and that's what vampires do to humans. Right?"

"Not necessarily. Unless we're feeding. Otherwise, it's . . . optional."

Tipping her head, she pondered that for a minute. All kinds of images spilled through her mind. Sexy ones, scary ones, ones that fell somewhere in between. But of course, she had no way of knowing how accurate they were.

"Is it good?" she asked with only a slight hitch to her voice.

"Very."

For him, sure. It was probably right up there with achieving an actual orgasm. But since he was the only one with fangs, she suspected he was biased.

"For both parties, though, not just the . . . heavy biter."

"I can make it that way, definitely."

"How?" she wanted to know, eyes narrowing with curiosity . . . and no small amount of self-preservation.

"I'll show you," he said, grabbing her up again and kissing her until she forgot all about being bitten, or losing too much blood, or even her own name. His fangs scraped against her lips, but she didn't care. If anything, knowing they were there, how dangerous they had the potential to be, turned her on even more.

Holding her around the waist, he got to his feet, lifting her as though she weighed no more than one of his empty bottles of wine. Turning, he stalked across the living room without bumping into a single piece of furniture. His lips never left hers, his tongue never stopped delving inside her mouth as he carried her down the hall.

And she was no wilting lily in this ballgame. Her arms and legs were wrapped around him like a squid's, and she was kissing him back. Trying to suck out his molars, to be honest—if he had any molars to suck out. She also couldn't seem to resist running her tongue back and forth over those pointed incisors. Testing, exploring, imagining what they could and would do to her before the night was over.

When they reached his bedroom, he tipped her backwards so that she hit his giant, feather-soft mattress with a bounce. Her breath whooshed out and he pulled away from her.

She nearly whimpered, wanting him back. Wanting her arms and legs still banded around him, his mouth still ravishing hers.

It amazed her that she was here with him at all when she'd gone so very long without male attention. And to think that he was a vampire. An honest-to-Transylvania vampire. She'd hoped, imagined, dreamed . . . but in the back of her head, she hadn't really believed it was possible.

The idea was both exhilarating and frightening at the same time, but the part that made her most anxious wasn't that Sebastian was immortal, or had come back from the dead, or needed to consume the blood of other humans to survive. It was that she was about to sleep with him.

She'd been celibate for nearly a decade, and she decided to break her dry spell *now?* *With a vampire*, of all things? (Things? People? Species? She wasn't even sure what the proper term would be.)

No way was she changing her mind now, though. Falling into bed with a near-stranger was unusual for her. She'd never done it before in her life. Had never even *considered* it or thought she would be the type.

But surprise, surprise. Turned out she was the type. Her sister would be so proud that she was shaking off her mourning for Matthew, her self-imposed celibacy. Of course, Chloe might not be quite as thrilled to discover that the guy Chuck chose to help rid her of her second virginity bit people for his survival.

But she *wanted* this.

Really, *really* wanted it, she thought again as Sebastian began systematically stripping her of the clothes she didn't remember putting on in the first place. Without permission or warning, he yanked the undershirt up her torso and flipped it off over her head. Her arms flopped back to the mattress and her hair flew in every direction as he tossed the bit of white cotton aside.

Then his hands moved to the elastic waistband of the plaid flannel pajama bottoms. They came off with one long sweep down her legs to fall to the floor, leaving her completely naked, bare to his hot, direct gaze.

A flicker of uncertainly swept through her, making her want to do the coy pinup girl thing and cover herself with one arm across her breasts and a hand over her hoo-ha. Never mind that she'd decided just a bit ago that she had nothing to be ashamed of, figure-wise. Knowing she looked okay didn't mean that butterflies didn't start flapping away in her belly when she was lying naked in front of a very attractive, fully dressed, dark and dangerous man.

But Sebastian didn't leave her feeling shy for long. Still devouring her with his eyes, he dug an index finger into the knot of his tie and slipped it loose. He shrugged out of his expensive suit jacket, then opened his collar and the front of his inky blue dress shirt.

Next he unbuckled his belt, the sound of metal clicking and leather sliding against fabric causing goose bumps to break out over her flesh. He unbuttoned his trousers and unzipped the fly, and this time, she shivered.

God, was there anything sexier than watching a man undress? The rasp of clothing. The sight of bulging muscles and bronzed skin becoming visible inch by delicious inch.

It surprised her, actually, how tan Sebastian was. Weren't vampires supposed to be pale from lack of sunlight?

But then, maybe he wasn't tan-tan. Maybe that had been the natural tint of his skin when he became immortal. Or maybe—despite wide-spread beliefs to the contrary—he was able to use a tanning bed to maintain a nice, human flesh-shade. She should have looked for one of *those* in the penthouse while she was snooping around. Because she doubted he went down on a regular basis to use the ones in the casino's on-site spa.

While her mind was wandering, his hands continued to work. His pants fell to the floor in a rustle of sound, and he kicked off his shoes at the same time he rolled his shoulders to dislodge his shirt. That left him in only a pair of black silk boxers with a noticeable tenting at the front.

Chuck licked her lips, imagining the exact length and width and breadth of the cause of that tenting. But she didn't have long to wonder at the details of his masculinity before he shed the boxers as well, showing her the full, burgeoning reality.

She didn't know how much time passed, but she must have been staring for the span of at least several seconds, because he suddenly stepped forward, and his low voice broke the tense silence of the room.

"Like what you see?" he asked.

When she dragged her gaze—reluctantly, oh, so reluctantly—up to his face, she found one black brow arched upward in amusement.

Licking lips gone bone dry, she gave a wobbly nod. "It's been a while, but I don't remember them being quite so . . ."

"Large?" he supplied with typical male arrogance.

Meeting his gaze head-on, she dug deep for a modicum of arrogance of her own. "Mouthwatering."

Full House

Sebastian's penis jumped at her stark admission. A second ago, his chest had been rising and falling with his even breathing. He didn't need to breathe, of course, but old habits died hard, and maintaining human attributes helped with the façade.

But now his chest was stone still, only his throbbing erection beating in time with the pounding of his heart. He was picturing her on her knees, her mouth—wet, hot, watering—on his cock.

What was it about this woman that turned him inside out? He wasn't exactly a green, unschooled youth. Far the hell from it.

He'd stopped counting birthdays long ago. Though if he were forced to do the math, his age would fall somewhere around the four-hundred mark. That was a lot of years to live. A lot of women he'd bedded.

A few he'd spent a good amount of time with. Decades with wild and wicked female vamps that had gone by in the blink of an eye. A few others—demure human females—he was sure he'd fancied himself temporarily in love, or at least in lust, with.

But they all paled in comparison to this statuesque tabloid reporter who'd discovered his secret and then been courageous and determined enough to go undercover as a showgirl at his very own club to prove it.

He couldn't explain it. He was rarely at a loss for feminine company these days, even if most of the women who spent the night with him—willingly, of course—rarely remembered the details by morning. But he couldn't recall the last time he'd been this hard, this eager, from nothing more than a little heavy petting and intense visual stimulation.

She was sprawled naked in the center of his bed, like a sacrificial offering. He wanted to stand there forever, just looking at her. Devouring her with his eyes.

He wanted to stroke her from head to toe. Let his fingers do the walking as he memorized the feel of her skin, every dip and curve of her beautiful body.

He wanted to crawl on top of her, kiss her from temple to toes. Kiss her, lick her, taste every inch of her, and then go back to the beginning and start all over again.

Stalking to the bed, he put one knee to the mattress and his hands to Chuck's waist, lifting her with no effort whatsoever to move her back a few more inches. She gave a small gasp of surprise, but otherwise didn't protest. Maybe because she knew that whatever he did with her, she would undoubtedly enjoy it. That was something even he'd be willing to bet the house on.

Wrapping his fingers around her narrow ankles, he spread her legs and pushed her knees toward her chest. She watched him carefully, uncertainty whispering across her violet eyes.

Mouth curving in a reassuring smile, he leaned up to kiss her hard and fast. "Don't worry, I won't hurt you. I'm not that kind of vampire."

That brought a smile to her face, as well as a short, breathless laugh from her generously proportioned chest. "I'm not afraid of you, it's just that . . . It's been a while since I've been this naked in front of anyone. Since a man has touched me. Or looked at me that way. Or—"

"Ah, so you're more nervous about having sex again than about being at the mercy of an unholy fiend of the night."

She raised a brow at his corny turn of phrase. "Why don't

we just say I'm slightly anxious about being in bed with a vampire, and leave it at that?"

He grinned. When was the last time he'd grinned during foreplay? He'd venture to say not in this century.

But Chuck Lamoreaux—what kind of name was that, anyway?—amused the hell out of him. Her boldness. Her tenacity. Her self-deprecating sense of humor.

"You've got nothing to be nervous about. I'll be gentle and make sure you enjoy it, I promise."

Her hair brushed against the satin duvet as she cocked her head. "I'm not worried about the last, but . . ."

"What?"

"What if I don't want you to be gentle?"

A fist of lust twisted inside Sebastian's gut so tight he almost doubled over. Christ, what she did to him.

Her words, an odd mix of coyness and bravery, made part of him want to be extra gentle with her . . . and part of him want to flip her over onto her stomach, raise her hips, and drive into her hard and fast from behind.

There was nothing gentle about that, or about the way he *would* take her once he got inside of her. But they weren't there just yet.

He covered her mouth with his own, kissing her, teasing her for a long, drawn-out moment. Trailing his lips along the line of her jaw, he murmured, "I'm going to be gentle. Then I'm going to be rough—and everything in between."

Her body jerked beneath him. Hiding his smile in the curve of her neck, he continued to suckle. Every once in a while, he nipped with his teeth, let the sharp tips of his fangs graze her soft, pale flesh and delighted in the shivers his attentions caused.

He kissed her throat, the dip at the very base when she swallowed, traced the sharp line of each collar bone with his tongue. Crossing her chest, he began showering attention on her breasts. First one and then the other, first pressing light butterfly kisses all around and then firmer, tighter ones as he neared the areolas and nipples.

"So what kind of name is Lamoreaux?" he asked against her skin, knowing his voice would vibrate through his lips, causing even greater sensation.

Chuck's slightly arched back fell and she blinked slowly, like an owl coming groggily awake.

"What?" she asked, her tone making it clear she thought he was crazy for wanting to discuss such a thing *now*.

"Your name," he commented, keeping his voice as lazy as his slow licks and kisses. "It's rather unusual. I'm wondering at its origins."

He ran his flattened tongue straight over one puckered nipple and her breath left her lungs in a long hiss.

"I can't believe you want to talk about this now," she panted.

"Hmmmm." He rolled the sound up from deep in his throat, but didn't stop licking.

"French, I think. Don't know."

"You don't know?" Plumping her breast with one hand to bring it closer to his mouth, he let her hear his amusement.

She groaned, wriggling under him, which only lifted her closer to his ministrations. "My sister and I made it up. Real name is Monroe, but we both"—another moan, followed by a small whimper—"wanted to work under a fake name."

So their real names were Charlotte and Chloe Monroe. That explained why he hadn't been able to learn much about her sister when Aidan had first started talking about her. He wondered what he would find now if he did a search under their real names.

Both of them.

His initial concern had been only for Chloe—the sister he'd *thought* he'd brought up to his penthouse this evening. How was he to know she was a twin, and that he'd inadvertently ended up with the best of the pair?

That was speculation, of course, but considering the *other* sister was the one sprawled naked beneath him right now . . . the one he was most attracted to, most intrigued by . . . he was almost certain he'd gotten the better end of the deal.

"Lamoreaux has a nice ring to it. Very romantic. Excellent for both a dancer and a writer like yourself."

He was at the underside of her breast now, laving the soft cushion with his tongue while at the same time using his thumb and forefinger to toy with the nipple of the opposite breast.

Without warning, his ears were pinched and his head was yanked up. Chuck held him by the hair, her own head tipped down so that she could meet his gaze straight on.

"Why are we talking about this now?" she demanded, giving him a little shake of frustration.

He liked it, this forceful side of her, but didn't think he should tell her as much. He also didn't think he should admit that he suddenly found himself wanting to know everything about her.

Big or small, important or trivial, he vowed to discover it all. And if that took the next four hundred years of his life . . . well, that was a prospect he thought he might just be more than looking forward to.

"Sorry," he said, though they both knew he didn't really mean it. "I guess I should find something better to do with my mouth."

Without giving her time to respond, he slid down the rest of her body and hiked her legs up over his shoulders. She gave a short gasp of surprise that turned into a long moan of pleasure as he parted her folds and ran two fingers along her damp slit, just grazing her over-sensitized clitoris.

She was amazingly responsive; his every touch had her twisting, wriggling, purring low in her throat and biting her bottom lip with her perfect white teeth. And he hadn't even gotten started yet.

His fingers played through the crisp, dark curls covering her mound—a bit of a novelty for him; so many of Vegas's modern lovelies were into waxing these days that he was usually met with "airstrips," cutesy decorative designs, or nothing but smooth, hairless skin of the so-called Brazilian variety. And that was nice, but the natural look was good, too.

He took his time, blowing gently on the swollen tissue, teasing her opening with the tip of one finger, using his tongue to taste everywhere but where he knew she needed it most. Her hands clutched the sheets on either side of her hips, her heels digging into his back.

"Se-bas-tian," she panted, dragging his name out to three distinctive syllables.

She was close . . . and so was he. The scent of her arousal, the feel of her pressing against him, shivering beneath him, made him want to bury himself inside her and come as much as she did. But he wanted to do something for her first.

Focusing his efforts, he filled her with two wide fingers, encouraged when her soft inner muscles stretched and then rippled around them. With his tongue, he stroked her silken labia and circled the tiny nub of her clit.

Her hips shot off the bed and then began a steady rocking motion as he drove her higher and higher with his lips, his tongue, and occasionally his teeth. All of them. She made tiny mewling sounds and murmured a litany of incoherent speech that he took to be, *Oh, God . . . yes, yes . . . no more . . . I can't . . . please . . . oh, yes, yes,* yes!

She came with a scream that nearly peeled the paint from the walls. Her head shot back, her spine bowed, and she bucked against his face as the orgasm shuddered through her. It seemed to last forever while he gripped her hips with strong hands and continued to lap at her juices, gentling his touch until she settled.

When she was completely wrung out, lying limp and boneless in his arms, he crawled up the length of her body to cradle her close. Her lashes fluttered as she struggled to open her eyes, and he smiled at how well he'd managed to wear her out in just a matter of minutes. Wait until she discovered how much more pleasure he had planned for her. For both of them.

"Wow," she breathed when she finally managed to open her eyes all the way. They were languid and unfocused, but glimmering with the after effects of sexual fulfillment.

"I take it you enjoyed yourself," he said with no small amount of smug satisfaction.

She gave an unladylike snort. And then, "Why did you do that?"

He quirked a brow. "You *didn't* like?" he asked, waffling between umbrage and disbelief.

She snorted again, this time adding a light slap to his bare shoulder. "Don't be obtuse. 'Like' isn't a big enough word for how good that was. But why would you bother when you could have just as easily gone straight to the main event and enjoyed yourself just as much?"

"My poor, beautiful, *obtuse* darling," he murmured, punctuating the words with a kiss to her temple, her nose, the corner of her rosebud mouth. "It's called foreplay. And in case you didn't notice, I enjoyed it *quite* as much as you did."

Her hair was a mass of chestnut curls splayed out across his bedspread, and he couldn't resist running his fingers through the silken strands. "I love your fragrance, and your flavor, and how you respond to my every touch."

He wouldn't have thought it possible after what they'd so recently shared, but she blushed. Two bright spots of scarlet actually bloomed on her cheeks, and her gaze skittered away, as though she could hide from him even while being pinned securely under his significant bulk.

"You don't believe me?" he pressed.

Lightly gripping her chin, he tipped her face back to his and forced her to meet his eyes. Lifting his other hand, he brushed the knuckles of two fingers—the same two that had been so deeply inside her—across her lips.

"Taste," he told her. "Then maybe you'll understand."

He continued to brush his fingers against her lips, then added his mouth, knowing her juices still coated him there, as well. Whether she responded to his prompting or simply the desire to accept his kiss, her lips parted and allowed his tongue to enter. He kissed her long and thoroughly until they were both breathless and the room filled once again with burgeoning passion.

Of course, his passion had never actually subsided. He was still as hard as a spike, grinding against the soft cushion of her lower abdomen. But her pleasure was more important to him, and he wanted to make sure her first experience with sex after so long without was everything she'd thought, dreamed, expected, and more.

"I want this to be good for you," he told her, smoothing the hair away from her face as she stretched like a cat beneath him. "Better than good."

A small smile raised her lips. "I don't think you have to worry. I'm like a sexual camel. I can live on that one orgasm for another ten years, easy."

Sebastian burst out laughing. His chest rumbled and he buried his face in the hollow of her throat until the chuckles subsided.

"I'm very glad to hear that," he managed after a moment, "but that won't be necessary, believe me. I intend to give you many more before the night is through."

Wrapping her arms around his neck, she flashed him a bright smile. "Oh, goody. I'll store them up for my next extended drought."

Slipping his own arms under her back and pulling her flat to his chest, he bit back a growl of feral possession. "Maybe there won't be a next time."

She didn't say anything, but he could see her thoughts flitting through her eyes like a movie on the big screen. She was thinking that he was a vampire—a real, live (ha! well, you know . . .) vampire—when she hadn't really believed they existed . . . that this was all moving way too fast . . . she didn't know him, he didn't know her . . . maybe it was just a dream, and she would soon wake up to a much more boring and much less pleasurable reality. . . .

All the same thoughts were ticking through his mind, and though he never would have expected to feel so strongly about a mortal woman in such a short amount of time . . . the fact was, he did. He was thinking forever, here, and for him, that was a very long time. It could be for her, too.

But that discussion would come later. At the moment, he had more pleasuring to do. For both of them.

Four of a Kind

"I don't have condoms on hand," Sebastian said. "I can get them, if it will make you feel better, but just so you know, I'm clean. Extremely so. Vampires—"

"Hey," Chuck interrupted, rolling her eyes even as she rubbed her leg lazily up and down his hairy calf. "This is not some run-of-the-mill Vegas chippy you're talking to. Or even a run-of-the-mill tabloid reporter. I've done my homework. Vampires can't carry blood-borne human diseases or transmit them to others. And pregnancy is a non-issue."

He looked both amused and impressed by her recitation of vampire factoids. Oh, yes, she was an ace reporter, all right. And when all of this was over, if he left her so much as a shred of her memories, she was going to write the mother of all exposés about spending the night with him. She would title it *I Slept with a Vampire* or *In Bed with a Bloodsucker*, or maybe *The Richest Vampire in Vegas*.

What a shock it would be for the world to find out that the owner of one of the busiest, most successful casinos on The Strip was really a lord-knew-how-old immortal who drank the blood of innocents to survive. Well, okay, maybe not innocents. She wasn't exactly sure what—or who—he "ate." They hadn't gotten that far yet, but she certainly intended to ask at the first nonsexual opportunity.

"Actually," he intoned, splaying his fingers behind her back to casually stroke the slope of her spine, "that last isn't entirely true. We have been known to reproduce. Rarely, and under very precise circumstances, but it can happen."

She raised a brow, her investigative instincts kicking in. Where was a notepad when she needed one?

"Really?" she asked, not bothering to hide her curiosity.

"Yes, really," he said with a grin, obviously enjoying her keen interest. "I'll explain it to you sometime. But *not . . . now.*"

Faster than she could blink, he had her up and over him, and he was flat on his back. His knees cushioned her bottom, his erection pressing eagerly between them.

Staring down at him through the curtain of her hair as it cascaded around her face, she did blink then. She wasn't even shocked by the move, by the suddenness of being horizontal one second and vertical the next. If anything, these little superpowers of his were growing on her, and she found them both fascinating and convenient.

"That was quick," she said. "I just hope being fast on the draw doesn't translate to *everything* you do."

He canted his pelvis, driving his arousal even higher against her. "Oh, I can go slow, believe me. And if you're not satisfied when I'm finished, I guess I'll just have to start over."

She envisioned his doing just that, and a shiver rolled through her. She could imagine him doing slow things and fast things and everything in between, and she wanted them all.

A tiny cheerleader inside of her that she'd never known existed gave her pom-poms a shake and whooped, "You go, girl!" Quite a switch from the bookish, four-eyed president of the debate club she'd been living with for the past ten years.

But if she was going to kiss her celibacy goodbye, she might as well do it in a big way. And doing the nasty with a hot, sexy vampire with wicked-sharp fangs and superhuman strength was about as big as it got.

Leaning down, she let her hair fall around them while she

kissed him with every ounce of pent-up passion she hadn't let loose with anyone else in a very long time. Her palms rested flat on his broad chest, feeling the warmth of his skin—were vampires normally warm-blooded, or did that mean he'd recently fed? Ick, better not to think about that right now— and the play of his sleek, hard muscles beneath her fingertips.

His own hands wandered along her buttocks, her thighs, her waist and breasts, and back again, over and over. Every inch of Chuck's skin tingled like it had pins and needles, her blood humming as though he'd already bitten her and imbibed her with a bit of his own immortal essence that gave her powers beyond her wildest imaginings.

She could certainly do with an extra dose of strength, heightened senses, the whole works. But at the moment, the only thing she was feeling was mega-horny. Was that a superpower? And if it was, did it come from her . . . or from him?

Vampire or not, Sebastian *did* have powers—the power to make her crazy with desire, senseless with wanting him.

Reaching between them, she grasped his erection and arranged herself so that she hovered just above him, teased the tip of that hard, hot length of satin-over-steel with her wetness. He moaned against her mouth, raising his hips in an effort to push farther inside her.

She thought about toying with him. Pulling away only to lower herself ever so slowly again, inch by excruciating inch.

But torturing him would only torture her, as well, and what was the point of that? He'd already given her a very generous orgasm; she not only wanted another—or another half dozen, if they could manage it—but wanted to give him a hefty dose of mind-blowing pleasure, too.

Curling her nails into the firm planes of his pecs, she blew the air out of her lungs in short little huffs as she moved her hips down and covered him all the way to the root.

When she was fully seated, when he was buried inside her as far as he could go, they both sighed. It was bliss. Complete and total satisfaction. Not in the big-bang way, but in a way that simply made her go *ahhhhhh*.

She could have stayed that way the rest of the night, the rest of her life . . . except . . . she didn't want to. She wanted to move.

Fast.

And hard.

Sebastian must have read her mind, because his hands went to her hips, gripping tightly. She bit her bottom lip, savoring the sensations as he lifted her slightly . . . and brought her back down. Lifted her . . . and brought her down.

She threw her head back, letting her hair dance down her back, letting her breasts lift and her eyes slide closed. His hands guided her movements, but she was more than a willing partner, using her knees and thighs to ride him.

They went slowly at first, a long, languid up-and-down glide. Something else she could have done forever, if not for the build of exquisite friction between them. It sped up her breathing and made her stomach clench in anticipation.

All of her muscles clenched—in her legs, her abdomen, her fingers as they curled like talons into his chest, and those that wrapped around him so intimately. He groaned, hitching his pelvis up as she came down, and they both hissed.

Next thing she knew, Sebastian's face was a hairsbreadth from her own, his warm breath dusting her cheeks and fluttering the ends of her hair. Shifting beneath her, he rearranged himself so that they were locked together like puzzle pieces.

Her breasts pressed against his chest. A fine sheen of perspiration coated them both, making their skin slick and salty. She smelled it when she inhaled, tasted it when she put her mouth to his shoulder.

She linked her arms around his neck and her legs around his hips, hugging him tight, while he clasped her back. They moved together in perfect symmetry—hot, grinding, X-rated symmetry, but symmetry all the same.

He used his hands, his arms, his entire body to lift her, then bring her down again, harder and harder each time. His thighs cushioned her. His lips brushed her throat, followed by the scrape of his tongue and teeth—those wicked, glorious fangs that scratched, but never broke the skin.

"Sebastian," she panted, even as the pounding increased, threatening to steal the breath from her lungs completely.

He grunted in reply, his fingers flexing at her waist, his hips tilting higher to meet her downward thrusts.

"Sebastian," she said again as the tension grew. Her arms and legs tightened around him while everything else tightened inside of her. She could feel the climax coiling at her center like a cyclone. She was almost there, so close, her head was beginning to spin.

But something was missing. Something scary and dangerous and elemental that she shouldn't be thinking about, shouldn't want . . . but did. Desperately.

"Bite me, Sebastian," she murmured, sure he could hear her no matter how soft the words because of his keen vampire hearing. "Please."

His entire body jerked in her embrace, head coming up and gray eyes piercing through hers. He stopped moving, making her moan with disappointment, but if anything, his grip on her grew even more taut.

"What?" he bit out in a strained, gravelly voice.

Tipping her head, she shook her hair back over one shoulder and bared her throat. Even she could feel the pulse beating there like a tribal drum. "Bite me," she said again. "I want you to."

He shook his head and pulled back slightly. His mouth was a flat line, and she could practically see the wall going up between them. Not that she had any intention of allowing it.

Running her fingers through the tousled black hair at his temples, she took hold of his head and held his face directly in front of her own. His gaze met hers, and she saw the battle taking place there, in his mind and his heart.

"No," he told her, shaking his head despite her hold on him.

"Why not?" she wanted to know.

"It's too soon. You're not ready."

"I am, and I want it, Sebastian. As much as I want you."

"No," he said again, trying to sound firm, trying to sound resolute, but Chuck thought she heard a waver of indecision there . . . of longing.

"If you're going to wipe my memory come morning, then we only have tonight. This is my one chance for the full 'hot vampire sex' experience. I'm not afraid," she reassured him. "And I know you won't hurt me."

Shifting in his lap, driving his rock-hard cock even deeper inside of her, she did her best impression of kudzu, wrapping around him like a sticky, swarming vine. She wasn't letting him go until she got what she wanted—what she knew they both wanted.

"I know you want to," she whispered, pressing her mouth to his ear and *his* mouth to the side of her throat. "Do it, Sebastian. Please."

A low, heartfelt growl rolled up from his chest. She could feel the fight of desire versus apprehension playing out within his conscience.

Desire won out. With a groan of defeat, his mouth opened wide at her neck, covering the muscles and tendons that ran along her jugular. His warm breath dusted her skin, his tongue darting out to taste the pulse point a second before the tips of his fangs ran over the same spot.

And then her skin was broken, his teeth were sinking deep, and her blood was pouring out, pounding through her veins and into his waiting mouth.

She moaned at the sensation, eyes sliding shut. It was like nothing she'd ever felt before. The room was spinning even behind her closed eyelids, making her lightheaded, but in the very best way. Heat rushed through her, making her fingers and toes and everything in between tingle.

And the "in between" was incredible. Rising up over her, Sebastian tipped her to her back, then pressed her into the mattress with his broad, heavy frame.

His mouth never left her throat, the slow, methodic suckling as he drank almost like another sensual invasion. She would have the mother of all hickies come morning, she thought dazedly, wondering if he could erase that as easily as he'd promised to erase her mind.

While her lifeblood filled him, he filled her, moving again, sending banked passions flaring to blazing life. He drove into her, no longer gentle, no longer solicitous of her response or weighing every touch and stroke.

Her blood—or maybe just blood itself, regardless of the donor—had changed him, turned him feral and sexually ravenous. And she loved it. He couldn't hold her tightly enough, bite her deeply enough, pound into her hard enough.

She dug her heels into his spine, twisted her fingers in his hair, met his violent thrusts with the lift and tilt of her own hips. And her lips urged him on, though she had no real concept of what she was saying. *Yes, yes . . . God, yes . . . please don't stop* sounded about right, but that might have been all in her head.

Her only clear thought was of the orgasm racing toward her like a tidal wave. She wanted to catch it, throw herself into it, ride it wherever it cared to take her for as long as she could . . . and to bring Sebastian with her.

And then she was there, screaming as ecstasy slammed into her, taking her over the edge and into the abyss. Surge after surge of pleasure struck her, rolled through her, making her writhe against the satin sheets and shout Sebastian's name.

He was there with her. A moment after her climax began, he clasped her close and released her throat as he stiffened and came. Shudders wracked him as he convulsed above and inside of her, and she welcomed every arch, every quake, every squeeze of his fingers on her buttocks.

Minutes ticked by before their bodies stilled and their breathing returned to normal, but even then, Chuck felt far from ordinary. Sebastian might clear her mind of any memory of tonight, but she suspected that deep down in her heart and soul, she would always remember that *something* had happened this evening. Something different and special and life-altering.

As heavy as they felt, she forced her eyes open, noticing the touch of color just beginning to spread across the far end of the night sky, well past the neon lights of downtown Las Vegas. Morning already, when it seemed only moments ago that she'd been squeezing into Chloe's costume.

Morning! The thought—as well as its implications for the man still draped on top of her—registered, and she started to sit up with a jerk. But then a sudden cranking sound filled the room, and thick steel panels slid down over the glass window-panes.

"It's okay," Sebastian muttered, levering himself up a scant few inches and rolling to his side. Fighting with the covers they were still sprawled on top of, he tugged them loose, then got the two of them tucked comfortably under-neath. "They're on a timer. Down just before sunrise, up just after sunset."

So that's how he managed to avoid sunlight in a penthouse framed by nothing but windows. What a smart man. Smart, and rich enough to afford the very latest in vampire safety technology.

"Gotta sleep," he said, sounding sleepier by the minute. Not that she blamed him; she was feeling all kinds of relaxed and ready for a nap herself.

His arm snaked around her waist, yanking her snug against him, her back to his chest. "Don't go anywhere," he mumbled, burying his nose in her hair and his lips to the nape of her neck.

"Aren't you going to erase my memory now?" she asked quietly. Now that he'd had his way with her, drunk her blood, given her more pleasure than any ten mortal men combined could ever dream of offering . . .

"Later. Sleep now," he slurred, his voice growing softer in the darkness. "Stay. Sleep."

She really wished she had some paper and a pencil handy. Or a micro-recorder. Or cell phone. Or even a Morse Code machine so she could tap out a few notes about her night with a vampire. He still intended to wipe her memory later, and it might be nice to have a few facts jotted down in case she ever did get the chance to write her article. Or even just so that she might recall a few valuable personal moments from this whole experience.

But then, if vampires were as accomplished at scrubbing brain cells as he claimed, she would probably only wonder what the heck she'd written down all that scrawled nonsense for, anyway, so what was the point?

With a yawn, she gave up—at least momentarily—on the idea of being some ace investigative reporter and stayed wrapped safely in his warm embrace. And she slept, more soundly than she could ever remember.

Straight Flush

It was the sliding rise of the steel window coverings that woke her. Until then, she had been so deeply asleep that she hadn't even been dreaming. Just floating in the ether, enjoying the quiet, endless black of post-coital bliss.

And maybe a small bit of blood loss from Sebastian's rather aggressive nibbling. But that was nothing she couldn't recover from—and wouldn't do again in a minute, if given the chance.

Stretching beneath the warm and satiny sheets, the crisp hairs on Sebastian's legs tickled the backs of her calves, his chest pressed along the length of her spine. Lower, clear evidence of his morning arousal nudged against her butt.

Or would that be evening arousal? And did vampires call erections "wood," or did they have an aversion to that word because of the whole stake-through-the-heart thing?

Wiggling around, she turned to face him and realized it was nearly dark outside. The Vegas skyline was once again inky blue, bleeding into black, dotted with spots of light and color and sparkling proof of The Strip's twenty-four-hour adult revelry.

Despite the amount of research she'd done before deciding to take her sister's place and stalk the elusive Sebastian Raines, she had a lot to learn. Being involved with a vampire was definitely going to take some getting used to. Sleeping all day, doing all the important stuff at night . . . eating her weight in red meat to keep her iron up so she didn't pass out in the middle of suckingly good sex. . . .

That was, provided she would actually *be* involved with a vampire. She had no problem admitting that she wanted to continue seeing Sebastian. They didn't know one another very well yet, but already she found him fascinating. Already, she found herself imagining a future with him. Maybe only a near future rather than a far-into-the-future future, but a future all the same.

And they both knew the sex between them was IN-CRED-I-BLE. That was worth exploring, at least, wasn't it?

The question was, did Sebastian want to keep seeing *her*? Was she, a mere human, worthy of a vampire's time and affections, or was she nothing more than a one-night amusement?

Dragging her gaze away from the view out the windows, she looked down at him only to find him staring up at her. She gave a small jerk, startled, realizing he hadn't moved a muscle when he'd come awake. She wasn't even sure he was breathing.

Not that he needed to, but . . . you know, it would have been nice. Less like lying in bed next to a corpse.

He didn't feel like a corpse, though. He was still toasty warm, whether from being tucked under the covers and against her or from feeding so heavily on her only hours before, she wasn't sure. And his flesh was smooth and alive over the hard planes of masculine muscle.

"Hi," she said softly, her tone tentative and weaker than she would have liked.

"Hello," he returned.

Raising a hand from beneath the sheets, he cupped her shoulder, then ran his palm down the length of her arm. Chill bumps lifted across her skin, but had nothing to do with being cold.

He tipped his head, studying her for a moment, then murmured, "Regrets?"

She shook her head. "No. You?"

One dark brow arched over smoky gray eyes. "Certainly not. In fact, I'm considering an encore."

With a tiny smile, she said, "I think that can be arranged." But first . . . "Just give me a second to use the bathroom, okay?"

His hand slipped away from her arm as she threw back the covers and rolled out of bed. But as much as they'd shared last night and as comfortable as she'd been sharing her body with him, she wasn't quite brave enough to traipse across the room in front of him bare-ass naked. So even though he teased her a bit with a lighthearted game of tug-o-war, she managed to walk away with the navy blue duvet wrapped around her like a toga with a very long train.

"If this were Olympus instead of The Inferno, you'd fit right in," he commented, lifting up on one elbow to watch her walk away.

She gave a cute little curtsy and even stuck her tongue out at him before shutting herself in the bathroom to the echo of his muted chuckle.

Sebastian's master bath was as luxurious as the rest of his penthouse, and probably every property he owned. Marble floors, double-basin marble vanity, giant Jacuzzi tub, and a separate marble-lined shower that was roughly the size of her entire bathroom at home. She could fit everything she owned in here, *live* in here, and she didn't think she'd mind it a bit.

Her daydreams of how the other half lived were fractured, however, when she used the restroom and saw red splotches dotting her thighs. For a minute, she thought maybe she'd started her period. But that couldn't be right, considering her recent cycle and how regular they typically were.

A tap at the closed door drew her from her confused distraction, and she quickly finished up, re-draped her make-shift toga to cover all the pertinent body parts, and went to answer it. Not that there was any question of who would be on the other side.

Was it his vampire blood or simply the normal Y chromosome men possessed that made him so comfortable standing there completely nude? Of course, he looked really good nude, so she wasn't exactly going to complain.

The fact that he was semi-aroused—which she noticed, but was trying scrupulously not to stare at—didn't help, either. It made her want to drop her coverlet and see what it felt like to make love with heated marble tile at her back.

"Everything all right?" he asked, looking genuinely concerned, making her realize she must have spent longer than she'd thought trying to figure out the mysterious stains on the insides of her thighs.

"Sorry," she apologized, inclining her head, "I was just . . . thinking."

Her response apparently didn't ease his worry. He reached out to brush a lock of hair behind her ear. "About what?"

Even before she decided to tell him the truth, her cheeks heated, and she could feel the flush climbing all the way to her hairline.

"It's a little embarrassing," she began quietly, averting her gaze, "but . . . I think I may have started my period."

"Why?" he asked, and when she looked back at him, she found one dark brow raised quizzically.

"Why do you think?" she practically squawked, hugging the blanket tighter to her chest, as though it could protect her from any more humiliating questions.

"Don't take this the wrong way, but I would . . . *know* if it was your time of the month."

It was her turn to lift a curious brow. "And how would you know that?"

His mouth twisted, half-amusement, half-chagrin. "I don't think you'd appreciate the details. Suffice to say it's a vampire thing."

Since she was beginning to suspect she *did* understand what he was talking about, she let the topic drop. But if he was right and that wasn't the case, then it still left the question of what the heck was going on.

"Oh, my God," she blurted out at the sudden thought that darted through her mind.

"What?"

"I think I was right. I think my virginity grew back."

He chuckled at that, but she cut him off with a stern look. "I'm not kidding. I told you how long it's been since I had sex, and I was just thinking that I wouldn't be surprised if my virginity was growing back. Then *we* have sex, and I've got blood on my legs, so you do the math. I'm a medical marvel," she murmured, half under her breath. "I can write a story about myself for the *Tattler*."

Though he wasn't laughing at her anymore, he still looked highly entertained. "I've been around a long time, and I've never heard of anything like that, not even in the vampire world. Let me see," he said, reaching for the portion of duvet covering her hoochie.

She gave a yip and jumped back. "Don't you dare," she told him, slapping at his hand.

"You can drop the modesty act, sweetheart," he said, taking a predatory step toward her. "I've already seen everything you have to offer. Seen it," he stepped closer, "touched it," closer still, "tasted it."

The low drawl of his voice rolled across her skin like warm honey, making her quiver. When he reached her, crowding her against the outside shower wall, he ran his knuckles along her bare arm from elbow to wrist. Taking her hand, he tugged her arm from her waist, carefully loosening the blanket until it fell away to pool at her feet. She tensed, expecting him to crouch down and start inspecting the goods, like some car mechanic checking under the hood.

Instead, he bent slightly and scooped her up, carrying her to the edge of the massive, step-up tub. Setting her down on the wide ledge—which was startling to her bare bottom, warm or not, but she bit her lip to keep from letting him know—he reached around to turn on the water. While the tub filled, he knelt before her and put his hands on her knees.

"Let me see," he repeated in a low, persuasive tone, keeping his eyes locked intently on hers. "Please."

Taking a deep breath, she let her legs fall apart, opening herself to his gaze. He studied her carefully, even sliding the pad of his thumb over one of the rust-colored smears.

When he was finished, he lifted his face to hers again and gave her a small, reassuring smile. "At the risk of frightening you with too much information about the secret lives of vampires all at once," he said carefully, "this is nothing you need to worry about. It's not your blood, it's mine."

Chuck blinked. She wasn't frightened, but she sure was confused. "I don't understand," she told him.

With a sigh, he reached around her, shutting off the water, then slowly got to his feet. Taking her hand, he pulled her up with him and helped her step into the tub.

She thought he would join her, but instead he saw her settled, then turned to sit on the edge of the tub ledge to face her. He grabbed a washcloth and a bar of fragrant soap, and dipped them into the warm water.

"Vampires are filled with blood," he began, working the soap into a thick lather within the dark terry of the cloth. "More so than humans. Which means that our bodily fluids tend to be tinged with red. Tears, sweat . . . et cetera."

It was the *et cetera* that caused her to blush, because she knew exactly what he was talking about. They hadn't used a condom; hadn't *needed* to use a condom, at least not to prevent pregnancy or disease. But apparently there were still a few fun side effects of letting a male vampire come inside of you. No wonder all of his bedclothes were so dark.

But even though there was a certain *ick* factor involved, she found his explanation fascinating. It was one more factual detail about real-life vampires that she hadn't known before. Something none of her extensive research had turned up, and that she could use to make her own article even more authentic and powerful.

At that thought, her brows drew down. Wait a minute.

"Tip your head," Sebastian said softly. "Let me see your throat."

She did as he asked, her head currently spinning like one of those brightly colored whirl-a-gigs people stuck in their flower gardens.

"Does it hurt?" he asked, wiping the washcloth gently over the abrasion.

She shook her head. She'd glanced at the bite in the mirror when she'd first entered the bathroom, and though it was possibly the most gnarly injury she'd ever had, it didn't bother her. Two small, round puncture marks that had already scabbed over, surrounded by a bit of tender, bruised tissue.

While it might mean turtlenecks and scarves for a while, the memory of how the marks had gotten there, why they were there, who had given them to her . . . Well, frankly, it made her hot, and she wasn't opposed to collecting a few more, either.

She might just need to increase her iron and orange juice intake to make sure she didn't turn anemic. Wasn't that what blood banks gave their donors to keep them from passing out?

"I'm sorry," he murmured in a low voice. "I was too rough with you."

Lifting her head, she met his gaze. "No, you weren't," she told him with stark honesty. "You were perfect. And I liked it."

She was surprised to see him flush slightly at her words, then felt her own temperature rise as she realized the blood rushing to his face was in part hers. *Their* blood was mingled in his veins. Talk about a turn-on.

"Still," he insisted, "I'll be more careful next time."

"Next time," she muttered, her knees unconsciously coming together when he slid the cloth down her chest and between her legs to dab at the stains he'd left there.

A part of her didn't want to say anything about "next time." Even though he'd brought it up. Even though the curiosity was killing her.

But if she mentioned it, if she asked, he might realize he'd made a fatal mistake and rectify it. If she kept her mouth shut, then she stood a chance of retaining her memories of her time with him for a while longer, at least.

But the curiosity . . . was . . . killing . . . her.

She needed to know. Couldn't stumble through life wondering what the next minute or day might bring—not where Sebastian was concerned.

So, much like removing a thick, sticky bandage, she took a deep breath and riiiiiiiiipped.

"Speaking of next time," she began, thinking for sure he would jump in and correct her, clarify, work his woo-woo vampire powers to turn her brain into a blank magic erase board.

Instead, he remained silent, continuing to stroke the washcloth over the soft flesh of her inner thighs and lower. He held her gaze the entire time, though, those fog-gray eyes of his never wavering.

Steeling herself, she waded back in. "I didn't think there would be a next time," she told him. "You said there couldn't be, that you were going to erase my memory first thing in the morning. Or . . . you know, whatever. As soon as we woke up."

His hand stilled beneath the water, on the inside of her knee. He blinked a couple of times, as though warring with himself over what to say, then blew out a resolved sigh. Pushing up from the edge of the tub, he moved around until he was at her back. Next thing she knew, the water sloshed and he slipped down behind her.

He pulled her close so that she was reclining against him, her back to his chest, his legs bracketing hers. The hand with the washcloth continued to make lazy circles on her stomach and around her breasts. She ignored the beading of her nipples, just as he ignored his mild erection. Both would be dealt with eventually, she suspected, but for now they were comfortable simply lounging, relaxing, being with each other.

"I've been thinking about that," he said just above her ear. His tone held an edge of uncertainty, despite the slow and easy motion of his hand. "Maybe I don't have to wipe your memory quite as soon as I'd planned."

Chuck's heart gave a little leap in her chest. Hope? Excitement? She was afraid of giving too much credence to either.

"Why not?" she asked cautiously.

"Because I like you, and I don't think I'm finished with you yet."

Royal Flush

She nearly snorted at that. The first part was lovely. She believed him, and knowing he felt that way about her made her feel warm and tingly all over. But then he'd had to pull the rich, powerful, mega-millionaire playboy attitude on her.

He wasn't *finished* with her yet? If she wasn't sitting in twelve inches of water that might splash all over and make the marble floor dangerously slippery, she'd be tempted to whip around and punch him a good one, right in the gut.

Then again, she sort of knew what he meant. Provided he left her with her memory and full I.Q., she wasn't sure she was finished with him yet, either. There was so much more she wanted to know, to do, to experience, and he was at the center of it all—both personally and professionally speaking.

So instead of smacking him, she said, "What does that mean, exactly?"

"It means . . . I wish I'd met you long before now, under different circumstances. But since even vampires can't go back in time, we have to accept the way things are now and deal with them as they are."

Well, that was clear as mud. "Sorry, Dr. Phil, you'll have to elaborate. That made about as much sense as feathers on a fish."

He tightened his arm around her waist and nipped the lobe of her ear with his teeth. His fangs were less prominent now, so she barely felt them, but she certainly knew they were there.

"Don't be cheeky," he warned her. "I'm trying to open up and share, here. Not something men—or vampires—do very often."

"Not well, anyway," she quipped, which only earned her another nip with more fang and a tighter squeeze.

She grinned. She was actually beginning to enjoy this. The intimacy, the teasing . . . the openness he wasn't quite as bad at as he seemed to think.

But she wasn't just being playful; she really was confused about what he was trying to say.

"I still don't understand."

At her back, she felt his chest expand and contract as he took a deep breath, then let it out. "I don't feel right asking you this, given who—and what—I am. Given who you are, and what you do."

Her stomach gave a tiny lurch of nerves and anticipation. Was he leading up to what she thought he was leading up to? And if he was—how would she feel about that?

Dragging his wet fingers through her hair, he tugged her head sideways to rest on his shoulder, continuing to bathe her slowly, sensually with the damp cloth. "You're the first woman I've met in longer than I care to remember who I can imagine being with for any length of time."

"Your 'length of time' or mine?" she had to ask.

At the back of her head, she felt his shoulder lift in a shrug. "Either," he said carefully. And then, "Maybe both."

That made her stomach tumble even faster.

"What are you saying, Sebastian?"

Seconds ticked by with nothing but the slosh of water and her rapid breathing filling the giant room.

"I was thinking that maybe I wouldn't work my vampire mojo on you just yet. That you might like to stick around, see how things play out."

"Are you asking me to date you?" she only half-teased.

"Something like that," he returned, doing a bit of teasing

of his own by running the cloth suggestively between her legs. She gasped, arching against his seeking hand.

"The only problem is," he continued, "you couldn't write about me. Or talk about me to others. Ever."

He said it quietly, almost apologetically, and she fell a little bit more in love with him for it. Because, yes, she could admit it, if only to herself—she was pretty sure she was falling for him, big time.

The intellectual side of her brain told her that was ridiculous. He was a vampire, for God's sake, and she'd known him for barely twenty-four hours. True, she'd fallen into bed with him in the blink of an eye, but she blamed that, at least in part, on her long, self-imposed abstinence.

But the other side of her brain, the side directly connected to her heart, didn't care what he was or how short their acquaintance had been. She never wanted to leave his side, and it had nothing to do with the fact that he had more money than Bill Gates and Donald Trump stacked together. (Although the lush digs *were* a total turn-on.)

What he said was true, though. If he let her keep her memories, and they ventured into an honest to goodness relationship, there was no way she could write about him for the *Tattler*. No way she could reveal his deepest, darkest secret.

For one thing, she'd feel like a total schmuck, if she did. And for another, she could never hurt or betray someone she cared about that way.

"What are we talking about, here?" she needed to know. "Just not writing or talking about you as a vampire, or giving up my writing altogether?"

He shrugged again. "I think we'd have to reassess that as we go along. You definitely can't write about me, or let anyone know what Aidan and I really are, but I don't care what you write about otherwise."

She sat up like a shot, twisting around to face him. "Your brother is a vampire, too?"

For some reason—which now made her feel like a dolt—that had never occurred to her. Although, now that he mentioned it, it made perfect sense. How else would he have gotten a brother who looked so much like him at his age? Adoption? Cloning? Now, that would have made a good tabloid story!

"Of course," he told her with an indulgent smile tipping his lips. "What did you think?"

"I didn't," she admitted, falling back against him with a tiny huff. "In case you haven't noticed, I've been a little busy."

He tweaked her nipple, clamping his legs tighter on the outside of hers. "I've noticed. I'm hoping you'll be busy again very soon."

As much as she wanted that, too, there was no point rushing into more of the fun stuff until this decision had been officially made.

"What happens if we try to build a relationship and it doesn't work out?"

"I'll have to kill you, of course."

She jerked away from him again, sitting straight up. But before she could turn on him with wide, shocked eyes, he chuckled and tugged her back into place.

"I'm kidding. I haven't killed anyone in centuries."

She chose to believe he was kidding about that, too, though part of her suspected it might be the truth.

"I would simply wipe your mind, the same as I can do now, if you'd prefer. The longer we're together and the more you know, the harder it will be to erase all the pertinent details, but it can be done."

She thought about that for a minute. "So we can go at it as sort of a trial run. If it doesn't work out, no harm, no foul."

It was his turn to pause while he considered that. And when he finally responded, he didn't sound entirely chipper about the idea. "Yes."

She thought about that for more than a minute. About what her life had been like up to this point—her marriage to Matthew, watching him die, getting the job at the *Sin City Tattler* that kept her busy and distracted for eight long years.

Her relationship with her sister, who was apparently involved with a vampire, too, though she didn't think Chloe realized it. And her relationships with pretty much *no one* else.

Writing far-out stories on subjects most people knew were completely made up was the perfect occupation to keep her isolated and alone. Which was exactly what she'd thought she wanted for her life after losing Matthew.

But maybe that wasn't enough for her anymore. Maybe stepping out and doing something crazy, something different, something slightly dangerous, was the way to go.

Oh, she wasn't afraid of Sebastian, even knowing what he was. He would never hurt her, physically, of that she was absolutely certain.

But pain to her body and pain to her heart were two different things, and he *did* possess the power to break that heart in two if a relationship between them didn't work out.

Then she thought about what her life could be like if she stayed with him. Mind-blowing sex aside, she had to admit that the companionship alone would be nice. Having someone to talk to, snuggle with, wake up with in the . . . evening.

And while they'd already had quite a heart-to-heart, revealing more to one another in a single short night than most couples revealed in months or years, she felt as though there was so much more to learn about Sebastian. She wanted to know it all, even if she could never write about him or tell another living soul.

So was it worth the risk? Was she willing to give up her chance for the Big Time and put aside all the work she'd done to discover his true identity for a shot at a truly larger-than-life romance, and possibly true love?

It was a frightening leap to contemplate, and she'd never been nearly as daring or happy-go-lucky as her twin sister.

But her heart was pounding in her chest, and she could swear it was telling her to *say yes, say yes, say yes.*

She didn't say yes, but she did pull away, twisting and sending the now lukewarm water splashing against the sides of the wide tub until she could straddle him. He dropped the washcloth and gripped her hips, balancing her rear end on the tops of his slick thighs.

Wrapping her arms around his neck, she leaned in, pressing her breasts flat to his chest. With her lips mere centimeters from his, she stared into his steel-gray eyes. If she hadn't already decided on her answer, what she saw there would have made up her mind for her.

"Okay," she whispered. "This is the craziest thing I've ever done . . . but then, so is falling into bed with a vampire on the first date."

"It wasn't really a date," he corrected her, but he hugged her close while he said it. "More of a fact-finding mission."

She smiled. "Then I guess you owe me one. You can take me out to a movie and a late dinner."

"Or maybe you can accompany me to the charity dinner I agreed to attend next week. It doesn't start until ten p.m. and is a thousand dollars a plate. That's better than a box of popcorn at some boring Hollywood flick, right?"

She shrugged her shoulder. "I was going to make you buy me a soda and a box of Sno-Caps, too," she teased. And then, in a more serious tone, she asked, "Are you sure you want to take me out in public so soon? You're not known for being seen out and about very often, especially with women."

"Which is how those rumors started about my being gay," he quipped with a wry lift of his lips. "But, yes, I'm sure. You aren't just some temporary amusement for me, Charlotte."

Her nose wrinkled automatically and he corrected himself with a chuckle. "Chuck. You know, I'm not sure that's something I'll be able to get used to—calling you Chuck. And think how it will look in print when the papers start linking us together. 'Sebastian Raines and his lady love, Chuck.'" Shaking his head, he said, "I much prefer the sound of 'Sebastian and Charlotte Raines,' if you must know."

Raking her fingers through his hair, she cupped the back of his head and tipped it toward her. "Keep talking like that, referring to me as your 'lady love' and implying we might one

day be married, and you can call me anything you want."
Her heart was already skipping beats just thinking about it.

He grinned at her. "Good. Then come here, my lovely
Charlotte, and kiss me. We need to make good use of this
water before it gets any colder, and then we should probably
get dressed and see if we can track down your sister and my
brother. I have a feeling they're up to no good and headed for
total disaster."

"Oh, I don't know. If I can find love with the vampire of
my dreams, Chloe might just manage to do the same."

But she kissed him, anyway, and when they finished, the
water was both cold . . . and all over the expensive marble
floor.

Married . . . with Fangs

Ante Up

"I think Aidan might be the one."

Chloe's identical twin sister, Charlotte—Chuck for short—lifted her head to meet Chloe's eyes, but then ducked back down as Chloe raised the gigantic feathered and sequined headdress to place on her sister's head.

Although they'd both spent their lives in dance classes, Chloe was the only one who did it now professionally. She'd been a showgirl for the Inferno Hotel and Casino's dance revue club, Lust, going on almost ten years now.

Sigh. Time sure did fly when you were a single mother living from paycheck to paycheck. She was *so* ready to give up her stilettos and skintight costumes for a more reasonable nine-to-five.

Or better yet, the life of a stay-at-home mom. If she ever got such an opportunity—which she was hoping she would very, very soon—she swore she'd be the best little housewife ever. She would wear an apron and a string of pearls. She would dust and vacuum and starch her husband's collars, bake cookies and pot roasts and homemade bread.

Okay, so her idea of a home-cooked meal was walking in the door with Chinese takeout, and the only way she normally knew dinner was ready was if the smoke alarm went off. But she was willing to learn.

"'The One'?" Chuck asked, wincing as Chloe drove hairpins into her scalp to keep the "Flames of Hell" headdress in place. "Capital T, capital O?"

"Uh-huh."

"Aren't you moving kind of fast?"

Chloe's stomach dipped at her sister's question and the thought of what was going to happen later tonight.

Was it the right thing to do? She had no idea. A part of her was hugely excited about it, while the other was scared stupid.

But she'd made her decision, and had every intention of following through with it. It was what was best for Jake . . . and hopefully for herself.

Adopting a flippant attitude she didn't quite feel, she said, "You know my policy—the faster the better. And this one is on the hook."

On the hook and about to be reeled in. She just hoped *she* wasn't the one who ended up flopping around on deck, gasping for air.

"Just be careful, okay?" Chuck told her.

"I will," she promised. "You, too."

Taking a step back, she studied her sister, feeling as though she was looking in the mirror. Her sister was dressed from head to toe *as* Chloe, because tonight she *was* Chloe.

It might not be the smartest plan in the world, but Chuck had insisted she wanted to take Chloe's place onstage tonight. They ran through Chloe's dance routine together on a regular basis—Chloe for her job, and Chuck simply for the exercise. (She had a small addiction to chocolate that she was trying to keep from settling for too long on her hips.)

Chloe wasn't worried about Chuck messing up as much as she was about her sister getting caught. If that happened, Chloe honestly didn't know what the ramifications might be. She could lose her job, and Chuck could go to jail, she supposed. Or at least be charged with . . . something.

But the more dangerous part of Chuck's plan was that she intended to stalk the Inferno's elusive owner, Sebastian Raines. The man was richer than triple-layer chocolate fudge cake, oozed charm like a sieve, and had danger written all over him. Even Chloe, who felt as though she spent ninety percent of her life at the Inferno, had only seen him a handful of times. And each of those times, he'd been surrounded by bodyguards who looked as though they'd recently escaped from the gorilla enclosure at the local zoo.

And her sister—intrepid tabloid reporter, more used to making up stories about potato chips popping up in the shape of dead celebrities or religious figures—had gotten it into her head to break through the veil of secrecy surrounding the casino mogul and prove that "something was up with him." She hadn't given Chloe a clue of what she suspected that something might be, but she'd been adamant about going through with her nefarious plan.

Chloe was concerned about her sister, but also knew Chuck could take care of herself. She wasn't about to pass up the opportunity for a night off, either—with pay. Especially since Chuck's plans just happened to play in perfectly with her own.

So she'd been more than happy to sneak Chuck backstage and help her wiggle into her "Flames of Hell" costume. The sheer stockings with the dark lines running up the back; the red-and-orange sequined body suit; the tall, feathered and sequined headdress. Not to mention the glitter eye shadow, long fake eyelashes, and enough sparkling rhinestone jewelry to wave in a fleet of 747s.

"If anyone finds out what you're doing and why . . ." she began, feeling the need to warn her sister one last time of the consequences of going through with this.

"They won't," Chuck insisted. "We're identical, remember? We used to do this all the time in school. I can pretend to be you almost as well as I pretend to be me."

They both chuckled, remembering all the fun they used to have as kids, trading places and convincing people they were the other twin. Everyone but their mother; the single mother and former showgirl herself had always been much too street smart to fall for her daughters' antics.

A shout from the dressing room on the other side of the bathroom door made them both jump. Their eyes met, and Chloe knew Chuck's heart had to be pounding as hard as her own.

"Showtime," Chloe said.

She gave Chuck a final once-over, checking the makeup, the jewelry, the headdress, the fit of the costume, and the straps of the high-high platform heels.

"All right," she said, blowing out a breath. "Break a leg."

Her sister winced, and she immediately regretted her choice of words. But they were good luck and might actually keep her from doing so literally, so she didn't take them back.

"You go out first," she told her, hand on the knob, "and I'll hide here until the coast is clear."

With a final hug, Chloe saw Chuck out, then locked herself back in the broom closet of a bathroom, listening to the stampeding *clack-clack-clack* of heels as dancers rushed toward the stage, the stage director's shouted orders, and the strains of the music *she* was usually out there shaking her money-maker to.

She loved being a dancer, really she did, but being a *show-girl* lifted the term to a whole new level. She and the other girls she danced with were all extremely talented. They could have danced on Broadway, if they'd wanted.

But working nights, in the heart of one of Las Vegas's most popular adult casinos—as opposed to those that catered to children in an effort to be family friendly and bring in even more tourist dollars—meant that people made a lot of assumptions about her character. Especially people of the male persuasion, who thought the word "showgirl" was synonymous with "high-priced hooker" and spent more time ogling her boobs than paying attention to what was taking place onstage.

It was to be expected. As were the pinches to her more-bare-than-not bottom and being propositioned multiple times a night. Even if she wasn't in costume, wasn't even on the clock, once folks found out she was a showgirl, she often got the exact same treatment.

It had been fine for a while. Her mother had been a showgirl, so long before she'd ever balanced her first thousand-pound headdress, she'd known what to expect. And some of it was even enjoyable. The attention. The flattery. The parties. The flowers and gifts that often showed up at her dressing table from not-so-secret admirers.

But things were different now. She was getting older, as were her knees and ankles and every other joint in her body.

And she had a little boy to think about. Kids hadn't been part of the plan—at least not in the short run—and her relationship with his father hadn't lasted much longer than it had taken her to get pregnant, but Jake was the love of her life. One of those things you didn't know you wanted or needed until it was thrust upon you. Which was why she could call him a surprise, but never an accident or a mistake.

Having a child made her rethink her priorities, though . . . and her future. Her family was great about Jake, and hugely supportive of her, despite some of the less-than-stellar choices she'd made. Her mother—retired now and living in Henderson—kept him overnight while Chloe was at work. And Chuck was not only her back-up sitter, but the world's greatest aunt. Between the three of them, it was a wonder Jake wasn't spoiled rotten.

But she was tired of dropping him off at her mother's every night, then being too worn out most of the day to give him the attention he deserved.

She was tired of feeling guilty that her son's only influences were women, and worrying about whether or not he missed—and needed—a good male role model.

And some days, she was just plain tired.

But all that was about to change. If tonight went as she hoped, she would soon have a husband for herself, a father for Jake, and enough money to make the need to dance ancient history.

Ace

Once she was sure everybody was onstage and the dressing room was empty, Chloe cracked open the bathroom door and slipped out. Sneaking over to her section of the long, lighted makeup table, she grabbed her small clutch purse, checked the drawer for anything else she might need, and hightailed it out of there, taking the back exit so no one would see her.

Of course, even if they did, she would merely claim to be her sister. As far as the rest of the world was concerned, she was onstage right now, shaking her feathered booty in front of a hundred-odd witnesses. And the way she was dressed, she didn't think anyone would suspect otherwise.

Where Chloe was a girly-girl, always madeup and perfectly coiffed, going for the fancy and frilly over sensible, Chuck was the opposite. Chuck went for simplicity above everything else; easy wash-and-go hairstyle, jeans and tees, and very little to no makeup. Oh, she cleaned up nice. *Real* nice, if her gorgeous, *identical* twin sister did say so herself, but only when absolutely necessary.

It had been kind of a thrill to dress her tonight, and spackle on about ten pounds of makeup. She wondered if Chuck knew how to get it all off when the time came, and made a mental note to leave a message on her cell, just in case.

So while Chuck was dressed like Chloe right now, in walking Sin City Barbie attire, Chloe was dressed like Chuck. Faded low-rider jeans, low-heeled ankle boots, and a black baby doll tee with the slogan *I'll try to be nicer if you try to be smarter* emblazoned across the front.

Taking a lesser-used entrance/exit at the rear of the club, she made her way out of Lust and onto the main floor of the casino. As usual, the place was bustling. Slot machines dinging and whirring, cards being shuffled and dealt, chips being laid down or collected, and scantily-clad waitresses in their short red skirts and devil horn headbands zipping around taking orders and delivering drinks.

The whole place was wired, cameras in the ceiling and security people milling around looking like Secret Service wannabes. There were a few dressed in street clothes, too, she knew, blending in with the crowd and keeping an even closer eye on Sebastian Raines's million-dollar interests.

But it didn't matter who saw her now. Not only did she fit in perfectly with the gamblers littering the floor, but she was on her way out, and no one really cared what guests were doing unless money, cheating, or impending violence were involved.

Wending through the casino, she headed for the hotel's main lobby, and straight out the front doors, avoiding the bellmen and other Inferno employees as much as possible. Vehicles came and went beneath the wide portico, making it easy for her to slink along the side of the building and onto the sidewalk.

She only had to go a couple of blocks. Even though Aidan's brother owned the Inferno, and he could come and go as he pleased, they'd agreed to meet down the street so fewer people would be likely to see them together. Aidan was too identifiable, and his presence tended to draw a crowd.

Tonight of all nights, she did *not* want to draw a crowd. Not until the deed was done and she had the younger Raines brother's ring firmly on her finger.

Skirting a group of boisterous fraternity boys who were whistling and sending cat calls in her direction, Chloe spotted

Aidan's sleek black Ferrari Scuderia Spider idling at the curb, and a wide smile stretched across her face.

He always made her smile. From the moment she'd met him—backstage after one of her performances—his carefree demeanor had kept her laughing and made *her* feel carefree for the first time in a long time. Being with him was easy, and she hoped it stayed that way, because she intended to be with him for a while to come.

Not for the first time, she wondered if she should have told him about Jake, introduced him to her son, and waited to see how they got along before thrusting them together indefinitely. But she was too nervous, too afraid that if she did that, everything would fall apart and she would lose her shot at the future she was trying to create for her son.

Reaching the snazzy sports car, she climbed into the passenger seat and leaned in for a long, liquid kiss. He kissed like a dream. And Chloe should know; she'd kissed a lot of frogs before finding this prince, and none of them could hold a candle to Aidan's lips—soft and smooth, but firm and masterful. Or his tongue—bold and seeking. Or his hands, which always seemed to be involved in his kisses, touching her, stroking her, soothing her.

When they parted, they were both grinning.

"How'd it go?" Aidan asked.

"Fine. Chuck's onstage now. I hope she's okay."

As far as he knew, Chuck had agreed to take her place so she could skip work and slip off to meet him. She hadn't filled him in on the fact that this whole thing had actually been Chuck's idea, giving Chloe the unexpected opportunity to get away without being missed.

"If she's half as talented as you are, she'll be fine."

Her limbs went warm and loose at his words. Oh, he was a charmer, all right. She just hoped he stayed that way, instead of being one of those men who was all sweet and kind before the wedding vows, then turned angry and controlling after them.

"Are you ready, then?"

Butterflies broke through their cocoons inside her stom-ach, flapping around and sending her pulse rate skittering. Was it excitement or trepidation? Or maybe just plain old generalized anxiety?

She nodded, and he offered her another dazzling smile that flashed a hint of dimple at each cheek. Checking the flow of traffic behind them, he waited for an opening before putting the car in gear and peeling out. Once his hand was free, he reached for hers and held it as they tooled down The Strip, wind blowing her loose hair into a tangled mess.

Before she knew it, he was slowing down and pulling in to the Little Blue Chapel—which was, as the name suggested, little and blue. And it looked like a chapel, small and square, with stained-glass windows, a steeple on top, and a short set of steps leading inside.

From the moment they'd concocted their plan, Chloe had let Aidan make all the arrangements. She didn't care where they did this, she just wanted it done before he had a chance to change his mind. So Little Blue Chapel, Chapel o' Love, or Hank's All-Nite Fish Fry—she didn't have a preference, as long as it did the trick.

Still, when he cut the engine and turned in her direction, she shot him a "really?" look.

He shrugged. "You told me to pick one, and as long as we're doing it this way, we're going to do it right. Vegas style," he added with a teasing wink.

They climbed out of the car, and he met her on her side be-fore she'd even gotten the door closed. Then he took her hand again and led her inside.

The Little Blue Chapel was known for its theme of "all things Elvis," especially of the "Blue Suede Shoes" persua-sion. The chapel itself was covered in blue aluminum siding, followed by blue walls, blue carpeting, and blue curtains sep-arating the vestibule from the main ceremonial room.

"Well, hi, there," a woman dressed in—you guessed it—blue chiffon greeted them with a wide, toothy smile. Her light blond, blue-washed hair was blown up into one of the biggest poofs Chloe had ever seen, a la Priscilla Presley, circa 1967 or 1970.

"We're here for the Raines-Lamoreaux ceremony," Aidan told her, obviously loving all the pomp and circumstance.

"Monroe," she corrected with a tug at his arm. If she was going to do this without being entirely sure it was the smartest thing in the world, she was going to make sure it was legally binding.

"Right, right," he agreed, then told the hostess, "Aidan Raines and Chloe *Monroe*."

The woman nodded and started digging around in her paperwork. "We've got you right here," she said, coming around a counter covered in Elvis memorabilia—movie posters, photographs, magazine covers.

"The first thing we need to do is get you changed. You step right in there and pick an outfit," she told Aidan, pointing to a door marked LITTLE BOYS. Then she took Chloe by the elbow and tugged her toward one that said LITTLE LADIES. "And we'll get you all decked out in a beautiful new gown."

Chloe let the woman lead her away with only a quick, backward glance at Aidan. She found herself in a room the size of a small closet, already half filled by a long rack of assorted wedding gowns.

It came as quite a surprise to discover that most of them were actually white. She would have expected blue. But apparently, the Little Blue Chapel was fully traditional—in this sense, at least. Priscilla had been married in white, so they wanted to give their customers that same option. But there were also a few off-white, and yes, blue, dresses to choose from, as well.

The hostess pulled gown after gown from the rack, holding each up to Chloe's neck in front of a full-length mirror tacked to the wall. And though she gave Chloe plenty of time to insert her own comments, Chloe got the feeling this was really the other woman's show, and she would wind up being married in whichever dress the Priscilla-wannabe found most fitting.

Sure enough, a moment later, she crowed, "Perfect!" and began helping Chloe strip down to her bra and undies. In five minutes flat, Chloe found herself standing in a pair of size eight, two-inch pumps—she wore sevens and would have preferred three inches, at least—and a high-waisted white gown with thin spaghetti straps and just a sprinkling of decorative beading across the front. The gown, too, was a size too large, but the other woman fixed that with a set of safety pins she pulled out of Chloe-didn't-know-where.

"Now wait here," the woman instructed after fiddling with her hair and attaching a lightweight veil with a pair of tiny combs.

The woman slipped out, and Chloe could hear her next-door, *ooh*ing and *aah*ing over Aidan's appearance, then hustling him into—oddly enough—the staging area. Something Chloe was more than familiar with.

Chloe stood there, heart pounding, palms sweating, as she studied her reflection. She looked like a bride. Maybe not a giddy, one-hundred-percent willing bride, but she was passable enough. And she would look good in the pictures, that was for sure.

"All right, dear," the woman said opening the door and ushering her out. "We're ready for you."

A moment later, "Love Me Tender"—but, of course!—began to play over hidden speakers, and a bouquet of blue and white artificial roses was thrust into her hands. She clutched them like a lifeline, squeezing until real flowers would have wilted and died.

Then the curtains were drawn back and she was shoved into the heart of the chapel, a room filled with more blue flowers, a blue carpeted aisle, and three parallel rows of short, white benches designed like church pews.

At the other end of the aisle stood Aidan, looking eerily like a young, handsome Elvis Presley. He wore a powder blue jumpsuit, open at the throat and covered with large rhinestones in various colors leading down to the wide, bell-bottomed ankles. When he noticed her perusal, he winked, then adopted a very Elvis-like pose, complete with curled lip and raised eyebrow.

She couldn't help but chuckle, and when Priscilla nudged her in the small of the back, she started down the aisle with only a twinge of trepidation. When she reached his side, Aidan took her arm and twined it with his own, then turned them both to face the minister, who was dressed in full, over-the-top, Elvis garb.

His jumpsuit was black, and stretched almost beyond endurance to cover his heavy bulk. His hair was shoe polish black and about as real as most of the boobs she danced with onstage each night.

Hers were *au naturel*, thank you, thank you very much, but most of her fellow dancers went the saline and silicone pump-up route. The largely male audience liked them, and an oversize rack was definitely easier to see from a distance. Not to mention a beacon for off-the-books tips and offerings of jewelry.

But the minster's obvious rug was styled into a giant, glossy pompadour that would have made The King proud. All of that, added to the man's natural flabbiness and heavy jowls, definitely put him well into the "Old Elvis" column.

He smiled widely, though, and welcomed them both to the—insert well-known Elvis drawl—Little Blue Chapel, then launched into a long, theatrical speech about love and romance and the sanctity of marriage.

Chloe's stomach somersaulted again at the knowledge that she wasn't going into this with the purest of motives. Not where Aidan's feelings were concerned, anyway.

Then the questions began. *Do you take this woman . . . ?* Yadda, yadda, yadda. And Aidan answered every one with a firm, decisive, "I do."

The minister turned to her. "Do you take this man . . . ?" Yadda—*gulp*—yadda—*gulp*—yadda—*gulp*.

She opened her mouth. Closed it. Opened it again, and the words came out.

"Yes. I mean, I do."

And again . . . "I do."

And again . . . "I do."

Aidan lifted her left hand and slipped a pair of rings on her finger that she hadn't even known he had. She would have thought he'd bought them here, tonight, since a display in the lobby area made it clear wedding bands were available for sale on the spot.

But she'd spent enough time in Vegas, enough time being wooed by men with more money than brains, to know the difference between fake gold and diamonds and the real thing. These rings—unless her eyes and the dull fluorescent lighting deceived her—were the *very* real thing, with a capital G, capital D.

The gold of the bands was traditional yellow, polished to a high gleam, while the diamond of the surprise engagement ring was not only gigantic—three carats was her best, on-the-spot guesstimate—but clear as a summer's day and sparkling in every one of its four million princess-cut facets.

Chloe swallowed hard. If the vows hadn't scared her enough and made reality sink in with a bone-deep chill, this certainly did the trick. This was not some cheap wedding set picked up on the fly at some—ha!—all-night chapel on The Strip. Money had gone into these. Big money, along with time and thought and emotional consideration.

Oh, God.

Once the rings were fit snugly on her hand, Aidan smiled and gave her fingers an encouraging squeeze. She hoped he didn't notice how cold they were, or realize that the iciness was *not* due entirely to typical bridal jitters.

Then he held out a matching band, the masculine version of her own. Her free hand shook as she took it from him and placed it on his left ring finger.

The reverend pronounced them husband and wife, invited the groom to kiss his bride, and the deal was done. Solidly, legally, irrevocably done.

As Aidan leaned in to brush his mouth against hers, she took a deep breath and let it out slowly. It was over. Everything had gone exactly as planned. No bumps, no kinks, no one running in at the last minute to scream their objections.

And now she was officially the wife of one of the richest men in Nevada. She was Mrs. Aidan Raines.

Two

H e was married. Aidan couldn't believe it.
Everything had gone off without a hitch, too, which
surprised him no little bit. He'd held his breath the whole
time, waiting for Sebastian to burst through the curtained
doorway and call a halt to the entire ceremony.

His brother's stance was that he was being foolish, rushing
into something with a woman he'd known for only a month.
But if anyone should understand that time was relative, it
was Sebastian. They had been around for hundreds of years,
been *through* things together that most mortal siblings couldn't
even fathom.

But Aidan knew his own heart, and his heart was telling
him that Chloe was the woman for him. She was beautiful,
and smart, and funny . . . and the fact that she looked freaking amazing both in her Lust costumes and out didn't hurt,
either.

Sebastian was too stern, too wrapped up in making money
and keeping their identities as vampires a secret. He needed
to loosen up a bit. Maybe find a woman of his own that he
could open up to, snuggle down with, and *not* zap with his
vampire mojo as soon as they were finished doing the nasty.

But who was he kidding? Sebastian was too set in his ways
to lighten up enough to really get to know a woman. To fall
in love.

Aidan, he was happy to say, was not. He loved love. Chloe

was the first woman he'd really fallen for in the last couple decades, but before meeting her, he'd still sowed his fair share of wild oats and been open to getting to know as many lovelies as possible. And in a town like Las Vegas, there were almost too many to count.

Blondes, brunettes, redheads. Leggy, busty, bootylicious. He'd always been a very open-minded guy, and didn't have a preference. He liked them all.

But Chloe . . . ah, his beautiful Chloe put them all to shame. It hadn't been her tits, her ass, or her high kicks that had caught his attention that first night he'd watched her perform at Lust. It had been her smile and the youthful exuberance glittering in her violet eyes.

People—especially performers—aged fast in Sin City. Hard living just didn't sit well with human beings. But from the moment he'd met her, it had been obvious to Aidan that Chloe loved her job and loved life.

For someone like him, who had been there, done that in just about every way possible for centuries, she was a breath of fresh air, and it hadn't taken him long to realize he wanted to spend the rest of his life (such as it was) with her.

No, he hadn't yet confessed to her that he was a vampire. He should have, he knew, but he was a little unsure of the dating protocol where something that monumental was concerned.

First date—kiss on the cheek. Second date, kiss on the lips. Third date, full French and a little over-the-shirt action. Fifth date, hot, sweaty monkey sex, if both parties were willing. Was it the eighth date when he was safe to say, "Hey, hon, I forgot to mention that I'm a vampire. I drink blood, can't go out in the sun, and when we sixty-nine, it's all I can do not to bite you in the femoral artery."

Eighth, twelfth, two hundred and second . . . He just hadn't worked up to it yet.

But it wouldn't matter. She loved him, and now they were hitched.

He'd managed to keep his fangs hidden from her—even

though simply being near her got him hard as a spike, which brought his fangs out even faster than desperate hunger—as well as his need for liquid sustenance and aversion to sunlight. Not terribly difficult when she worked nights and most of the time they were together was spent horizontally. Or vertically, but also bare-ass naked.

Other than going for drinks at Dante's, the Inferno's most popular on-site cocktail bar, after a show, he didn't think he'd ever actually taken her out for a meal or to a movie.

Hmm, he should probably rectify that now that they were man and wife. Men did things with their wives other than boinking twenty-four/seven, didn't they? He might even have to take her shopping and hold her purse while she tried stuff on.

Shifting a glance to where Chloe sat beside him, he reached across the Spider's console to take her hand—her left hand, the one with his rings adorning her slim finger. She lifted her head and offered him a soft smile, and it was all he could do not to pull over, drag her onto his lap, and take her right then and there.

They were back on The Strip, headed in the opposite direction as to when he'd first picked her up. He zipped past his brother's casino without a second glance.

He had a suite of rooms there, just like Sebastian, but had never taken Chloe to them. They were too close to his brother's, too risky. The last thing he needed while in the middle of an intimate and X-rated seduction was to have his brother burst in, lecturing about what a mistake he was making spending time with a lowly showgirl—and a mortal one, to boot.

So instead, he was taking her to his *other* place. He didn't think Sebastian knew about it, but that didn't mean he couldn't find out in the blink of an eye.

Still, Aidan thought it would be a safe enough spot for them to stay for a while.

A few minutes later, he steered his Ferrari into the underground parking garage of The Heights, his very own upscale apartment building. His brother might think he was capricious, needing to be taken care of and watched over like a green adolescent, but he wasn't entirely dependent or without business acumen. He'd learned enough from Sebastian, at least, to put away a little money of his own and actually build this place from the ground up.

Which was how he'd managed to design an extra-large living space *under* the underground garage. It was just as luxurious as any of the other apartments the building had to offer—maybe even more so, since he was the one holding the purse strings—but with zero risk of sunlight entering, and special key cards and fingerprint authorization required to get inside.

Easing into his reserved space, he let go of Chloe's hand so he could turn off the engine and pocket the keys. Then he went around the rear of the car to open her door and help her out. The wind had blown her long, chestnut hair in all directions, making her look as though she'd just been thoroughly tumbled. It made him want to tumble her, right here in the parking garage.

He could do it, too. There was no one around. The place was completely deserted, and if anyone did show up, he'd know it long before they got close enough to see anything.

Moving in, grinning like an idiot, he crowded her, backing her up against the Spider's front side panel. She leaned away at first, almost nervously, as though trying to avoid him. Then she shook her head and smiled, lifting her hands to his shoulders.

Bodies pressed together from chest to thigh, he brushed her nose with his, and then settled in for a long, hot, wet kiss. This was the kiss he'd wanted to give her back at the Little Blue Chapel, right after the preacher had told him he could kiss his bride. He'd wanted to sweep her back over his arm and taste her, eat her, devour her. Only their audience of Grampa Elvis and Grandma Priscilla had precluded the consummation of their marriage right then and there.

But they didn't have an audience now. They were all alone, with nothing to stop him from taking her the way he wanted.

Deepening the kiss, he bent her backwards, tugging the hem of her snug black T-shirt from the waistband of her jeans so he could feel the warm, smooth skin of her abdomen. Running his palms up her ribcage, he cupped her breasts through the lacy material of her bra.

She moaned, and for the first time began to actively kiss him back. Her own hands went to his belt, unbuckling the thin length of expensive leather, but not pulling it free of its loops. Instead, she undid the top of his slacks, her knuckles brushing the tip of his straining erection.

His hips arched toward her touch, but before he could make contact a second time, she took her hands away, going to work on the buttons of his shirt. She had it open in a matter of seconds, pushing the sides apart to stroke his bare chest.

It was all he could do not to whimper. Grasping her waist, he lifted her onto the car's hood, nudging her knees apart and stepping between them. He pressed his hard-on into the notch of her thighs. Even through the layers of their clothing, he could feel her heat, the pulse of her longing.

In seconds, he'd pushed her shirt up and over her breasts, dragging the cups of the bra with it, leaving her gloriously bare to his gaze and his hands and his mouth. Her nipples were dark raspberries, tightened with pleasure, and he wasted no time rolling them between his fingertips, snagging them with the pads of his thumbs.

Her own hands were busy at his crotch, one sliding inside his pants to cup his cock, the other lowering his zipper. She toyed with him through his cotton briefs, squeezing, stroking, running *her* thumb across the sensitive tip. He sucked in a breath, pressing himself more firmly into her hold.

He was about to go to work on her pants, pull them down just enough to get inside her, when he heard the hum of an engine, the squeak of tires. They were still far off in the distance, just entering the garage at the other end of the building, but it still wasn't safe to be here. The last thing he needed was for headlights to whip around and spotlight their carnal activities.

With a muttered curse, he broke their kiss and reluctantly—so damn reluctantly—pulled Chloe's hand from his pants. Blinking in confusion, she merely stared at him.

"Car," he said by way of apology. "Come on."

Not bothering to straighten his own clothes, he tugged her shirt back down to cover her—*groan*—gorgeous breasts, then took her hand and led her a short distance to his private elevator. Instead of going up to the lobby or other levels of the building where apartments were located, this one went down and led to only one destination—his place.

Using his personal key card to call the elevator, the doors opened and he guided her inside. His key card got the doors open, but the only way to get the car to move was with a thumbprint. *His* thumbprint.

He pressed it to the I.D. panel, making a mental note to update the system with Chloe's print, as well. After all, she was his wife now, and would be living here with him. He wanted her to be able to come and go as she pleased.

It took just a few seconds for the car to glide down to the sub-basement level and the doors to open on his private living quarters. Much like Sebastian's top-floor penthouse, Aidan's apartment took up the entire lower floor of the building and contained everything he could ever need or want. Gourmet kitchen, large living room area, a handful of bedrooms and bathrooms, an office, home theatre, even a workout room and sauna, though he didn't use them nearly as often as a human male might.

The only thing it lacked was windows. There wasn't a single one in the entire place. Instead, he'd used a number of paintings and pieces of artwork to decorate the walls, and bright colors for the walls to give the illusion of daylight and access to the outdoors.

"Wow."

As he'd hoped, Chloe seemed impressed by what she saw. She was tucked up against him, his arm wrapped snugly around her waist, their clothes still tellingly askew.

"You like?" he asked, smiling proudly.

"It's . . . great," she offered slowly, her gaze still taking in the unique construction and expensive décor. "But where are we?"

"My place. The secret one no one knows about." Leaning in, he nuzzled her hair and pressed his lips to the side of her throat.

"Like the Bat Cave."

He chuckled. She didn't know how right she was. And he was inordinately proud that she'd picked up on the fact that they'd come down instead of going up, and that there was no view other than the ones a handful of local art galleries had provided.

"Something like that."

Turning her toward him, he hugged her close, opening his mouth over the pulse of her neck. "Mind if I give you the grand tour later? Right now, I have a few more important things on my mind."

Rather than answer, she wound her arms around his neck, driving her fingers into the hair at his nape. Then she pressed herself fully against him from pelvis to breastbone and lifted a leg to hitch over his left hip.

With a groan, he cupped her ass with both hands and scooped her up, taking her mouth as he turned for the master bedroom. He didn't need lights or even open eyes to navigate his apartment. If his vampire super-senses hadn't been enough to guide him, his familiarity with the floor plan and every stick of furniture would be.

Tongues tangled and sparred as he carried her to his bed. The crux of her thighs rode him the same way he hoped she would ride him when he had her naked and writhing above him.

His bed was king size and low to the ground, covered in a

plain beige coverlet. He dropped her to the center of it, following her down, sending the mattress bouncing.

Picking up where they'd left off on the hood of his car, he began stripping her of her clothes. Too many of them. Too many arm holes, neck holes, leg holes, buttons, and zippers, all working against him to keep her dressed when he desperately wanted her *un*dressed. He yanked her shirt up and over her head, and she lifted her arms to help him, dark hair spilling out around her as she fell back against the bed.

Next he dealt with her bra, unsnapping the hooks at the back and drawing the straps down her arms. It wasn't the first time he'd seen her bare breasts; not by a long shot. But still the sight of them had his diaphragm clenching, his gums throbbing around his already rapidly descending fangs.

Careful not to let her see his razor-sharp incisors, he said, "Have I ever told you how much I love your tits?"

Her nose wrinkled. She hated that word, which was why he enjoyed teasing her with it. And she knew he meant it in the most reverent of ways.

"You, and every guy who's ever walked into Lust during one of my shows."

"Yes, but I'm the only one who gets to see them in all their naked glory," he told her, cupping them in his hands and pressing them together. "Or feel them. Or taste them. Ever again."

With that, he lowered his head and took one of the plump, ripe points into his mouth. She had beautiful breasts, big enough to fill a man's hands, but not so big that she looked like she was about to topple over. They were also full and pert, sitting high on her chest in a way that usually required plastic surgery.

He suckled one nipple, tracing the tight flesh of her areola and rolling the gumdrop tip with the flat of his tongue. When she arched beneath him, her breath growing choppy, he moved to the other and gave it equal treatment.

"Aidan," she panted, tugging at his hair. But he didn't stop, so she decided to fight dirty.

Releasing his head, she put her hands at his waist and started tugging at his slacks. This time, as she pushed them down, the briefs went with them. She released his cock and balls, left his ass bare, and then used her feet to wiggle the pants lower so her hands would be left free. She used them to grip him, tug him, drive him crazy.

With a gasp, he abandoned her breast and glanced between their bodies to see her long, nimble fingers playing him like a flute. He would have called foul, but it felt too damn good. Besides, he intended to play foul soon enough, too.

Kicking off his shoes, he shrugged out of his already unbuttoned shirt, then his pants and underwear before going to work on hers. He flipped open the front snap of her jeans and lowered the zipper, hooking his fingers into the waistband to drag them off.

Her shoes took some time to deal with. Normally, she wore heels, the strappier and sexier, the better. The kind that slipped right off. But since she'd dressed like her sister tonight, not only were her clothes less revealing, her shoes were of the pedestrian variety. Plain white tennis shoes that took a bit of hard-won dexterity to untie.

Once they were gone, it was easier to peel away the denim and scrap of material that made up her thong underwear.

And then she was naked.

They were both naked.

Three

Grasping her elbows, he tugged her up, reveling in the feel of her bare breasts pressed to his bare chest; her soft, bare stomach pressed to his hard bare abdomen; her bare (*really* bare—waxed to glossy perfection) mound pressed to the length of his rigid, almost painful erection.

He kissed her lightly, smoothed a hand down the line of her delicate spine into the cleft of her buttocks. She shivered at his touch, and he wasn't far behind.

"Turn around," he murmured, pleased when she did so immediately, without a word, without trepidation.

Climbing onto the mattress behind her, he knee-walked them closer to the center of the bed to give them more room to maneuver, then tugged her back against him once more. With one hand, he cupped her breast, the other hand trailing down the center of her slim torso.

While his mouth nipped and nibbled at her throat, his fingers dipped into her damp, feminine folds. Chloe sucked in a breath and stiffened against him as he cruised over her tight little clitoris. He held her more firmly and continued his erotic exploration, adding the tweaking of her taut nipple to the mix.

He loved the feel of her, all warm and supple like pulled taffy, as well as the scent of hot, highly aroused woman. Finding her center, he slowly teased the opening with two rough fingertips, stirring her juices, preparing her for his entry, both now and later.

Filling her to the first knuckle, he twisted his fingers, enjoying the sound of her hitched breaths and the cushion of her swollen, sensitized flesh. At her neck, he sucked gently, giving her a small hickey of the innocuous human variety.

What he really wanted, though, was to taste her there. To sink his fangs, which were pulsing in tandem with the throb of his cock, into her skin and the tiny vein lying beneath, pumping all that delicious blood to her heart and through the entire rest of her anatomy.

He already knew how she would taste. His heightened senses took him well past the sexy floral fragrance of her favorite perfume—lilies and ginger and a touch of honey—to what lay beneath. The way she tasted when they made love—tart and musky and feminine—would carry into her bloodstream, along with that wonderful copper tang.

He craved it, just as much as he craved being inside her, stroking them both to a quivering, mind-blowing climax. But to have her body and her blood at the same time . . .

He shuddered, driving his fingers even deeper so that she clenched around him. Now *that* would be ecstasy.

Promising himself he wouldn't bite, wouldn't even come close, he ran his teeth over her in the direction *opposite* to what it would take to break the skin. He knew the sharp tips would scratch, but they wouldn't do any damage, and *damn* did it feel good.

Between her legs, he drove his fingers deep, as far as they would go. His thumb rode her clit while he pressed into all that soft, tender tissue, searching for her G-spot and knowing he found it when she gave a sharp cry.

With his hard cock rubbing into her buttocks, he fucked her with his hand, playing with her breasts, rolling that swollen, overly sensitive nub, and nibbling at her neck like a starving vampire.

In only seconds, she came with a scream no one but he

would ever hear. She arched against him, spasmed around his fingers, and nearly took him straight over the edge right along with her.

Drawing his hips away just in time, he managed to hold back. Barely. He waited for her to calm before tipping her head and kissing her sweet, rosy lips.

"Bend forward," he commanded, knowing full well she was too loose and wrung out to do anything else once he let go of her.

Grabbing the pillows from the headboard, he folded one in half and tucked it under her belly. The other he used to cushion her head and chest.

Poor darling was so sated, she draped herself across both without a word, practically without a breath. And he should know—he only used his lungs out of long habit and to keep from freaking out mortals who might notice his chest hadn't moved in an hour and a half—but he tended to be very aware of other people's breathing habits.

"You aren't falling asleep on me, are you?" he teased.

She rolled her head on the pillow and gave a muffled, "No."

He grinned. He didn't quite believe her, but in a minute, she would once again be wide awake. Guaranteed.

Staring down at her delectable ass, he grabbed the twin porcelain globes and gave them a squeeze. Chloe made a noise partway between a grunt and a sigh, and his smile got even wider. She really was adorable.

And sexy as hell.

He flicked the tip of one fang with his tongue. They were throbbing like the dickens. Fully extended . . . longer than he could ever remember them being.

The same could be said for his dick. Baseball bats, marble pillars, and railroad spikes all came to mind.

Taking one hand from her buttocks, he gripped himself, squeezing near the base and then stroking slowly upward. Tempting fate, to be sure. At the same time, he smoothed his fingers through her crease, finding her creamy moisture and running it up and down.

She was plenty wet. More than ready for him. And he was certainly ready for her.

Normally, they used a condom. It wasn't necessary—he could no more give her something than he could catch it from her, and vampires were notoriously disease-free. But she didn't know that, and since he hadn't yet told her he *was* a vampire, there was no other way to convince her that her idea of safe sex was redundant.

Just trying to weasel out of using a rubber would have made him sound like . . . well, a weasel, and she probably would have run a hundred miles an hour in the other direction. He didn't want to be that guy. Even though it was an added step and an added barrier neither of them needed, he wasn't willing to come across as being even remotely unconcerned about her health and welfare.

So he'd suited up like a good little boy each and every time they'd been together.

This time, though, he'd already given her a nice, head-spinning climax that had left her drowsy and satisfied. And she was facing the other direction, which meant she wouldn't know whether he'd donned protection or not.

Oh, there would be plenty of explaining to do later, especially given the pink, blood-tinted stain his semen would leave on her thighs, but he'd planned to tell her everything at some point this evening, anyway. So there was no time like . . . a couple of hours from now.

Nudging her legs apart with his knee, he used his damp hand to spread her wetness over his cock and balls. Then he moved closer, lining up his plump, swollen tip with her slick opening.

She moaned and arched her hips slightly. He eased in, first just an inch, and then another and another.

Soon, Chloe was pushing herself up to her elbows, then onto her hands. He heard her still-silent breathing speed up and felt the tension growing in her muscles and tendons.

"I love you, you know," he told her, gathering up the long, loose strands of her hair and draping them down the center of her spine.

Her response was a low, guttural groan. One he reciprocated wholeheartedly.

With a single forward thrust, he buried himself to the hilt, closing his eyes on the tight, wet heat that surrounded him. He moaned. Took short, shallow breaths, even though it was a totally human thing to do.

Chloe wiggled her behind, making him grit his teeth.

"God, you feel good," he ground out.

Panting, she dropped her head and curled her fingers into the bedclothes. "Stop being cruel, Aidan. For God's sake, *move!*"

Oh, she didn't know from cruel. Not really. But he intended to show her pleasure.

Grasping her hips, he pulled out almost all the way, then glided back in. Withdrew and pressed forward, parried and retreated. Slowly at first, drawing plaintive whimpers from her as she kneaded the covers like a hungry kitten and pushed back, trying to meet his thrusts and hasten his movements.

He tried to hold on, tried to keep his plunges slow and easy. But he was already primed well beyond even his usual immortal limits. Hard and aching, his balls drawn up and tight.

Snaking an arm around her waist, he hauled her up, letting her head loll on his shoulder. He swept her hair to one side, out of the way so that he could press open-mouth kisses to her collar bone, the taut muscle running from her shoulder to her neck, and that sweet, thrumming jugular vein that rested just beneath her sweat-dappled skin.

His hands moved from her waist to her breasts and back again. Over her hips, her thighs, between her legs. He touched her everywhere he could reach and in whatever way kept her close to him, aided their movements, brought her up and down on his rampant cock harder and faster.

She bounced against him, tiny mewling sounds passing her lips and echoing through the room. Slipping his fingers over her belly and into the slit of her mound, he found her hot button and pressed.

With a scream, she came around him, flexing, tightening, bringing him with her like a backdraft. While the orgasm ripped through him, making him gasp, making him stiffen inside of her, he tipped her head and couldn't resist any longer. The truth would come out soon enough, and she would know everything.

Opening his mouth, he skimmed his teeth—fangs and all—across her skin, finding just the right spot. And then he sank them in, bit deep, letting her blood spill over his tongue even as he filled her with his essence.

It was everything he'd dreamed of and more. She tasted like honey and flowers and sunshine—or what he imagined sunshine might taste like, since he hadn't actually seen the big ball of fiery gas in decades. For long, drawn-out moments, he simply held her, drank her, absorbed her into himself as much as he could.

Suddenly, though, he realized she wasn't moving. Was perfectly, almost deathly still, and not just in the post-orgasmic, too-sated-to-budge way. Loosening his grip, he took a last sip and ran his tongue over the two pristine puncture marks in her throat, using his unique vampire enzymes to seal the wound. Then he cupped her chin, brought her face around to his while still caressing her stomach and between her breasts.

"Are you all right?" he asked softly, bussing her cheek.

She licked her lips, the tendons of her neck convulsing as she swallowed. "You bit me," she said, sounding a little dazed, a little confused.

"Yes," he admitted, not wanting to have this particular conversation right here and now, but knowing he had no one but himself to blame for the timing and circumstances.

She licked her lips again, moving away from him slightly so that he slipped out of her warm, wet body. He bit back a groan at the loss of her heat, her nearness, but didn't try to stop her.

"You bit me," she repeated. This time, her voice carried a note of astonishment edged with anger.

Uh-oh.

Lifting a hand to her throat, she felt the marks, violet eyes widening when she realized it was a hell of a lot more than the average love bite.

"You bit me—" Her accusations were all annoyance now, any signs of perplexity gone. "—and you broke the skin."

"I'm sorry," he told her, and he meant it. He'd loved drinking from her, having her share that part of herself with him, but he had dropped the ball on the whole red light/green light asking permission thing beforehand. "I should have told you sooner. I should have explained instead of just jumping in like that."

Looking at her fingers, rubbing the red-smeared pads together, startlement flashed across her features. "I'm *bleeding*."

Still on her knees, she turned to face him. "What the *hell* were you—"

Lifting her head, she stopped in mid-sentence, shock causing her eyes to pop. She went white as a sheet, her mouth dropping open.

"Oh, my God," she breathed, and Aidan knew his belief that she would understand and accept him, and that they'd live happily ever after had been *sorely* miscalculated.

And then her eyes rolled back in her head, her body went slack, and she hit the sheets in a dead faint.

Four

Chloe's eyes fluttered open. For a couple of minutes, she didn't know where she was.

Judging by the cushioning beneath her and the blankets on top of her, she guessed she was in bed, but the room itself was dark, and it took a moment for her vision to acclimate.

When it did, all she saw was a blank ceiling and slightly less blank walls. She thought she could make out a few doors here and there. One, she assumed, led to a bathroom, the other out into the rest of the . . . house, apartment, whatever . . . and the double set was likely a closet. In her best estimation, anyway.

Lying there, she let the silence surround her and tried to remember how she might have gotten here. It came back to her in a flash, at the same time she realized whose arm was around her waist.

Aidan.

Her husband.

They'd run off to get married at one of Vegas's many all-night wedding chapels, then come back to his apartment (in the basement of an otherwise very nice building, which she admitted was slightly odd for one of the richest men in the state), and had truly incredible sex. That part wasn't so surprising—sex with Aidan had always been off the charts.

But then things had gotten weird. She must have drifted off right after she'd climaxed, because she'd had this bizarre dream about him biting her neck from behind, and then of turning around to find his eyes glowing red, and giant, razor-sharp fangs protruding from between his parted lips.

Ha!

Normally, she would blame such strange imaginings on consuming too much spicy food before bed. But since she'd been a nervous wreck most of the day, worrying about how her sister's bait-and-switch plan would work out, and then about sneaking off to elope with her own white whale, she hadn't eaten all day.

So maybe hunger was the cause of her post-coital night-mares.

Wondering if Aidan had any quick and easy food in the house, she rolled to her back, shifting his arm lower on her waist. His face rested against her shoulder, but she didn't feel him breathing, which was a little peculiar. Then again, it's not like she was overly familiar with her new husband's sleeping habits.

Had they slept together before? Well, yes and no. They'd certainly heated up the sheets, usually going at it like a couple of howler monkeys every chance they got. But any time they might have spent sleeping was more to recover than to catch some zees.

She really was attracted to him. From the moment they'd met, he'd sent her blood boiling. She'd spent the better part of their first date—which had actually been just drinks at Dante's, one of the Inferno's most popular cocktail bars—picturing him naked and squeezing her knees together to keep from embarrassing herself.

But her willingness to jump into bed with him so quickly was also due to the fact that she'd been desperate to snag him. Once she got to know him a bit and realized she actually liked him, trusted that he was a decent guy, she'd thrown herself into the relationship wholeheartedly. The more he wanted her, and the more she'd wormed her way into his head (Cos-*tanza!*), the better her chances of catching and keeping him.

And that's exactly what she'd done, wasn't it? She'd landed herself a nice, rich husband.

Which meant that if he wanted to live underground and do it doggy-style every night, so be it. She certainly wasn't going to complain about the sex—she was a fan of pretty much every position, and happily, Aidan never failed to bring her off. Sometimes in multiples.

As for living here . . . that's something they'd have to discuss later. Jake would definitely love that his new stepfather had his very own Bat Cave, but she wasn't entirely comfortable with the idea of her son being in a basement apartment that she didn't know quite how to get safely in or out of, that he could get trapped in, or that might turn him into one of the Mole People if he spent too much time here.

Then again, she hadn't told Aidan about Jake yet, had she? So discussions and decisions about where they would live and how he would be raised could wait.

Pushing back the covers, she sat up, careful not to disturb her bed buddy. But he never moved, didn't even draw an extra breath.

So he was a heavy sleeper. That was good to know. And might come in handy living under the same roof as a rambunctious four-year-old.

Scrounging around on the floor, she found Aidan's black silk shirt and shrugged it on, buttoning it down the front while she searched for her undies. She found them—miraculously—just behind the dust ruffle at the foot of the bed.

Barefoot, in only her new husband's shirt and her ironically matching thong panties, she padded out of the bedroom and down a long hall to the living area they'd passed through when they'd first arrived. All the lights were off, making the underground quarters pretty much pitch black, but her night vision kicked in enough to keep her from stubbing her toes or walking into a wall.

Finding a lamp to turn on so she didn't have to familiarize herself with the apartment like she was reading Braille proved slightly more complicated, however.

She padded around, feeling for an end table or a light switch, finally locating one on the other side of the wall that separated the kitchen from the living room. When she hit it, bright light exploded, blinding her for a minute as it bounced off all the glossy chrome and stainless-steel surfaces filling the large kitchen.

She covered her eyes, then blinked a few times until they acclimated. When they did, she zeroed in on the giant refrigerator almost as though it was calling her name. Her grumbling stomach must have been fitted with a homing beacon where food was concerned.

Padding across the cool tile floor in her bare feet, she yanked open one side door, ready to grab just about anything she could find. Cheese and crackers, maybe a bit of wine, or even a bowl of cereal would do.

Well, it looked like she could manage the wine part, at least. Inside the fridge, the shelves were nearly bare except for a couple of onyx wine bottles.

The produce drawers were empty, as were the narrow shelves lining the inside of the door. There was no milk, no eggs, not even a container of leftover Chinese takeout. Opening the freezer side, she found even less—just empty shelves behind a puff of icy air.

Well, darn. What the heck did her new husband eat? Apparently only *out*. Of course, with his money, he could not only afford to eat all of his meals in five-star restaurants, but hire a private, 'round-the-clock chef to cook for him, if he liked.

Still, there had to be *something* here she could nosh on. Moving from the refrigerator, she started checking the cupboards. The ones above the countertops . . . the ones beneath the countertops . . . even the one under the sink.

She found glasses—juice glasses, wineglasses, highball glasses—plates and bowls in every size imaginable, even silverware in one of the drawers and cooking utensils in another. But not a damn thing more. No ingredients to cook anything, not even a box of crackers or cereal.

Seriously, what the hell was going on? How could the man not have so much as a Fruit Roll-up on hand? Didn't he believe in midnight snacks or get hungry at all when he *wasn't* trolling up and down The Strip in his fancy sports car?

With a huff, Chloe actually stomped her foot. She considered opening one of the bottles of wine and drowning her sorrows, but knew better than to drink on an empty stomach. Especially one as empty as hers was right now.

She didn't particularly want alcohol, anyway, she wanted *food*. A turkey sandwich. A big plate of spaghetti and meatballs. No, a trucker's breakfast—eggs, sausage, hash browns, toast and jam . . .

The more items she added to her mental menu, the hungrier she got. Hands on hips, she whirled around. Either she was going to start beating on Aidan until he woke from his comalike stupor, or she was going to find his car keys, find her way out of this underground tomb, and take *herself* out for breakfast.

But she didn't get far. Drawing up short, she yipped to find her groom towering in the doorway.

For a man who slept like the dead, he sure did wake up bright-eyed. And sexy as hell.

Looking wide awake and not the least bit rumpled, he was naked except for a pair of black silk boxers. Which, in her current mood, annoyed her to no end.

Crossing her arms over her chest, she glared at him, successfully wiping away a shade of the chipperness written all over his face.

"Hey," he said cautiously, eyeing her from head to toe and back again. He put his hands on his hips, then down at his sides, then across his own chest, then dropped them again. The male version of fidgeting. "Are you okay?"

"No, I'm not okay," she answered quickly. "Why don't you have any food in your house?"

For a minute, he simply stared at her, his expression blank. Then he croaked out, "What?"

She huffed out a breath and rolled her eyes. Making an

eating motion near her mouth with her hand, she said, "Food. *Food.* Something to eat. I'm *starving*, and you have nothing but a couple bottles of wine in your refrigerator."

He blinked, still looking dumbfounded.

Throwing up her hands in frustration, she moved to the hanging cupboards and threw open the doors. Then she did the same to the refrigerator, sweeping her arms in every direction like Vanna White turning letters on *Wheel of Fortune*. Only Chloe's phrase was beginning to read *My h_sb_nd is _ d_mb_ss*, and she didn't need to buy a vowel to figure it out.

"You're hungry," he murmured, finally catching a clue.

Her shoulders sank and she fell back against the edge of the counter. "*Yes*," she breathed. "I'm very, *very* hungry. You failed to feed me last night before you dragged me off to the chapel and then dragged me back here for the wedding night. And why the heck don't you have any food in the house?" she demanded. "That's the most bizarre thing I've ever seen."

"You're hungry," he said again.

He must have seen the murder in her eyes and how close she was to smacking him, because he put his hands up and said, "Okay, okay. I'll get you something to eat. Do you want to go out or order in?"

"Out. And then we go grocery shopping and stock your cupboards."

With a brusque nod, he started to turn away, presumably to go get dressed, only to stop and turn back.

"That's all you're upset about?" he asked. "The food situation?"

"What else would I be upset about?" she said, tipping her head to the side quizzically.

"I thought maybe . . ." He paused, his glance flicking to her throat before once again meeting her eyes. "Maybe you were mad at me about last night."

Chloe went still, a sudden chill washing over her. Why would he be worried about how she'd feel after they had sex?

They'd done that a few dozen times already. Last night had been hot enough to singe their eyelashes off, sure, but then, it usually was.

"What about last night?" she asked slowly.

"You know . . ." He looked uncomfortable, as well as confused when he gestured toward her neck. "The biting and everything."

A low hum started in her ears and spread throughout her entire body. Slowly, she lifted a hand to the side of her throat, feeling for the mark she'd thought was nothing more than a dream.

At first, she felt nothing but smooth, normal skin. Then her fingertips found a rough spot. She couldn't tell exactly what it was, but it felt bumpy and scabby . . . two small spots right beside each other.

As far apart as, say . . . a pair of fangs.

The scene from last night, the one she'd thought was some bizarre dream brought on by stress and low blood sugar, flashed through her memory. Aidan behind her, having just given her one of the top five greatest orgasms of her life . . . the sharp pain in her neck that she hadn't quite been able to identify . . . touching the spot and bringing her fingers away to find them smeared with blood . . . accusing him of biting her . . . then turning around to find his eyes glowing red and drops of blood on his mouth.

Had it really happened? And if it had, what the hell did it mean?

She hadn't yet found the bathroom in this place, and hadn't seen any mirrors on the walls during her brief glance around last night or her stumble through the dark today. So instead of trying to get past him to look for one, she turned back to the glossy silver refrigerator. Twisting this way and that, she found the best view of her throat she could manage and studied it for a moment.

Yep, there it was. Two small dots that looked like puncture wounds. Even given the cloudy reflection, she could make out dark circles of scabbing with lighter pink irritation around them.

W-T-F?

"So you really did bite me," she accused, spinning back to face him. She'd be surprised if *her* eyes weren't glowing red this time.

He had the good sense to look sheepish, his mouth turning down and his cheeks coloring slightly. "I'm sorry. I should have explained sooner."

Explained? Explained what? That he was a total perv?

"Please tell me I didn't marry one of those Anne Rice/ Vampire Lestat cultlike freaks who believes they really are a bloodsucking creature of the night. If you had your teeth cosmetically altered or actually drink blood, not only will I divorce you, I'll stake you in your sleep."

He flinched, a couple of times, though she couldn't be sure which part of her tirade disturbed him most.

"This is something we should probably talk about *after* you've had something to eat. And since there's a good chance you'll want to try that staking thing once you hear what I have to say, we should probably order in."

Narrowing her eyes, she crossed her arms back over her chest, this time to stave off the goose bumps that were breaking out along her skin.

"You aren't going to kill me down here and make this apartment my underground tomb, are you?" she asked, and she was only half-kidding.

He let out a bark of laughter, which surprisingly made her feel better instead of worse. It was real laughter, the laughter she was used to hearing from him. Not crazy, maniacal, serial killer laughter. She hoped.

"Definitely not. We don't kill for food anymore. It's not necessary."

Okay, so maybe it was crazy, maniacal, serial killer laughter.

"Who's 'we'?" she asked, not entirely sure she wanted to know.

Holding her gaze, Aidan shifted his weight from one foot to the other, then lifted a well-muscled shoulder before giving her an answer she really didn't want to hear.

"Vampires."

Five

Aidan wasn't sure what to expect next from his lovely new bride. And she was lovely, standing there in his dress shirt, her long legs and feet bare.

But there was also an element of Frankenstein circling her normally pleasant personality. As in "Bride of . . ."

Not that he could blame her. She was running on an extremely empty stomach—something he knew more than a little about, in a manner of speaking—and it wasn't every day you learned you'd married a vampire.

He really, *really* should have mentioned that small detail to her before they'd tied the knot.

Since Chloe was just standing there, looking more than a little shell-shocked, he carefully backed out of the kitchen and returned to the bedroom. In the pocket of his suit coat, he found his cell phone and flipped it open.

Reception down here wasn't as great as he'd have liked, but it would do. He did a search for nearby restaurants that offered home delivery and picked one he thought Chloe would approve of. Making a quick call, he placed an order, then made a mental note to meet the delivery person upstairs in the parking garage in twenty minutes.

Dragging on his pants, he grabbed a loose T-shirt from one of his dresser drawers and pulled it over his head on the way back to the kitchen. He was relieved to find Chloe right where he'd left her, back to poking and prodding at the bite mark while she studied her reflection on the refrigerator door. It was better than having her race around the apartment, ranting and raving like a loon, even if he knew that reaction was probably coming.

"I ordered some food," he told her quietly. "It should be here soon."

Turning from her perusal of what he'd done to her . . . in a weak moment and without her permission, he was chagrined to admit . . . she glared at him.

"First I eat, then you tell me what the hell is going on," she told him in a firm voice, leaving no room for argument. Not that he intended to try.

"Absolutely." He should have done it much sooner, but was infinitely grateful she was willing to let him feed her first so her temper wasn't balancing on quite such a hair trigger.

Up until this moment, he hadn't even realized she had a temper. All the time they'd spent together had been filled with fun and laughter and hot, sweaty sex.

Not that that was anything to complain about, but it apparently chalked one up in the Sebastian Was Right column. Rushing into marriage without telling her about his little "condition" and without experiencing every aspect of her mood spectrum maybe hadn't been the wisest decision he'd ever made.

"I'm going to get dressed," she said, slipping past him.

He stepped out of the way, didn't even try to stop her.

"And don't forget what I said about the stake," she called back from halfway down the hall. "I know how to take care of myself, and I am not afraid to drive a pointy object into your heart."

Aidan flinched, raising a hand to rub his chest over the delicate organ she'd just threatened to puncture. Jeez, who would have thought she'd have such a nasty streak?

And people thought vampires were bloodthirsty.

Chloe took her time gathering up her sister's clothes and putting them back on. She tossed Aidan's previously comfortable shirt to the foot of the bed like it was on fire, kicking herself for being such a blind, stupid, bobble-headed fool. Chuck had been right to be concerned, to warn her not to do anything rash.

Well, it was too late for that. She'd gone so far past rash, she was ass-deep in a flesh-eating disease.

A vampire. Her husband—one of Las Vegas's wealthiest, most renowned local celebrities—thought he was a vampire. A nightwalker. A blood drinker. A sun-phobic, neck-biting, Dracula-wannabe undead creature of the night.

Fabulous. She'd thought she was landing a big fish. Turns out she'd only managed to land a lunatic.

The question was: How did she escape from this window-less, underground bunker and rid herself of her gruesome groom without letting him catch wind of her plan? The last thing she needed was to pique his curiosity or anger and send him into a killing rage.

No, she needed to bide her time, hold her temper—well, maintain her temper, anyway, since she'd already threatened him with that whole stake-through-the-heart thing—and convince him to take her topside so she could make a break for it.

Using his master bath, she relieved herself, brushed her teeth, and ran a brush through her hair. By the time she finished, she looked at least moderately better than a homeless person.

In no hurry, she traipsed back into the main room only to find it—and the kitchen—empty. She spun around a couple of times, looking high and low, checking all the dark corners and nooks and crannies she could find. For all she knew, Aidan had secret passages built into this place, or a coffin where he took his "eternal rest."

She was getting dizzy from all the up-and-down whirling around when the elevator doors slid open. Straightening with a jerk, her vision blurred and the room spun. She had to reach out and latch on to the counter to keep from tipping over again.

By the time the lightheadedness passed, Aidan was back inside, his arms laden with white paper takeout bags, and the elevator had closed.

Dammit. She may have actually had a chance to escape if she'd been paying better attention.

But then the scents of Italian wafted over, filling her nostrils and making her stomach twist and churn like it was trying to leap out of her body to get to the food. Oh, my God, she loved Italian! Although, as hungry as she was right now, she could probably eat dirt and convince herself it tasted like tiramisu.

She was across the room in a blink, falling on him like a ravenous . . . well, vampire, at least judging by the movies she'd seen. She grabbed the bags from him, taking them directly to the low coffee table in front of the white suede sofa. Tearing into them, she pulled out aluminum containers, plastic silverware, napkins, and a loaf of steaming-hot garlic bread.

She inhaled deeply. It smelled like heaven. And even better when she took the top off an order of manicotti. Without waiting for him to join her, she dug in, taking bite after delicious bite.

After she'd downed one whole ricotta-filled manicotti and three slices of garlic bread, she finally paused long enough to take a swallow of the Diet Coke that had been included in one of the bags.

Taking the manicotti and bottle of soda with her, she sat farther back on the sofa and crossed her legs to use as a makeshift table.

"This hits the spot. Thank you," she told Aidan, who continued to stand where she'd left him after ripping the food away from him like a purse snatcher.

"You're welcome." Slipping his hands into his front pockets, he rocked back on his heels, still watching her with the utmost caution. "I hope you're feeling better now."

She nodded. Her stomach was definitely filling up, her

blood sugar and electrolyte levels rising, her mood evening out, and her panic fading.

Around another mouthful of butter-soaked bread she was *so* going to see on her hips by the next day, she said, "Italian is kind of an odd choice for breakfast, though, isn't it? I expected eggs and pancakes, or maybe some ham and French toast."

He shifted uncomfortably, pulling one hand from his pocket to rub it up and down his thigh. Gaze locked on his, Chloe took another sip of her soda and simply studied him for a minute.

He really was a cutie. He had all the same main physical traits as his older brother, Sebastian—the black hair, tall and muscular frame, strong bone structure. But where his brother gave off an arrogant, almost dangerous air, Aidan was always smiling. He was lighthearted, fun-loving . . . the playboy type, right down to his showy, uber-expensive luxury sports car and willingness to invite hordes of complete strangers into his hotel room for an impromptu party or buy rounds of drinks in whatever club he'd happened to wander into.

Standing there now, though, he looked far from carefree and self-assured. He looked as though he were waiting for her to sprout horns and attack him like a demon spawned from Hell.

She didn't feel like attacking him, not anymore. But he didn't need to know that. Let him stay on the defensive until she understood who it was she'd really married.

"I thought dinner might be more appropriate, given the time," he began slowly. "I know you can't tell without windows, but it's about six o'clock at night."

With a forkful of manicotti halfway to her mouth, she froze. A dollop of sauce dripped off and went *splat* right on her left breast.

She looked down, then scooped it up with the tip of her index finger, plopping it in her mouth while her mind played over what he'd just said.

"Excuse me?" she asked somewhat dumbfounded, letting her fork fall back into the aluminum takeout container.

"Here's the thing," he murmured, sounding less than willing to tell her whatever he was about to tell her. Walking forward, he lowered himself to the coffee table, staying perched on the very edge in case he needed to beat a hasty retreat.

"I sleep during daylight hours. I can stay awake, if I have to, but tend to be groggy and slow. Whether I can see dawn coming or not, sleep pulls at me, and I don't wake up again until nightfall."

Resting his elbows on his knees, he rubbed his hands together, looking at the floor between his feet rather than at her. "I suspect you slept alongside me nearly as long because of the shock you had when I bit you . . . and the blood loss. I was too eager. I took too much. Especially for your first time."

Okay, so maybe stuffing herself with pasta and cheese covered in a thick, red sauce that looked entirely too much like the blood he was talking about hadn't been such a great idea. Swallowing hard, she leaned forward and set the food back on the table. She kept the soda, though; she might need it to settle her stomach if the pitching and rolling didn't stop.

"I think you're going to have to explain this to me—whatever it is you believe you are—from the beginning," she said softly.

So softly that she caught him off-guard. He'd apparently been expecting her to flip out and try to stab him with her little plastic fork. Which was still an option. And she had a little plastic knife, too. . . . She might be able to do some serious scratching with that, if she needed to.

His head jerked up and he met her eyes. When she only held his gaze, waiting quietly, he seemed to relax. Shifting on the corner of the table, he turned to face her more fully.

"I should have told you before," he said. "Before we got married, before we even got involved. I'm sorry for that."

A stab of guilt went through her, her fingers tightening on the bottle of soda in her hands. She was keeping something from him, too, wasn't she? Something *she* should have told *him* before they got married. Before they'd gotten so seriously involved.

So she owed him the benefit of the doubt, at least, right? He might have bitten her last night—so hard he broke the skin. Maybe he really did believe he was a vampire. There were psychologists who treated those kinds of delusions, right?

As his wife—as shiny and new, fresh out of the wrapping as she was—it was her job to listen to him, support him, get him help if he needed it.

At least within reason. If he tried to bite her again, all bets were off. It was slice and dice with her cheap plastic takeout silverware all the way.

Taking a deep breath, she inclined her head a fraction. "Tell me what?"

She sounded so normal! So *not* freaking out inside her own head. Two points for Chloe Lamoreaux, showgirl and actress extraordinaire.

It was Aidan's turn to lick his lips. He did that, then swallowed, his hands flexing and releasing where they rested on top of his thighs.

"That I'm a vampire. Sebastian and I both are."

Her eyes shot wide a second before she blinked. Hard.

His brother was crazy, too? Or was that simply part of Aidan's delusion? Did Sebastian even know Aidan was running around saying these things? Believing them?

"I don't . . ." She paused, rethought what she wanted to say, then shook her head and tried again. "There's no such thing as vampires."

Possibly not the best thing to say when one was sitting across from a man nearly twice her size who thought he *was* a vampire and already had a track record of flashing spiky fangs and chomping her on the neck. Especially when she was trapped alone with him in this windowless, single entrance/exit (that she knew of), dungeonlike apartment.

When, oh, when would she learn to keep her mouth shut?

Instead of being angry or defensive, Aidan nodded. "That's what most of the world thinks, and we're happy to let them believe it. But as hard as it is to process, I *am* a vampire, Chloe."

Her expression must have told him she was still having trouble accepting his declaration as truth.

"I'm not evil, or a demon, or any of the other misconceptions horror movies make us out to be. I need blood to survive, but I don't have to kill to get it. I can't go out in sunlight, but I do have a reflection and show up in photographs, and I don't turn into a bat." His mouth twisted. "Although, technically, I suppose I could. My brother can shift when he really, really wants to."

Oh, goody! Now he wasn't just talking about the *I vant to suck your blood* stuff, he was throwing shape-shifting into the mix.

She shook her head again—to clear it or rattle some sense into herself, she wasn't sure which. "I'm sorry, but this is all just a little much to absorb."

"You don't believe me." It was a statement, not a question.

She didn't think anyone would believe such an outrageous claim.

Taking a deep breath, he stood. "I guess I need to prove it to you."

Six

Chloe jerked back into the overstuffed cushions of the sofa, her hands shooting up to cover the pulse of her throat on both sides. Aidan rolled his eyes at her knee-jerk reaction, as justified as it might be.

"Don't worry, I'm not going to bite you again," he assured her. And then he raised a brow, sending her a hotly sensual look. "Not unless you ask me to."

Without waiting for her to respond to that, he put his hands on his hips and began to pace. Back and forth, back and forth, he wore a path in the small space between the sofa and matching armchair.

"The problem is, I'm not sure how to do that. Especially since you've already seen the fangs and the eyes and the . . . you know," he said, flipping his hand in the direction of the jugular veins she was protecting so diligently, just in case he was overcome by sudden bloodlust.

If she only knew. He was much more likely to be overcome by plain old lust-lust.

She was fully clothed again, in the same jeans and top she'd filched from her sister and been wearing when he'd first picked her up in front of the Bellagio so they wouldn't be seen outside the Inferno. She was even wearing a bra, more's the pity.

But even though she was no longer traipsing around in his shirt, with her legs and those sexy dancer's feet bare, she still turned him on. Yeah, she could be wearing twenty pounds of concrete or the Big Top tent from Circus Circus, and he could be blind as the proverbial bat, and he would still be turned on just standing in the same room with her.

There had been another woman, a very, very long time ago, who'd touched him the way Chloe did. One he'd been this attracted to, cared for this strongly. She was long gone, though, and despite the thin thread of loss that would always run through him, Chloe was the first woman in decades, possibly centuries, that he'd opened himself up to in such a deeply emotional way.

He wasn't ready to use the L-word quite yet.

Was it possible? Yes.

He thought about her often enough. Thought about being with her, making love to her, simply talking with her over a glass of wine or while they were lying in bed.

When they weren't together, he wished they were. At dawn each morning, as he was preparing for The Deep Sleep, he pictured her in his mind, knowing she was likely getting ready for bed, too, after a long night of being onstage. When he awoke again at dusk, he thought of her once more, wondering if she was up yet and what she might be doing. He didn't usually wait long to call and find out, either.

So the L-word was on the horizon, he was aware of that. And, frankly, he thought it would be rather nice to be in love with the woman he was going to be married to for the next several years. Possibly eternity, if it worked out that way.

He hoped it did. Sebastian might enjoy his lone wolf lifestyle, but Aidan needed more.

He was charming and intelligent, sure. He wasn't too shabby when it came to business dealings, either. Sebastian might be the casino mogul, the one who owned million-dollar properties all over Las Vegas and the world, but if Aidan had wanted to, he very easily could have followed in his brother's footsteps. He'd built this high-end apartment complex, hadn't he?

The problem was, big business and real estate didn't interest him. It was sad to realize, this many years into his existence, that he wasn't sure what did.

No, he hadn't spent his entire life—before or after his turning—aimless and uncertain. He'd had jobs. Careers, even. Hobbies and passions and money-making ventures. Sebastian had always been the more focused of the two brothers in that respect, but Aidan was no sloucher.

At the moment, though—for quite a while now, actually—he was floundering a bit. Nothing seemed to catch his interest, or at least didn't hold it for long.

Nothing, that is, until Chloe.

She had caught his interest in the blink of an eye. The sparkle of a sequin. The twitch of a tail feather. And unlike everything else that had come and gone, she was still holding on strong.

Meeting her had been the catalyst to Aidan's beginning to think about what he *did* want for his life these days. It wasn't money; he had plenty of that. Or fame; he was no Brad Pitt, and the attention he got just from being a frequent party-goer was plenty enough. Or immortality; he had that, too, in spades.

What he wanted—he was pretty sure, anyway—was a home. Family. All of those things that came to mind when studying a Normal Rockwell painting or watching a scene on television of a busy park full of playing children and parents watching them with eagle eyes.

He couldn't have all of that, he knew. It was possible for vampires to procreate, but not easily. And no children had ever been born of a vampire/human mating, which meant kids were off the table entirely unless Chloe agreed to be turned. Or they adopted, but that opened a whole other can of worms.

But that wasn't even the issue. If he'd wanted kids alone, he could have limited his dating to other vampires. There weren't a lot of them out there wandering around—certainly not as many as there were sun walkers—but they did exist, and he'd had his fair share of affairs with several of the fanged-and-female variety over the decades.

What he wanted was the home and hearth and haven of being with someone he truly cared about and who cared about him. Someone to come home to, to wake up with in the evening, to maybe adopt a shelter dog with so they could take long, leisurely walks in the moonlight.

Plus, Chloe was the first woman in a hell of a long time who had sent all of his wheels spinning to a million-dollar jackpot. So he'd met her first, then started feeling the tugs toward commitment.

And she'd seemed just as eager to settle down with him. Sure, he realized his wealth was a heady lure. She could very well have been a gold-digger, out to hitch her wagon to his star and live extremely well off of her husband's millions.

Something told him, though, that wasn't the case. She was too open, too genuine for those kinds of games or deceptions.

Which made him think they might actually have a shot at making things work. Yes, he was a vampire and probably should have told her that before he'd popped the big question and talked her into eloping. But once she came to terms with his little condition and accepted the changes that would have to be made to adapt to his unique lifestyle, they could still do the modern blood-drinker's version of the white picket fence, right?

A vampire could hope.

Of course, there was still the small problem of Chloe not believing one hundred percent that he *was* a vampire.

He'd already bitten her, drained her of enough blood to send her reeling, and given her any number of amazing, otherworldly orgasms. Did she think she could come like that with some lame-ass mortal man? Yet she apparently required further proof.

Not an easy feat, considering how well his kind blended with the rest of humanity. With the exception of being allergic to the sun, sleeping rather soundly during the day, and needing to ingest blood to survive, he doubted anyone could pick a true vampire out of a lineup.

"We're going to have to wait until morning," he said suddenly, spinning around to face her. The crack of his voice in the otherwise dead silence startled her so that she jumped and finally let go of her neck.

"What?"

"Going into the sunlight. It's the only thing I can think of that will convince you. But obviously we'll need to wait a while, since it's dark outside right now."

"What are we going to do until then?"

An easy smile spread across his face and he waggled his brows at her. "I've got a few ideas."

Her own brows rose to her hairline above her Frisbee-wide eyes. "Doubtful, Bite Boy. You really are crazy if you think I'm going to let you touch me after being told I married a vampire. One who bit me on my wedding night, no less."

"I told you I was sorry about that."

Her mouth twisted wryly. "I don't know if you can apologize for putting a hole in someone's jugular. *Two* holes."

He didn't know quite what to say about that, so he said nothing.

A minute later, her nose scrunched. "How do you go around biting people and not leaving big, ugly, very *obvious* wounds on their necks?"

She wasn't cowering in fear anymore, which he took as a good sign. And if she was asking questions, wanting to know more about how he lived, then maybe she was opening up to the idea of exactly what he was.

Moving slowly, he stepped to the sofa and took a seat at the opposite end to her, making sure not to spook her by getting too close. No throwing up his arms like he was wearing a cape and doing the whole scary Count Dracula thing.

Stoker *really* hadn't done them any favors with that one, the jerk-off.

"We possess an enzyme. In our saliva," he explained.

"After we drink, we lick the wound to close it and begin rapid healing."

Her fingertips once again traced her own fang-dots. "These don't seem to be healing all that fast. And that still doesn't explain why people aren't walking around with bite marks everyone and their mothers can see."

Eyes going wide, she sat back and gave a small gasp. "Unless that's the motivation behind the whole scarf fad. I never understood the point when only about three of every ten women can pull it off. And turtlenecks . . ."

She gave a small shudder to show how she felt about that particular fashion statement. Of course, Chloe was far from a turtleneck kind of woman. She was every man's fantasy, with a body Hugh Hefner only *wished* he could get in his magazine. She rarely did long sleeves, let alone anything that hid her amazing cleavage.

"I'm sure scarves have come in handy a time or two," he told her. "But most times the enzymes begin to heal the wound within only a few hours."

She gave him a look he had no trouble interpreting. Licking his lips, he returned a sheepish one of his own.

"I was too eager, too rough with you. I did give the wound a cursory swipe, but because of my . . . over-enthusiasm, I may not have done it carefully enough, and it may take longer than usual for you to heal completely."

"So I'm what? Scarred for life?"

He winced at that, considering the expression's double meaning. "No. At least, I don't think so. The marks should heal the same as any cut, leaving behind maybe just the tiniest hint that they were ever there. And I promise, next time I'll be sure to patch you up properly."

The minute the words were out of his mouth, she was up and off the sofa. Her turn to pace, apparently.

"I told you, there isn't going to *be* a next time. I'm not entirely sure I believe there was a last time. This is all just a little too bizarre for me, you know?"

"I know. I'm sorry. I never should have let things between us go as far as they have without telling you. I didn't mean to lie to you, but that's exactly what I've done. It was a lie of omission, and for that, I apologize."

With a huff, she threw up her hands. "Stop it!" she nearly yelled at him. "Just stop apologizing."

"But I truly am sorry," he continued. He didn't know how else to convince her. "I should have come clean with you from the very beginning, or at the very least before we ran off to that Little Blue Chapel and tied the knot. It wasn't fair to you, and I need you to believe that I really am—"

"*Don't* say sorry," she ground out. Putting her hands to her temples, she rubbed as though fighting the beginning of a headache. "Don't apologize to me one more time."

"But I need you to understand—"

"I do," she interrupted him again. "I do understand. But every time you apologize for keeping your secret from me, you make me feel like a piece of crap."

That brought him up short. Narrowing his gaze, he thought about it for a minute, then asked warily, "Why?"

Chloe let her arms fall to her sides, gave a long-suffering sigh, and turned her head to meet his gaze. "Because I lied to you, too."

Seven

This was so not how she'd wanted to break the news to him. Then again, she hadn't exactly wanted to be married to a man who claimed to be a vampire, either.

He was so adamant about it, too. And she'd seen the fangs, the inhumanly glowing eyes, and had a tender, scabby bite mark on her throat.

If it looked like a duck, quacked like a duck, waddled like a duck . . . Let's just say there was a part of her that was beginning to believe he was a duck.

She also believed he was sorry for not breaking the news to her sooner. He couldn't have been more convincing on that score. But the fact that he'd admitted something personal and questionable to her meant she couldn't stay here any longer and pretend she hadn't been lying to him, too.

Releasing a pent-up breath, she returned to her spot on the sofa, sitting down with her head bowed and her hands clasped together between her knees. She continued to breathe, sucking air into her lungs like an asthmatic, then letting it out. Sucking in, blowing out.

"So here's the deal," she said, trying to work her way up to the whole shebang. "I'm not exactly who you think I am, either."

Slanting a glance in his direction, she saw that there was no censure on his handsome face. Where she'd flipped out, gone straight for the "you lied to me!" crazy white woman banshee response, he merely looked curious. His expression was eager and interested, but otherwise blank. Which only made her feel worse.

Tamping down on her guilt, she took another deep, stabilizing breath, squeezed her eyes shut, and blurted out, "I have a son."

Eyes still squinted tight, she waited. For what, she wasn't sure. Questions, accusations, a violent outburst? When none came, she slowly pried open one eye, then the other.

He wasn't angry. If anything, he looked positively gleeful.

"You have a son?" he asked.

She nodded. "His name is Jake. He's four years old."

When those details were met with more silence, she shifted on the sofa and began wringing her hands. Fidgeting. That's what she was doing. Her stomach was in knots and her heart was pounding harder than it had when she'd thought Aidan was going to bite her again.

"I had an affair with this guy a few years ago," she began, knowing she was about to ramble, but somehow unable to stop herself. "He was rich and attractive, and I really thought we had something. I thought he might be The One. Then I got pregnant."

With a sigh, she leaned back, pulling her legs up and wrapping her arms around them, her chin on her knees. "I didn't do it to trap him, in case that's what you're thinking."

And then to herself, *Sound defensive much, Chloe?*

Yes, she did. For good reason, she supposed. She *hadn't* gotten pregnant on purpose, even though she really had believed Peter was her Prince Charming.

Just like she'd said, he'd been everything she wanted in a man—rich, attractive, charming, successful. Marrying him would have saved her from a life on the stage and dying covered in sequins and feathers, the same as she was now hoping marriage to Aidan would do.

Of course, the minute she'd told him the stick had turned blue, he'd dropped her like a flaming bag of dog poo.

Dumped her, and broken her heart a second time on his way out by telling her she'd been a nice piece of ass, but he'd never seen her as anything other than a temporary amusement, considering he was already married with other *legitimate* children at home.

She'd cried herself sick for two weeks after that. Cried and puked, cried and puked, and she didn't think it'd had the least bit to do with morning sickness. That hadn't really kicked in until Peter was far enough away to be little more than a dot on the horizon.

Now here she was, making the same mistakes all over again. Only this time, she wasn't knocked up, and the most eligible bachelor she'd managed to find was a self-proclaimed bloodsucker.

"That's not what I was thinking," Aidan assured her.

She gave herself a mental head shake, glad to be dragged out of her maudlin thoughts. Not that their current conversation was much cheerier.

"I was actually wondering why you didn't say anything before now. All the times we were out, talking about our pasts and our families. Admittedly, we both skipped over *a lot*, but I'm surprised you never mentioned you had a child. Or that you needed to get home to take care of him."

"Are you implying that I'm a bad mother?" she asked in a deceptively low, steady voice. If he thought she'd gone off the deep end when he'd confessed to the whole unholy, unnatural, unbelievable undead thing, he wouldn't even want to be in the same county when she reacted to the implication that she was an unfit parent. Because that's one topic she *was* defensive about.

"Of course not," Aidan replied, as though that had been the furthest thing from his mind.

Blowing out a breath, she let the tension leak from her muscles and bones. She really needed to stop jumping to conclusions and getting her panties in a bunch before she had all the facts, but where Jake was concerned, she was a complete mama bear.

Bad enough she worked nights and slept much of the day while Jake was awake.

Bad enough she worked on The Strip, in a casino where drunks and gamblers and all manner of lowlifes hung out to watch her shake her bon-bon, proposition her, or pat her on the ass.

Bad enough that one day, when Jake was a bit older, his friends and schoolmates would likely start to think as their fathers did—that "showgirl" was just a fancy term for "whore"—and torment him with cruel jabs aimed at his mother's job and reputation.

She had enough to feel guilty about, but where her son's health, happiness, and well-being were concerned, she took her job as his mother *very* seriously.

"Most people who have children love to talk about them, though," Aidan continued. "Brag about them. Show off their pictures. I'm just surprised you were able to keep him a secret for so long."

He was right, it hadn't been easy not to talk about Jake. A thousand times, his name had leapt to her lips, and she'd nearly let the cat out of the bag. Nearly pointed to a game or toy in a store window Jake would have loved . . . nearly let his picture in her wallet be seen . . . nearly said she needed to call it an early night so she could get home to her little boy.

Licking her lips, she ignored the gooseflesh breaking out over her arms and told him the truth. "I was afraid you wouldn't be interested in me anymore if you knew I had a kid."

For a second, he said nothing. Then he blinked like an owl—a really sexy owl—and said, "Well, that's just stupid."

Chloe didn't know whether to be offended or relieved by that response. She chose to be relieved.

Before she could say anything, though, Aidan asked, "So where is he now?"

That wasn't quite what she'd expected, so it took her a second to answer. "At home. With my mother."

Startling her once again, he hopped to his feet and clapped his hands in front of him. "Let's go see him."

"What?"

"I want to meet him. He's my stepson now, right? So I should get to know him."

He looked positively giddy at the very prospect, but all Chloe could think was that Aidan was a vampire . . . or at least claimed to be one . . . and taking a vampire to meet her little boy didn't exactly scream Mother of the Year.

"It's late," she told him. "You said it's nighttime already. He might be asleep by now."

"What time does he go to bed?"

Her mouth popped open, then she closed it again. Should she tell him the truth or lie? She didn't even know what time it was now, so she wasn't sure what bedtime to make up.

Unsure of what else to do, she reluctantly went with the truth. "About nine o'clock."

"Great!" Glancing at his watch, he said, "It's only seven now. That should give us plenty of time to get there and have a little visit before Jake needs to go to bed. Besides, we have quite a bit of time to kill before the sun comes up and I can prove to you once and for all what I am."

Aidan didn't think a short trip to Henderson should be such a production, but from the minute she'd agreed to take him to meet her son, Chloe had done nothing but chatter away about how she expected him to behave.

Don't tell my mother we ran off and got married.

Don't tell Jake you're his new daddy.

Don't say anything *about being a vampire.*

And for God's sake, don't say or do anything vampire-ish!

What she meant by "vampire-ish," he wasn't entirely sure. They'd been dating for a month now and *she'd* never suspected that about him, had she? He certainly didn't go around flashing fang or hissing like a rabid dog. And he'd never once bitten anyone in public.

Thanks to his sleek little Ferrari Scuderia Spider, they made the trip in no time. It only seemed like forever because of Chloe's nervous rambling.

Aidan found it kind of adorable, though. She was the hottest thing going—sexy and sensual and completely uninhibited in bed, as well as her everyday life. But when it came to her family, and her kid in particular, she turned defensive, possessive, and protective all in one.

Truth be known, he wouldn't mind having some of that passionate emotion directed his way.

And maybe one day it would be. They had a lot to work through; she, especially, had some rather major, life-altering facts to come to terms with. But he was confident that once she did, they would be okay, they would have a future together.

One could hope, anyway.

With Chloe giving him turn-by-turn directions, they pulled up in front of a modest ranch home nestled into a middle-class community. Since it was already dusk heading toward dark, it was hard to make out the exact color of the wide aluminum siding, but he thought it was probably a light yellow or beige with black shutters on the windows.

There were potted plants on the small front porch with the twisted iron railing, and chain-link fence all around, enclosing the entire yard. In that yard were clear signs of childhood play—a brightly colored ball, a Big Wheel, one of those miniature plastic basketball hoops, a sandbox shaped like a pirate ship . . .

The items made Aidan smile. He pictured a tiny little male version of Chloe out here, laughing and playing, yelling, "Mommy!"—or perhaps "Gramma!"—"Watch this!" while he tried to stand on his head or sink a ball into the plastic netting.

And he wanted nothing more than to get down on the ground and play along. Toss a baseball around, play hide and seek, maybe teach the little boy to ride a bike.

He wouldn't be able to do any of those things during the

day, of course, but there was always early evening or indoor activities they could busy themselves with. Heck, aside from what Aidan could provide on his own, there were hotel/ casinos all along The Strip that catered to children; ones that housed arcades, bowling alleys, and Chucky Cheese-like playgrounds that offered children not only their weight in pizza, but entertainments rivaled only by Disneyland and the main Mouse himself.

And The Inferno itself held a movie theatre and Olympic-size swimming pool—complete with diving boards and water slides. He might have to convince Sebastian to close those areas down to public traffic once in a while so they could screen G-rated flicks or play Marco Polo without some Play-boy Playmate wannabe's silicone ta-tas falling out of her too-small bikini top.

He had no doubt he could find a million-and-one ways to interact with Chloe's son and be as much of a father to him as any mortal, sun-loving man.

Leaving the car, Chloe beat him up the walk to the front door. As he reached her, she turned on him once more.

"Please, *please* be careful," she begged him in a harsh whisper. "I don't want Mom to get suspicious about us and start asking questions, and I'm definitely not ready to tell her what's going on. Not until I know for sure myself."

He nodded sagely. Inside, he was chuckling, amused by her high anxiety. But outside, he made sure to keep his expression serious and solemn.

To his surprised delight, he'd inadvertently walked into just about everything he'd ever wanted in this eternal existence of his, and he had no intention of jeopardizing it by doing something stupid in front of his new mother-in-law.

"And be careful around Jake," she continued. "I don't want him getting all excited about you, thinking you're going to be his father from now on, when you might burst into flames at sunrise."

Aidan flinched. Where vampires were concerned, that was hitting well below the belt. The very idea had him breaking out in a cold, pink-tinted sweat, even though that's exactly what he intended to do in a few more hours, just to prove his true identity to her.

Ouch. He hoped he'd remember to stop off at an all-night drugstore on the way back to pick up some extra-strength burn ointment. The stuff didn't really help all that much, but it would provide a modicum of pain relief until his rapid healing process kicked in and vanished the scars completely.

"Don't worry," he said, taking her wrist and pressing a soft kiss to the back of her hand. "I promise not to embarrass you or say anything that will alert your family to our true relationship."

She seemed to consider that, then dragged in a deep breath and let it out again, her stiff posture and rigid tension going with it.

"Okay. I'm sorry, it's just . . . I'm really careful with Jake. I've never brought a man home to meet him or my mother before, and if this doesn't work out . . . I just don't want to have to explain, or for my baby's heart to be broken."

He inclined his head, giving her his silent agreement and understanding. Inside, however, his own immortal heart clenched. She didn't realize it, but if things didn't work out between them, her son's wasn't going to be the only heart in pieces.

Eight

When Chloe turned back to the door, he was surprised and delighted that she kept hold of his hand. With the other, she tapped lightly, then used a key she'd pulled from her pocketbook to let them in. He'd noticed, too, that she'd slipped off her sparkling new wedding band and engagement rings—the ones he'd paid a cool quarter of a mil for—to hide them from her mother and leave her left hand once again bare and unclaimed.

They were inside, front door closed behind them, when footsteps sounded from the rear of the house. A lovely older woman appeared from around the corner, smiling widely when she saw her daughter.

"Chloe! What are you doing here?"

"Hey, Mom," Chloe greeted her. "We came to see Jake. Is he still awake?"

The older woman nodded and tipped her head in the direction from which she'd just come. "He's in his room, playing."

She answered readily enough, but Aidan saw the interest gleaming in her eyes. She was happy to see her daughter, but curious as all get-out about the man at her side.

Chloe must have noticed her mother's subtle body language, too, because she said, "Mom, this is Aidan. We've been seeing each other for a while now, and I wanted to introduce him to Jake before we . . . got too serious. Aidan, this is my mother, DeeDee."

Aidan held out his hand—the one Chloe wasn't holding like a lifeline. "Pleased to meet you, Mrs. Monroe."

Was it possible he was actually nervous about meeting Chloe's family? He was so old, had met so many people and been in such a wide variety of situations over his many, many years on this earth, that he wouldn't have thought anything could truly shock or rattle him. But it seemed he would have been wrong. Because standing here, shaking hands with his new bride's mother, had his palms sweating and the rest of him feeling clammy and jittery.

DeeDee took his hand in a firm grip, testing him, he suspected. Her indigo eyes, just a few shades darker than Chloe's own violet ones, were sharp and intense. She was sizing him up, and he could only hope she approved of what she saw.

At least he'd remembered to use Chloe's real last name instead of the more flamboyant one she used professionally. He'd also cleaned up a bit and changed clothes before leaving his apartment, so the pants and shirt he wore now weren't as wrinkled as the ones that had lain on his bedroom floor all day after he'd ravished the woman's daughter six ways from Sunday.

"Aidan," DeeDee intoned. Not coldly, but not fireplace warm, either. "I'm afraid Chloe's never mentioned you."

He offered a small smile. "I hope that means I hold a special place in her heart." Tipping his head more in Chloe's direction, he winked. "One can hope, anyway."

DeeDee offered a low, non-committal hum. "So what do you do, Aidan?"

Slapping a hand over her face, Chloe groaned. "Mo*ther*."

"It's all right," Aidan told her, giving her hand a reassuring squeeze. "Your mother has a right to know how the man who's interested in her daughter makes his living."

Turning his attention back to DeeDee, he said, "Actually, Mrs. Monroe, I guess you could say I dabble."

She didn't look terribly impressed by that bit of information.

"My brother is Sebastian Raines," he added, only to watch her eyes go wide. Oh, yes, Sebastian's name had a tendency to impress just about everyone the world over.

"He has his fingers in quite a few pies, as I'm sure you probably know, and I mostly help him with those. I don't have anything quite as large or impressive as the Inferno under my belt, but I do all right for myself."

That was certainly an understatement. He didn't mind being linked to his brother most of the time, but he also didn't like people believing he relied on Sebastian for everything he did and owned. No, Aidan had a few of his own projects going, and his own money in the bank . . . as well as other, much more secret and less impenetrable hidey-holes.

"Don't worry," he added. "If your daughter and I stay together, I'm more than capable of taking very good care of her."

Chloe's mother arched a dark brow. Down to the curve of her lips and her long, lithe dancer's figure, she was nearly a perfect cut-out of her younger daughter. Which made him wonder just how much of their father's DNA had made it into the gorgeous twins.

"I should say so, Mr. *Raines*."

The stressing of his surname let him know he'd passed the first familial hurdle. He would have released a pent-up breath, if he had any, but he'd been so wired since stepping inside the house that he'd forgotten that part of his human persona.

Picking up with some even breathing before anyone noticed he hadn't been using his lungs, he continued to curve his lips in an easy smile. He was careful not to flash his fangs, even though they were recessed enough at the moment not to pose much of a problem.

"Well, you two go back and see Jake while I get us all something to drink," DeeDee told them. "What would you like, Aidan? Coffee, tea, maybe some iced tea? Or something stronger?"

"Whatever you and Chloe are having will be fine," he replied. "Thank you."

Almost before he got the words out, Chloe was grasping his sleeve, dragging him out of the entryway and through what looked to be a small family room. He barely had a chance to see more than lemon chiffon carpeting and sand-colored walls dotted with framed photographs before she was steering him down a narrow hallway also decorated with family photographs.

"My mother never offers guests something to drink," she all but snarled back at him. "She doesn't like them to over-stay their welcome."

He wasn't entirely sure how to respond to that. Was she angry that her mother seemed to like him well enough to offer him refreshments, or because now that she had, they might be forced to stay longer than Chloe had planned?

"I'll bet you anything, when we come back, she'll not only have a pot of hot tea brewing, but a plate of cookies set out on the table. She'll try to pass them off as homemade and hope you don't notice the word 'Keebler' stamped into the center of the little elves' shortbread butts."

He nearly chuckled at that, then thought better of it.

"I'm . . . sorry?" he offered instead, hoping like hell it was the right thing to say.

Coming to a complete halt at the end of the hall, she turned on him and lowered her voice even more. "It's be-cause you're loaded," she told him. "She thinks I've landed myself a nice, big fish and doesn't want me to blow it, so she's going to pretend to be Miss Manners in hopes of show-ing you that we deserve to be part of the vast Raines empire."

"You do," he readily assured her.

She rolled her eyes, letting him know precisely what she thought of that declaration.

"I don't deserve a bank vault full of money or my weight in jewels just because I'm good in bed. And I don't want to spend the rest of my life listening to her bitch and moan about how I 'let you get away' if we don't end up growing old together."

He raised a brow, silently reminding her that there was pretty much zero chance of that, even if they stayed married for the next millennia.

"Oh, you know what I mean," she huffed with the flip of her wrist.

Knowing it probably wasn't the wisest question to pose at this point, he asked cautiously, "Do you and your mother not get along?"

Chloe blew out a breath, all of her steam and annoyance seeming to seep away with it. "I love my mother," she told him. "Normally, we get along very well. The problem is, we're a little *too much* alike, so she sometimes thinks she should be allowed to make decisions for me . . . or badger me into doing things the way she thinks I should."

"Should I simply write her a check for a million dollars or so to get her off your back for a while?"

Chloe's eyes went as wide as Lake Tahoe a second before she realized he was teasing.

"Don't you dare," she warned, punching him in the arm with far more force than he thought necessary.

Offering her a confident smile, he pulled her close, kissing her hard and quick right on the mouth. "Stop worrying so much. Your mother likes me. Now let's see if Jake does. Come on . . . introduce me to your son."

It occurred to Chloe suddenly and out of the blue that she didn't really need Aidan's money. All she had to do was devise a way to bottle his kisses—infused with his minty, masculine flavor and unwavering confidence—and she would be a zillionaire overnight.

But he'd done exactly as he intended; rather than being a bundle of nerves and anxious energy, she was beginning to calm down and realize that having him meet her mom and little boy was not the end of the world. They met new people every day, right? Some who stuck around, some they never saw again. Whichever category Aidan eventually fell into, they—all of them—would deal. She would just have to have faith in that.

"All right," she said softly.

At the end of the hall, Jake's door was open a crack and she went to it, tapping softly to keep from scaring him if he was deeply involved in some imaginary game or another.

He was on the floor in his sea-blue and yellow Spongebob Squarepants footie pajamas, pushing a toy train around in front of him and making soft *chugga-chugga-chugga* noises, punctuated by the occasional *whoo-whoo!*

As always when she saw him—especially after a long night at work or off trying to seduce a rich daddy for him—her heart turned over inside her chest. Most mothers probably thought their children were the sweetest, cutest, most adorable children on the planet, but Chloe knew for a fact that hers was. He was also—thankfully—her spitting image, getting only his two-shades-lighter-than-her-own hair and possibly the curve of his nose from his deadbeat of a father.

When he heard her knock, he turned his head, and when she pushed the door open and he saw her, his eyes lit up like the stage lights at Lust.

Jumping to his pajama-bootied feet, he yelled, "Mommy!" and raced straight for her.

"Hey, beanpole." Dropping to one knee, she caught him up in a giant bear hug, rocking him from side to side and nuzzling the side of his neck until he giggled.

After a minute or two of tickled greetings, Jake pushed her hair away from one ear and leaned close to whisper, "Who's the fancy man?"

Chloe smiled, cocking her head a few degrees until she could see Aidan from the corner of her eye. "This is my friend, Aidan. He wanted to meet you before you went to bed."

"Me?" Jake asked, sounding surprised. "Why?"

"Why do you think, silly? Because you're cute and smart and funny, and he didn't believe me when I told him you had a pair of Spongebob pajamas." She plucked at the light-weight material, making sure to tweak his tummy in the process.

He giggled, covering his stomach and wiggling away. Then he turned his attention up to Aidan, tipping his head like a museum curator studying a particularly interesting new acquisition.

Seconds ticked by, and Chloe waited to see what her son's reaction would be to the first man she'd ever brought home to meet him. To his credit, Aidan merely stood where he was, offering Jake a friendly smile and letting him lead things wherever he wanted.

"I'm Jake," he said, with a hint of challenge to his voice.

"Hello, Jake. I'm Aidan."

Then Aidan did a truly remarkable thing—he stepped forward, tugged at the razor-sharp seams of his slacks, and dropped to the floor, sitting cross-legged beside her. Not something she ever would have expected from a man like him, especially given how much she was sure his clothes must have cost. And this was his casual look.

"I like your pj's," Aidan told Jake.

Jake glanced down at himself, then back at Aidan. "Did you really want to see them before I went to bed?"

"Absolutely. I love Spongebob. He's my favorite."

Jake beamed. "Me, too. I have more, you know."

"You do?" Aidan said, feigning awe.

"Uh-huh."

Running to the dresser, Jake pulled open one of the drawers and started pulling out every set of pajamas he owned. Well, the ones they kept at Grandma's house, at any rate.

"Spongebob, and Elmo, and Buzz Lightyear . . ." As he ticked them off, he laid them over Aidan's lap so he could get an up-close-and-personal look at every animated character known to man. ". . . and cowboys and trains and motorcycles. I have *Finding Nemo* at home, but I don't like them as much anymore. They have a hole in the knee Mommy keeps saying she's going to fix."

Aidan cast her a glance, and she pulled her mouth to one side, caught between amusement and chagrin.

"Little Suzy Homemaker, I'm not," she muttered with a shrug.

Better for him to find that out now, before he started expecting her to cook and sew and walk around with a feather duster permanently attached to her hand. Yeah, she was *so* not going to be that kind of wife, regardless of what she'd thought she would be willing to do before he'd actually slipped a ring on her finger.

Besides, he was rich; let him hire a cook and a seamstress and a maid, if he wanted that sort of work done. Come to think of it, she might ask him to hire a few of those folks so they could do that stuff for her, too.

If they remained married, of course. Nothing had been decided for certain yet. Although, if his interaction with Jake so far was anything to go by, the Magic 8 Ball was definitely bobbing around *all signs point to yes.*

A shiver stole through her at the thought. When had she started leaning toward making their impromptu marriage permanent? When had she begun to think that maybe being tied to a vampire for life—hers, his, however that whole deal worked—might not be so bad, after all?

Turning back to Jake, Aidan fixed him with a solemn gaze. "Can I ask you something, Jake? It's kind of important, so I'm going to need an honest answer."

Jake's eyes widened slightly and his face got tense, the way it did when he thought he might be in trouble.

Chloe went tense, as well. She didn't know what Aidan was about to say, but if he did anything to hurt or scare her child, she would not only hand him divorce papers on his way out the door, she'd also hand him his head on a silver platter. Maybe even literally, if he was telling the truth about the whole vampire thing, and that's what it took to kick his undead butt.

Mimicking Aidan's serious demeanor, her son nodded.

Aidan waited a beat, then lifted one of the pairs of pajamas from his lap and said, "Do you think they make these in my size? I'd *really* like a pair. Especially if they were just like yours. Then we could be pajama buddies."

For a second, Jake didn't respond. Chloe knew that hadn't been what he'd been expecting at all. Neither had she.

Then he threw back his head and laughed, and Aidan chuckled with him. So did she. She couldn't believe how well they were getting along. Or how good Aidan—a self-professed vampire who drank human blood and had been around for what she assumed was a really, *really* long time—was with her little boy. He didn't mind getting down on Jake's level, both literally and figuratively, and seemed to know just what to say and how to say it.

Yes, he could be playing a game, being nice to her kid only long enough to convince her he was father material. Behind her back, he might be a total jackass, the kind of guy she never, ever wanted anywhere near her son.

But something told her that wasn't the case. If he were that much of an all-around jerk, she thought she would have seen some of the signs before now.

Bouncing up and down a little on the pads of his feet, Jake said, "We could have popcorn and watch movies. Do you like *Despicable Me?*"

"I *love* it," Aidan replied with all the gusto of a man who'd just won a bundle on the ponies.

Of course, Chloe was pretty sure he was lying. If he'd ever actually sat through *Despicable Me*, she'd eat the feathers off her headdress.

"Do you like popcorn?" Jake asked, sounding a little worried. As though not liking popcorn might just be a deal-breaker in this new friendship they were forming.

"Only if it has lots and lots of melted butter on it," was Aidan's heartfelt reply.

Clapping his hands together, Jake threw his head back and did a little happy dance. Then, without warning, he threw himself against Aidan and arranged himself soundly on his lap.

Chloe blinked, shocked at Jake's open and enthusiastic response to Aidan. He was a happy and exuberant boy, but tended to be much more reticent around strangers.

Aidan, too, seemed more than comfortable with Jake. He held him on his lap like it was the most natural thing in the world. Like Jake was his very own son, and he'd been doing it for years.

Emotion clogged her throat and tears began to prick behind her eyes. This was the kind of relationship Jake should have had with his biological father from the very beginning, what he'd been missing all of his life. And now maybe, just possibly, she'd be able to give it to him.

"Speaking of late-night snacks," Aidan mock-whispered, "your grandmother said something about having cookies. Do you think we could talk your mom into letting us have a couple before you go to bed?"

Jake's face lit up, and both males turned baleful expressions on her. Normally, she wouldn't let Jake have sugar before bedtime, but since he was already so riled up, he would probably be awake half the night, as it was. What would a couple of cookies hurt?

Pushing to her feet, she wiped her hands on the back of her jeans and said, "I can't make any promises, but I'll see what Gramma says. Will the two of you be okay up here by yourselves?"

She was mostly asking Aidan, and he knew it. Grinning up at her, he nodded. "We'll be fine. Especially if Jake lets me play with his awesome train set."

That was all it took to have Jake bouncing off his lap and leaping over to the trains he'd been playing with when they first came in. A second later, he and Aidan had their heads together, so immersed in their conversation that even if she wasn't going for cookies, she still would have been invisible to them.

Nine

No two ways about it, Aidan was in love. Chloe's son was the cutest, smartest little tyke he'd ever met.

Granted, he didn't have that much experience with kids—vampires didn't tend to be a parent's first choice of babysitter—but with Jake, he seemed to be a natural. From the minute he'd met the young man, all the right words had simply fallen out of his mouth. Getting down on the floor and playing with him had been some of the most fun he'd had in a very, very long time.

Excluding the time spent with his mother, burning up the sheets, of course.

Glancing in her direction, he wondered what his chances were of ever seducing Chloe into bed again.

They were on the roof of his building. It was about five a.m., and despite the heat the Las Vegas desert could put off during the day, nighttime could be downright chilly, especially eighteen stories up.

He'd draped his suit jacket around her shoulders to keep her warm, and they were sitting on the ground with their backs against a giant metal box, most likely a heating or air-conditioning unit. He'd been involved in the construction of the building, but that didn't mean he knew what every nut and bolt was.

Maybe when the sun came up, he'd be able to tell. If he

wasn't a smoldering pile of ash by then. But that was, after all, why they were there.

They'd stuck around her mother's house until after midnight. Chloe had brought them cookies and milk, and he'd played with Jake until the boy had started yawning and could barely keep his eyes open. Then, with Chloe's assistance, they'd tucked the child into bed.

It had been one of the most special, familial experiences of his life, and as he'd stood in the doorway, watching her press a kiss to her son's forehead, he'd realized *this* was exactly what he wanted.

He'd thought marrying Chloe would be something, that it would be enough. He honestly hadn't given much thought to an actual family—as in, attempting to have children with her. That process, for a vampire—let alone a human/vampire match—could be very difficult and drawn out. He wasn't sure he would ever even have brought it up with her.

But now it turned out Chloe already had a child. By marrying her, he'd essentially bought himself a ready-made family.

Things would have been just about perfect, if not for the small issue of his being somewhat less than human. He was okay with it, but he wasn't so sure about Chloe.

The good news was, she hadn't run screaming yet. Minor freak-out down in his apartment notwithstanding, she'd been handling the situation fairly well.

Of course, he knew she still didn't quite believe him. Which meant he had to prove it to her. And after that . . . well, after that, he guessed they would have to wait and see.

Would she freak out on him again, this time grabbing up her son and her mother and maybe even her sister, and heading for the hills? Or would she freak out on him again, but only momentarily, before deciding she might be able to handle being married to a vampire, after all?

Either way, he figured the freak-out part was inevitable, but the rest . . . the rest was anyone's guess.

"You still awake?" he asked quietly when she'd been silent for nearly twenty minutes.

He felt her head roll on his shoulder. "Mmm-hmm. I still don't know what we're doing up here, though."

"You will, in another hour or so."

"But why do we have to be on the roof now?"

Letting his head fall back against the metal wall, he swallowed. "Because if we go inside, I'm not sure I'll have the courage to come back out when it's time."

She lifted her head at that. Even in the darkness, he could see her perfectly. He could see everything perfectly. Hear everything, too, from the slight wind blowing past the multitude of tall buildings and neon signs that made up downtown Vegas, to the voices and noises of people milling about far below.

Her eyes locked on him, confusion brimming in the violet depths. "Why are we up here, then? I don't want you to do anything you're afraid of."

"I'm not afraid, exactly." Horrified, petrified, sick to his stomach, maybe, but not exactly afraid. "And you need proof. You won't believe me unless you see for yourself, and we can't move forward until you know everything. Believe everything."

To his surprise, she snuggled back into the curve of his arm.

"I have to tell you, no matter what happens when the sun comes up, you've done a pretty good job of winning me over already."

He remained silent, waiting for her to elaborate even as blood—part hers, part his own—pumped hard and fast through his veins.

"The way you were with Jake tonight . . ." Her voice grew thin and she stopped to swallow. "I can't thank you enough. I haven't seen him that happy in a really long time. He's usually much more reserved around people he doesn't know, especially men."

"His father has never been involved in his life?" Aidan asked.

She shook her head. "As soon as I told him I was pregnant, he left skid marks getting away from me."

"His loss," Aidan replied quickly and fervently. And he meant it. As far as he was concerned, the guy Chloe had been involved with and who had fathered that adorable child was a complete ass for abandoning them. He didn't know what he was missing.

But his loss was Aidan's gain, and if he had his way, he was going to take full advantage of it.

"Thank you," she murmured. "I think so, too. But Jake doesn't know any better. He only knows that a lot of his friends at pre-school have daddies and he doesn't, and he doesn't understand why not."

"I'm not going to ask you for a decision now, but in twenty-four hours or so, after you've seen for yourself what I truly am and have had a chance to absorb that knowledge, I hope you'll consider letting me step into that role. I know I'm probably not anyone's first choice as father material, but I'll be a good one, I swear. And even though we'll face a few difficulties a normal man—a normal family—wouldn't, I promise I'll do everything I can to make you both happy."

Tipping her head back, she smiled at him. "No matter what the dawn brings, you're a very good man, Aidan Raines."

He shifted beside her, not because her words made him uncomfortable, but because his skin was starting to tingle. One of the first signs that dawn was approaching. It was an early warning signal that he needed to get to safety and tuck himself in somewhere nice and dark before the sun began to rise in earnest.

Another couple of minutes and his blood started to get warm, bubbling in his veins almost like water being brought to a slow boil. And the tingle crawling over his skin grew more and more uncomfortable until it itched and then burned.

When he spoke, his tone was rough, his throat dry and tight. "I hope you'll still feel that way in a few more minutes."

Far off on the horizon, dancing behind the mountain peaks and Vegas skyline, black gave way to blueish black, and then gray, and then the pastel colors of dawn: lavender and pink, with a hint of orange and yellow.

Aidan's chest rose and fell in rapid succession. He might not need oxygen to survive, but highly stressful situations apparently caused hyperventilation in vampires and humans alike. He licked his dry lips, squeezing his eyes shut as they began to burn and tear.

He couldn't see Chloe anymore, but he felt her shift against him. She came up on her knees beside him, her hands resting on his upper thigh.

"Aidan?"

She sounded concerned, and he knew he was probably scaring her, but he couldn't help it. He also couldn't reply. Hands clenched in his lap, it was all he could do to sit still and let this happen when his instincts and every cell in his body was screaming for him to get inside and away from impending danger.

"Aidan, are you all right?"

Not all right, not all right, rolled through his brain, but he still couldn't strangle out a response.

Bringing his arms up, he pressed the heels of his hands into his eye sockets, hard, and began to rock like a child. He hated this. Hated the pain wracking his body, yes, but hated the defenselessness even more. Hated her seeing him like this.

And then he smelled the burning. His skin was beginning to smolder. The intense heat battering his face and the back of his hands must be where his flesh was turning black and crisp and beginning to peel.

"Oh, my God," Chloe breathed. "Aidan, you're burning."

She sounded frantic, but his first inclination was to laugh. Isn't that what he'd told her would happen? Isn't that why they were up here—so he could show her what happened to a vampire when they didn't find a dark hole fast enough and were met with the agony of sunrise?

"Okay, that's enough."

Her voice was firm and decisive as she threw his jacket over him and started tugging him to his feet.

"Get up. I believe you, now get up right this minute," she said, yanking until he found his footing and let her drag him away.

He didn't know where they were going, but he hoped it was inside, away from the big ball of burning gas that was broiling him alive. He also hoped she meant what she said about believing him. Because if he had to go through something like this again just to convince her of what he really was, their marriage was going to be a short-lived one, indeed.

One minute, the sun was scorching him. The next, he felt blessed shade encompass him, and nearly sagged with relief. He shrugged off the jacket and lifted his head just as the heavy metal door leading to the roof slammed closed behind them.

Dropping onto the steps, he leaned back against the wall and let the cool darkness seep through him, soothe him. His skin still prickled and throbbed, the burns still aching, but at least things weren't going to get any worse.

Lowering herself to the step beside him, Chloe was shaking as badly as he was. "What the hell was that?" she asked, somewhat breathless.

Rather than answer, he arched one dark brow.

"I know, I know. I just can't believe . . . You told me, and I was halfway ready to agree with you, even if you were in need of shock treatments and a Thorazine Big Gulp, but I don't think I really believed it could be true."

Which was the number-one reason vampires weren't integrated into human society; the myths and legends were too scary to begin with, and they probably wouldn't believe it unless it slapped them right in the face. Chances were, human beings came in contact with vampires a lot more often than they realized. Especially at night. Especially in downtown Las

Vegas. They didn't call it Sin City for nothing, and vampires did have a tendency to be drawn to all things sinful.

Her gaze ran over his face and arms and hands, taking in what he assumed were some rather nasty burns. The ones on his hands were bright red in places, bubbling and white in others, and he knew his face must look similar.

"Are you all right?" she asked, sympathy tingeing her voice. "I mean, I know you're not all right, but . . . will you be okay? Is there anything I can do for you?"

"Do you believe me now? What I am, how I have to live?" he asked instead, answering her question with what he considered a more important one of his own.

Silence echoed through the narrow stairwell for several long seconds while she considered that, studied him, mentally ran through the very short list of other possible explanations.

"Yes. I believe you," she said softly.

With a stiff nod, he held out his hand and started to push up, wincing as his scalded skin stretched and pulled. "Then help me downstairs. I could use a nap, a drink, and some burn ointment—not necessarily in that order."

Being very careful in her movements, she hooked his arm over her shoulder and propped him up as they made their way down the single flight of stairs to the first level with elevator access. From there, they zipped down to the parking garage and shuffled the short distance to the private elevator that would take them to his apartment.

Once inside, he stumbled toward the sofa, dragging Chloe more than she was guiding him, and dropped onto it with a long, ragged sigh.

"Don't you have any light switches in this place?" she grumbled.

Forcing his eyes open, he saw her as clearly as summer morning—or what he remembered a summer morning looking like, at any rate. Around her, every detail of the apartment was equally clear, but he'd forgotten that her night vision didn't stand a chance of comparing to his own.

"Sorry. There's a lamp over there. And a wall switch over there." When he raised an arm to point, he was embarrassed to see that it shook, and quickly lowered it back to his side before Chloe noticed.

She flipped on both, and he clamped his eyes shut, hissing as the bright light stung his still-sensitive eyes.

"Sorry." It was her turn to apologize, and she immediately flicked off the overhead, leaving only the lower-watt lamp to wash the room in a dull yellow glow.

"Now where's the burn ointment?"

"I don't actually have any," he replied.

She gave an annoyed, motherly *tsk* that almost—*almost*—made him smile.

"What about a first aid kit?"

Not like he had any use for one of those most days, either.

"I don't know," he muttered from beneath the heavy shield of his arm thrown over his face. "There might be one in the kitchen or the bathroom."

Was a first aid kit something a designer would have supplied when she outfitted the place with everything from dishes and flatware to toothbrushes and toilet paper? He'd hired someone to fill the apartment from top to bottom before he'd moved in, then he'd slowly added some of his own belongings, but he hadn't removed much of anything. It sort of made him wonder what all he would find if he started poking into nooks and crannies.

He heard Chloe moving around, and then she called out, "Found it!"

A minute later, he felt the sofa give as she settled beside him.

"Move your arm," she told him a second before gripping his forearm and slowly prying it away from his face.

He let her, opening his eyes in time to see her wince at the condition of his face. Flipping open the tube of burn cream, she squeezed a little onto the tip of one finger and lifted it to his cheek.

More gently than he would have thought possible, she

spread a thin layer of the cool medicine over his marred skin. Cheeks, brow, the tip of his nose. Then she started on the tops of his hands and backs of his fingers.

"I thought vampires were supposed to heal instantaneously or something," she murmured, her gaze intent on what she was doing.

"Rapidly," he replied, "not instantaneously. All of this will be gone by tomorrow morning, after I've had a chance to feed and rest."

Finished playing Nurse Betty, she sat back to study her work, searching for any spots she might have missed.

"So this is the deal, huh?" she asked. "You're a vampire. A real, authentic vampire. Up all night, sleep all day, can't go near sunlight, need blood to survive. I get it. I can even accept it, as surreal as it still feels at the moment."

Leaning away from him for a second, she set the tube of first aid cream on the coffee table before wiping her fingers off on her jeans. "But what does it mean for us? For, you know"—she gave an all-encompassing wave of her hand—"our marriage and everything."

Ten

Chloe held her breath, waiting for Aidan's reply . . . and she wasn't sure why.

What did she want him to say? What did she *expect* him to say?

She was pretty sure she was in love with him. For real this time. Not just pretending to be in love because she was looking to hook the big fish, land herself a rich husband who could provide not only the necessities, but a lavish lifestyle for both her and her son.

And not just because he was a novelty. Being married to an honest-to-goodness vampire . . . ? That *was* pretty awesome, if she did say so herself.

Not that she could ever tell anyone. She might not be completely schooled in the dos and don'ts of immortality, but she was pretty sure keeping it under wraps was a must. Otherwise, everybody would already know about vampires, and Aidan wouldn't have had to work so hard to convince her, right?

So she understood that if they stayed together, there would have to be some adjustments to her routine and basic mindset—not to mention Jake's and the rest of her family's. She might not tell them the whole truth about Aidan, if his "condition," as he called it, was something he preferred to keep to themselves, but she suspected excuses would have to be made when Aidan couldn't attend daytime functions or passed on a second helping of Christmas dinner.

Despite the burns on the back of his hand that must hurt, even if they were preternaturally on the mend, he stitched his fingers with hers and pulled her hand to rest on his firm abdomen.

"I guess that depends on you," he said in a low voice, his coffee-brown eyes glittering intently into hers. "I'm in love with you. I want our marriage to work. But I also know I lied to you . . . or at least deprived you of some rather pertinent details. So if you want an annulment or whatever, I won't blame you."

A heartbeat passed. Or in her case, half a dozen. Her heart was pounding in her chest like a hummingbird's wings, her palms sweating. And she could only wipe one on the seat of her sister's pants because he was clasping the other.

"What if I don't?" she asked quietly.

His fingers flexed on hers, the only outward reaction to her words.

"Then we'll stay married. It won't be easy. There are things you'll need to know, certain things we'll need to do that you may not be used to. But I'll do whatever I can to make you more comfortable. Answer any questions you have, and try my best to fit into your life, though I realize there will probably have to be more changes made on your part to fit into mine."

His mouth twisted at the last, taking her stomach with it. How had he lived until now? she wondered. How long had he been a vampire, and what kind of family, what kind of life, had he experienced? Good, bad, indifferent?

There really were so many questions she had for him, and was glad he'd offered to answer them all. She suspected there would be a lot of very long, intense discussions in their future while she grilled him like a shish-kabob. But that would come later, after this first and most important decision had been made.

"You're really good with Jake," she murmured, loud enough for him to hear, but mostly to herself as she worked through her own thought processes and myriad emotions.

"He's a great kid."

"You're good to me."

His free hand rose, and he ran his fingers lightly through the hair at her temple, tucking a strand behind her ear. "You deserve to be treated well."

That made her throat tighten and her eyes grow damp. "Maybe not," she whispered.

His brows knit, and he looked at her askance, waiting for her to continue.

In a rough, watery voice, she said, "I have one more confession to make. I . . ." She paused, swallowed hard, tried to school her rushed breathing. "I married you for your money, Aidan. I cared about you, I had fun with you, but I don't know if I'd have gone through with it if you weren't a millionaire Raines."

Dropping her head into her hands, she covered her eyes, trying to hide from the wave of shame that washed through her. She'd been so stupid, convincing herself that she was doing the wrong thing for all the right reasons . . . that she cared enough for him to make a marriage work, even if it was based on lies . . . that he was flush with cash, and if she didn't take advantage of that, some other woman would.

But he wasn't quite the man she'd thought he was. He wasn't just a man at all, really—he was that and so much *more*. And even though he'd kept that from her, she understood why. He'd certainly had a better reason for lying to her than she had for lying to him.

"I'm sorry," she said, nearly weeping into her hands. "I'm a terrible person, I know. I'm just so afraid of being trapped as a showgirl all my life, of never being able to give Jake anything more than he has right now, when he deserves so much! And I convinced myself that we got along well enough, were sexually compatible, that you wanted to marry me, and we'd do okay."

With a sniff, she straightened and forced herself to meet his gaze. "If we didn't, I figured we could always get divorced, and I'd still be left with a very comfortable settlement, at the very least."

"And alimony?" he asked in a low voice.

Her chest hitched and tears spilled over her lashes to trail down her cheeks. She nodded weakly. "I know, I'm horrible!" she cried.

For a minute, Aidan simply stared at her, his eyes dark, his gaze unreadable. She hoped he wouldn't lose his temper so much that he flew into some sort of murderous, vampiric rage and bit her to death.

And then he threw back his head and laughed.

Chloe pulled away, her eyes going wide at such an unexpected reaction. Was he going crazy? Was this what the beginning of a murderous, vampiric reaction looked like?

But still he laughed. Deep guffaws that rippled the muscles of his tight abdomen.

When he settled down to mere chuckles, she licked her lips and said, "You're going to kill me, aren't you? Drain me dry and leave my lifeless body in an alley somewhere for the rats to nibble on."

He chuckled again, a single low rumble of amusement. "I'm not that kind of vampire," he teased. And then, "Actually, I was just thinking that we make quite a couple. First we dash off to elope after one of the shortest courtships in history, then we kick off our honeymoon by admitting all of the secrets we've been keeping from each other."

He didn't sound angry at all, which frightened her a little.

"You aren't mad?" she asked warily.

He shook his head. "No, I don't think so. I think it's kind of funny, actually. My one big secret probably trumps your two smaller ones, anyway."

She blinked hard, her shoulders going back. "They aren't *that* small," she muttered, knowing even as she did that she sounded like a pouting child. And why she would want to call attention to her big, giant whopper secrets when he seemed more than willing to offer her a pardon, she'd never know. But once again she'd opened her mouth and inserted her size-seven stiletto.

Sitting up, Aidan twisted his legs off the sofa and pulled her onto his lap all in one smooth move. However painful his sunburns were—and already, the cherry red was fading to more of a hot pink—they obviously hadn't impacted his flexibility.

"I know they aren't," he told her, snuggling her closer. "I'm just saying I think they even out. And that if you're prepared to overlook mine, I can certainly overlook yours."

The out-of-control pace of her heart began to slow as she let his declaration and what it meant sink into her brain. She didn't think another man on the planet would be willing to overlook the fact that she'd kept her child a secret until after he'd slipped a ring on her finger. Add to that her admission that her original intention had been to marry him for his money, her admission that she was a *gold digger*, for heaven's sake, and she was surprised he wasn't in the next county already.

How had she gotten so lucky? Aidan might be a vampire—and how wild was *that*? she thought for about the six thousandth time—but he was also possibly *the* most perfect guy for her. Ever. She could search Las Vegas—heck, the entire country—from now until the next millennium, and she didn't think she would ever again stumble across someone who suited her so very well.

"So now that we've both come clean," she said, "do you think we should start fresh?"

"I think I'd like to," he murmured softly. "If you would."

Toying with the inside of her lip, she took a deep breath, then let it out with a firm nod. "I think I might, too."

A slow smile spread across his face. When his lips parted, she spotted the sharp tips of his normally hidden fangs, and a ripple of dangerous awareness washed over her. Life with Aidan Raines was definitely going to be interesting.

Then, as quickly as it appeared, the smile vanished. His eyes darkened, the pupils going a fraction wider, and he fixed her with a serious, solemn stare.

"There is one more issue we should probably hash out," he told her.

Oh, no, she thought with a silent groan, dread dropping to the base of her stomach like a lead weight. How much more could she possibly take? She'd handled his big, unbelievable news rather admirably, if she did say so herself, but she wasn't sure how many more direct hits her internal bomb shelter could take before crumbling to the ground and sending her into a straightjacket.

"Please don't tell me there's more to the whole vampire thing. That you're also a shape-shifter or some sort of badass *Underworld* vampire-werewolf hybrid." Although, she did have a bit of a thing for Scott Speedman, so that could turn out to be really hot.

A strange expression flitted across his face. "Um . . . no. I mean, my brother can transform into a cat, yes, but I haven't mastered the art quite yet." His mouth twisted, and he took on a mocking tone. "He says I would if I'd only apply myself."

Aidan rolled his eyes, and she nearly chuckled. Ah, the joys of family dynamics. She'd been there, done that with her own sister, which only went to show that when it came to sibling relationships, it apparently didn't matter if you were human or vampire or little green leprechaun.

Of course, how he interacted with his brother shouldn't be the foremost thought bouncing around in her brain. He'd just admitted that vampires could shift into other forms. How freaky was that?

And even though Aidan might not be proficient at it yet, one day he could be, then she'd be living with . . . what? A wolf? A lion? A two-headed sheep?

No, no, no. She couldn't deal with that right now. She added it to her mental list of topics to discuss later, then blinked the thought away and turned her attention to the hand that was slowly gliding up the outside of her thigh toward her butt.

"Actually," he continued in a low, seductive tone, "I was thinking we should test our sexual compatibility again. Considering everything that's happened, and all the life-altering confessions we've made to each other, we should probably make sure we're still attracted to one another . . . that way." He punctuated the last with a lascivious wink.

His hand reached her rear end, gliding over one cheek before snaking beneath the hem of her top to touch bare skin. She didn't think he *really* doubted how well they got along between the sheets, but since her pulse was already speeding up, her blood heating and pooling low in her belly, she had no problem playing along.

His palm was curled beneath the curve of her breast now, his thumb flicking her nipple through the lacy material of her bra. She wiggled on his lap, teasing the hard line of his erection pressed against the fly of his dress slacks.

"Mmmm," she hummed from deep in her throat. "You're right. There's nothing worse than a sexless marriage. We really should make sure we haven't messed up that side of our relationship before we commit to the 'till death do us part' thing."

One corner of his mouth lifted. "You don't have to worry about that, at least not on my end."

"Yeah," she muttered, her nose wrinkling in one-quarter distaste and three-quarters puzzlement. "How is that going to work, exactly? Do I just grow old and gray and wrinkly, then keel over, while you stay young and hot and perpetually limber?"

"That's one of those details we'll be discussing down the road. And I'll fill you in on all the options, believe me," he said, tugging her against him as he fell back on the arm of the sofa, taking her with him to drape across his chest.

It might have been the time of morning . . . or the events of the day (and past two nights) . . . or Aidan's hot, hard body sprawled beneath her, primed and ready for action . . . but she found herself feeling strangely agreeable. The future was a giant, blank, fang-covered canvas that she should probably be having all kinds of qualms about, but she just wasn't. Whatever happened, whatever he told her about his past or present or how he had to live, she'd deal.

"Okay," she said with a shrug, her fingers deftly beginning to undo the buttons down the front of his shirt. "I suppose I can accept that for now. And we really should get down to the business of finding out if everything still works the way it did before I found out you were a bloodsucking fiend and you found out I'm a gold-digging, formerly single mother."

"Bloodsucking fiend, huh?" he asked with a raised eyebrow.

She nodded. "And former single mother gold digger."

"I like that term—'former,' " he said in a low voice. "I like even more that I'm the one to help you put those things behind you. The 'single' and 'gold-digger' parts, not the mother part," he clarified with a sexy half-grin.

"Me, too. Although, I could use a little less talk and a lot more action here," she told him, tucking her hands inside his now-open shirt and running them over the flat planes of his chest. His firm pectorals with their light dusting of hair, his tight, well-defined abdomen that went concave as her nails scraped along his flesh and he sucked in a sharp breath.

For the first time ever, she noticed the slight glow to his eyes. Not just the typical gleam of arousal, but an actual reddish glow. It was odd and otherworldly, and both frightening and fascinating at the same time.

"Show me your fangs," she whispered.

He pursed his lips, and for a moment she thought he might refuse. Then the tip of his tongue darted out to wet the thin line of those lips before he opened them, slowly and cautiously.

Millimeter by millimeter, his top lip peeled back until his teeth were revealed. All of them, including two thin, sharp, pearly-white incisors.

Touching one with the tip of an index finger, she marveled at how real they were. How intimidating, and yet practically invisible most of the time.

"Why haven't I seen them before?" she wanted to know. "I mean, we've talked and laughed. Kissed and done . . . all kinds of things with your teeth and mouth. Why didn't I ever notice them when they're so long and . . . *obvious* now?"

"I didn't want you to see," he told her, his lips brushing her fingers while she continued to probe and explore this interesting new aspect of his anatomy.

"So . . . what? You wished them away?"

He grinned at that, making the fangs even more evident.

"Not exactly. For one thing, they retract, so unless I'm hungry and about to feed, or feeling some extreme emotion, they pretty much align with the rest of my teeth, and as long as I'm careful, they're fairly easy to hide. For another, vampires have the ability to . . . distort human perception, if you will."

"Distort," she repeated slowly, "human perception."

His mouth closed, and he nodded. "Mm-hm."

"As in . . . mind control?"

He winced slightly at her candid choice of words. "Yes. Sort of."

"How 'sort of'?" she asked, raising a brow.

Her brain was already racing over every interaction they'd ever had. Did he hypnotize people? Could he read minds? Had he ever intruded upon her thoughts, or made her do or say something against her will?

To Aidan's credit, he didn't shy away from the question or try to change the subject.

"It depends on the vampire," he said. "The same as with mortals, the level of power and ability varies. Some are psychic. Some can control others' actions and thoughts. But most of us simply use a kind of glamour to protect ourselves. To keep humans from noticing the fangs or our sometimes anemic pallor. . . . Or to daze them when we feed, dull the pain of our bite, and wipe the memory from their minds afterward."

She waited a beat, wondering if the sensation filling her chest was dread or mere curiosity. "Did you ever do any of that to me?"

"Definitely not."

His response came so quickly, and with such a decisive shake of his head, she knew he was telling the truth.

"I may have hidden a few of the nuances of my appearance from you at first, but by putting a mental veil over myself, not by doing anything to you."

"So no reading my mind?"

"No."

"Or persuading me to do things I wouldn't have done on my own?"

"No."

"Or making me feel attracted to you when I didn't really?"

Everything from his chin to his forehead crinkled as he frowned. "Absolutely not. What man wants to be with a woman who doesn't truly desire him? If I turn you on, that's all you, babe. Well, it's partly me," he teased, arching his hips so she could feel even more of the turgid arousal pressing between them.

He did turn her on. He always had. But all the same, it was nice to know her feelings for him really were genuine, and had been from the beginning.

Even now, she had no doubt he could get her juices flowing in a way few other men ever had. His proposal that they go for a test run to see if everything was still working properly intrigued her, though. It was a little like role-playing, and if they really could go at it like horny minks after all they'd been through since last night, all the revelations and secrets revealed . . . well, then, she might believe they really could have a happily-ever-after marriage.

Granted, it would probably be the most bizarre marriage in history—a vampire and a mortal raising a young son together. Not to mention the fact that they lived in Las Vegas, and Aidan was one of the city's most recognizable residents, which meant prying eyes and wagging tongues galore.

She didn't know how he'd managed this long without questions and rumors and speculation running rampant about him and his brother. How had she—not to mention the entire rest of the world—never noticed that they didn't go out in daylight? That they didn't seem to age? That neither of them seemed to be connected to anyone—particularly companions of the feminine variety—for any length of time? Normally, the tabloids would sink their teeth into that sort of thing like a pit bull and not let go until they had answers or sold a hundred zillion copies, whichever came first.

So maybe this marriage would actually help him. She'd thought she was using him—for money, security, stability for Jake. But now she realized that he could use her, too. To convince people he was just an ordinary, run-of-the-mill, *mortal* guy. A family man. To turn away speculation that he was anything other than perfectly human.

Given her occupation as a showgirl—which she might not keep up forever, but had no problem sticking with for the time being—it would probably be even easier to explain why they were seen only at night and spent the day tucked away. And who would ever suspect that a couple raising a young son were anything other than exactly what they seemed?

Oh, yes. She was starting to see the up side of this bargain already. And if that wasn't reason enough to jump his sturdy, undying bones, she didn't know what was.

Jack

Lifting herself up slightly from his chest, she toyed with the buckle of his belt.

"You know, I think you're right. I feel completely different about you now that I know what you really are." Pursing her lips into a disappointed moue, she slipped the tail of the thin leather snake through one side of the buckle. "I'm not sure I'm attracted to you at all anymore."

Just as she'd hoped, he took the bait. One dark brow went up and he said, "Oh, really?" in a tone filled with pure masculine challenge.

She held her expression and nodded, blowing out a long-suffering sigh.

"Hmm. We'll just see about that."

Sitting up, he ripped his shirt the rest of the way off, then he grabbed the hem of her top and yanked it straight up over her head. Her arms lifted, then flopped back down as she let him do whatever it was he planned to do.

Next thing she knew, they were on their feet and he was unsnapping her jeans, dragging them down her legs. Unfastening his own and kicking off his shoes as he stepped out of them. She stepped out of her own shoes and left her pants a pile of inside-out denim on the floor.

She was still in her bra and panties, but Aidan was gloriously naked, his erection standing out in front of him, tall and proud. Fighting the urge to lick her lips—or fall to her knees and make a grab at him—she raised her head and met his piercing, sable-brown gaze.

Without a word, he hooked his hands under her arms and lifted her straight off the ground like she weighed nothing. Superhuman strength brought on by lust or simply super-vampire strength? Oh, she was going to have to put this man through his paces until she knew all his vampy little secrets and the limits to all of his preternatural attributes.

He started walking, taking long strides with great purpose, and she thought he would carry her to the bedroom. Instead, he crossed to the far wall and backed her up against it, none too gently.

Her bare back hit with a thump, driving the air from her lungs, and she couldn't even drag in more because he pressed right up against her, keeping her from drawing another breath. Holding her there with the solid wall of his torso alone, he hooked his thumbs into the elastic band of her panties and swept them down her legs as far as he could reach, letting them float the rest of the way to the floor on their own.

Then his attention came back up, zeroing in on her face. He looked at her like a starving man at one of the Inferno's all-you-can-eat $9.99 buffets . . . and she was the dessert bar.

Taking her mouth, he kissed her with a heat and passion she'd never felt from him before. His tongue slowly scalded her from the top of her head to the tips of her curling toes. His lips took possession, laying claim to every quickly melting cell of her body.

As pleasurable as the sensations bombarding her were, for a second, she tensed. It was too much too fast. He was overpowering her, trying to take over her thoughts and feelings, and drowning her senses with devastating sensations. Where was her judgment? Where was her control over her own actions?

Was he brainwashing her with some of his hypnotizing vampire woo-woo?

But, no, he swore he'd never done anything like that to

her, and she trusted his word on that. Which meant all of this —what he was doing to her now, making her feel and think and believe—was real.

The realization washed over her like a warm, comforting ocean wave, and she let herself go, riding along with the gentle lull. Lifting her arms, she wound them around his neck and hugged him tight, actively kissing him back with everything she had in her.

Her breasts were pressed flat between them, but that didn't keep her nipples from pebbling into hard, pointed peaks. Sliding his hands down either side of her hips and thighs, Aidan caught her behind the knees and lifted her legs to circle his hips.

She locked her ankles to hold herself in place while he ran the palms of his rough hands over every inch of bare flesh he could reach. Her waist, her back, the curve of her bottom and globes of her breasts. And then his fingers trailed down her abdomen, snaking between to find her pulsing center. Without pause, he parted her folds, letting the heel of his hand knead her bare mound while he spread her juices and readied her to take him.

Not that she needed it. She was burning up, a five-alarm fire blazing through her veins, threatening to make her explode with or without his active participation.

But as he opened her, nudged her with the tip of his cock, she threw her head back and moaned, doing her best to hold on. Aidan panted over her, his own desperation clear in the pinpricks of his pupils and the sweat beading his forehead. The little dots of dampness had a slight pink tinge to them, and she assumed it was another one of those "vampire things."

How had she never noticed that before, either? There were so many details about him she'd apparently missed, but that she was now going to be on the lookout for. Fangs sprouting from nowhere, eyes glowing in the dark, bloody sweat, plasma protein shakes . . . All that was missing was lack of reflection and turning into a bat.

She didn't have long to contemplate that, though, because instead of teasing and prodding with just the head of his hungry erection, he was now pushing forward, filling her in one long, powerful thrust. She bit her lip and held her breath, taking him, *loving* the feel of him so big and hard inside of her.

Whether she needed a minute to get used to his incredible size or to get her lungs functioning or not, he didn't give it to her. As soon as he was seated to the hilt, he began to move. Grasping her ass, he tightened his hold and hiked her higher, holding her in place while he pounded into her again and again.

It was brutal, primal, on the verge of violent . . . and Chloe loved it. Sex between them had always been wild, sometimes even acrobatic, but it had never been like this.

Aidan seemed freer, more uninhibited than ever before . . . and apparently hornier and more desperate than ever before, too.

Not that she minded. It wasn't her first time being banged against a wall like a Chinese gong, but it was the first time she'd enjoyed it quite so much. If he kept it up, she wouldn't mind him taking her this way every night of the week—and twice on weekends.

She was wrapped around him like ivy, close enough to share skin. Each upward drive of his cock had him rubbing the swollen bud of her clitoris, creating just the right amount of friction to have her teetering on the edge of almost constant orgasm.

Grasping the back of his head, she wound her fingers through his hair, hanging on tight and simply riding the sensations. She let him do whatever he wanted to do. Set the pace, the force, the timing of what promised to be a climax of cataclysmic proportions.

Just as she'd hoped, he took the lead. Her back and shoulders were braced against the wall, her head making the occasional semi-painful crack into the paint-covered plaster. But he let her take his mouth, kissing her back like he wanted to swallow her whole.

In a matter of seconds, the tension coiling inside her built to a fever pitch. Every bone, every muscle, every drop of blood in her veins grew tight with anticipation.

"Yes. Oh, God, Aidan . . ." she panted into the curve of his neck.

Her tongue darted out to lick his skin, and she tasted spicy, slightly metallic male perspiration, as well as the throb of his arousal, his single-minded resolve.

Locating his jugular vein, she ran her teeth lightly over it and the cablelike tendon running alongside. When she bit down—gently, she'd never done this sort of thing before and didn't want to hurt him—he groaned. A long, drawn-out sound that let her know he liked it. A lot.

Growing bolder, she bit him again, harder than before. This time, not only did he moan, but his body arched with pleasure and his hard length jerked inside of her. For a moment, she thought he'd come, but then he loosened up again and continued his quick, brutal thrusts.

With the building of her own pleasure, she knew there wasn't much time left. Seconds, possibly, before they both went screaming into that orgasmic abyss.

But there was something she wanted to do first—for him, but also for herself. Because though she wasn't entirely certain, she thought she understood now. Understood why he'd bitten her the last time they made love. Understood the added high it must provide for someone like him, if the mere act of nibbling at the side of his throat with her tongue and flat, human teeth was such a turn-on for her.

She nipped him one last time before moving her mouth to his jawline and across his lips.

"Aidan." It wasn't easy to speak past the squeeze in her chest or the cascade of rippling pleasure growing low in her belly and between her legs.

"Aidan," she breathed again. And then without waiting for a response, "Bite me. Please."

He stilled, almost as though she'd flipped a switch, making her whimper. She'd wanted more of him, not less, and the lack of movement caused the passion that had been building at a nice, steady pace to ebb.

His eyes met hers, dark and intense. When he spoke, his voice was scratchy and thick with exertion. "What?"

"Bite me," she repeated, toying with the hair at the nape of his neck and tightening her legs around his waist. "Do what you did before. Break my skin and drink my blood."

He started to shake his head, but before he could refuse, she gave his hair a sharp tug. "Yes. I want you to. Please."

"Chloe . . ." Her name passed his lips on a strangled breath of sound.

"Do it, Aidan." Her own voice was little more than a whisper, but she made it as much of an order as she could manage.

And it must have worked, because she felt him shudder a second before he leaned into her, put his face to her throat, and licked the pulse point throbbing there. Lower, he began moving again, returning the friction, the slow burn, the sharp climb toward ecstasy.

Chloe let her head fall back and her eyes slide closed. The feel of those razor-sharp incisors scraping along her skin when he opened his mouth sent tremors down her spine.

Never in a million years would she have thought something like this would appeal to her. More than appeal—it charged her up like a wind-up toy. She'd been so upset when she'd first discovered he'd bitten her last night, and now she craved it, was begging for it, wished he'd get on with it already.

No sooner did the thought trickle through her brain than he widened his mouth over her jugular. His hot breath grazed her skin, his tongue branded her with damp heat, and the tips of his fangs pricked like pins.

And then they did more than prick. They sank in, breaking the skin and making her jump at the sudden stab of pain. But as quickly as it came, the discomfort eased, replaced by a hazy, almost drugging fog of sheer pleasure. It filled her, surrounded her, made her feel as though she was floating in a cocoon of cotton gauze.

She didn't know how long she hung there, suspended by the overwhelming and unfamiliar sensations, but at least she hadn't passed out this time. Little by little, they began to lift, replaced once again with the heightened awareness of really good sex—only better.

All the usual feelings were there, but they were tinged with something more, something she couldn't quite define. When she opened her eyes, everything seemed brighter, sharper, larger than life. She smelled Aidan's scent more clearly, nuances she'd never noticed before. And his body inside and against hers . . . it was amazing. As though every pore of her skin possessed a zillion tiny little nerve endings, and all of them were alive and awake and humming like a buzz saw.

Chloe could hear him slurping at her throat, sucking the blood straight from her vein and swallowing it down almost as though it were a fine wine. A mewling sound rolled up from somewhere in her throat, and even without aggressive thrusts or direct stimulation to her clit, only the slow slide of his cock along her swollen folds, she started to come. With a gasp, her back bowed and she contracted around him, clutching him tighter and tighter, and driving him into his own orgasm.

Still latched on to her neck and drinking from her, he grasped her hips, canted her just so, and pounded into her once, twice, a third time before stiffening and spilling inside of her. She took everything he had to give, cushioning him when he collapsed against her, doing her best to buttress him when he started to go limp, even though she was the one with her back to the wall and no part of her touching the floor.

A moment later, he lifted his mouth from her throat, gently licking the abraded area . . . to speed healing, she remembered him saying . . . and then they were moving, sliding down the wall and onto the floor. They lay there in a tangle of arms and legs, and she, at least, was breathing heavily, her lungs burning as they attempted to re-absorb much-needed O_2. Aidan's hand hovered around her hip, stroking from waist to rear end and back again.

"I'm sorry," he mumbled, his chest rumbling beneath her cheek as he spoke.

Her limbs still felt rubbery and weak, but she managed to bend her free arm and touch the spot on her neck with the tips of her fingers. "I wanted you to."

He grunted. "Not that. I meant the sex. You were right— it was terrible. We've obviously lost any spark we had, and should probably go our separate ways."

Rearing up, she twisted around to stare at him with wide eyes and an even wider open mouth.

"Are you kidding me?" she demanded, unable to believe he could feel that way when the sex *she'd* just had had nearly blown the top of her head off. "That was *incredible*. Mind-blowing. My eyes are still rolling in their sockets like the cherries on a slot machine. Were you even in the same *room* as I was?"

With every other word, her voice rose half an octave, and she honestly thought she might reach out and smack him in a minute. Then his lashes fluttered and his eyes popped open. They were glittering with amusement, and the corner of his mouth twitched, telling her he'd been teasing all along.

"Oh . . . *you!*" She gave in to her annoyance and slapped him on the stomach, making him yelp.

"See if I ever let you bite *me* again," she grumbled, climbing less-than-gracefully to her feet.

Padding to the sofa, she started gathering up her clothes and slipping back into them piece by piece. Behind her, she heard Aidan getting up and moving to join her.

"Come on," he whispered, brushing aside her hair to kiss the nape of her neck. "Admit it—the biting was your favorite part."

The mere memory of his mouth on her throat, his teeth piercing her flesh, his ecstasy at the taste of her, sent a shiver through her and raised goose bumps over her half-naked body. Doing her best to hide her reaction, she shrugged a shoulder. "It was okay."

"It was more than okay," he murmured, wrapping his arms around her waist from behind and tugging her against him.

He was still completely naked, and she only had on her bra and underwear. She could feel a fresh erection blooming against her butt and thought that was a pretty quick turn-around time, even for an otherworldly, supernatural being.

"It was . . . how did you put it? . . . incredible, mind-blowing, eye-rolling. So admit it," he pressed, snuggling her close, "we belong together. We suit each other in every possible way, give or take a few sunrises."

Still moderately annoyed, Chloe pressed her lips together and shrugged again. She felt him brush a kiss across the offending shoulder.

"So we should stay married, right? Do the whole vampire version of a white picket fence and happily ever after."

She waited a beat, mulling that over. "What's the vampire version of a white picket fence?" she asked grudgingly.

"I don't know, but you can bet it doesn't involve pointy wooden stakes of any kind." He shuddered at the very thought and hugged her tighter.

She chuckled. As offensive as the image might be to him, for some reason, she found it quite funny. She could just see him avoiding picket fences all over whatever cozy, family-friendly neighborhood they decided to settle in, tiptoeing along the far edge of the sidewalks and turning into a bat just to fly into his own house.

No, he was right—his dank, windowless, underground apartment was probably the better choice for their particular happily-ever-after. And as cynical as she'd always been about that sort of thing, she actually believed they might have a shot at it.

They'd proved, after all, that they *were* still sexually compatible. "Combustible" might even be a better word.

"Fine, yes, I'll stay married to you." Turning in his arms,

she ignored the head of his penis, prodding her like a five-star general, and forced him to meet her gaze. "But there are things we're going to have to discuss and work out, especially where Jake is concerned."

His lips curved and he grinned like an idiot. "Absolutely. Whatever you want, Mrs. Raines."

She raised a brow. "That might be the topic of our first big fight. What if I want to keep my name?"

"Which one?" he asked flatly.

Hm. He had a point there, she supposed. "I don't know yet."

"Well, then, whatever you want, Mrs. Chloe Catherine Monroe Lamoreaux Raines."

Queen

A long time later, after another two or three more hot and heavy, better-safe-than-sorry, let's-do-it-again-just-to-be-sure-we-really-are-still-sexually-compatible rolls across the floor, the bed, the dresser, and back on the bed, Chloe stretched out along the prone length of Aidan's very smooth, very attractive, very *all hers* naked body.

She sighed, rubbing the arch of her foot along the inside of his calf. He gave a sleepy grunt, and his arm tightened at her waist.

With a grin, she tipped her head back on his shoulder to take in the strong line of his jaw, his closed eyes, his mouth slack in near-sleep. "Are you awake?" she whispered.

He made another rough, drowsy sound from deep in his throat, but didn't stir. She knew he was awake, though. For one thing, they'd gone at it again like rabid monkeys only about twenty minutes before. And for another, he'd slept soundly through all twelve daylight hours in a way she was learning only vampires could.

So now it was time to wake up and get a move on. If being involved with Aidan meant that most of her life was going to have to be lived during nighttime hours, there were things she'd need to get used to, and things they needed to take care of.

Pushing herself up on one elbow, she hovered over him,

tracing her fingers through the fine layer of crisp hair dotting his chest. "I've been thinking," she murmured.

He remained perfectly still, her statement having no impact whatsoever.

"I *said* I've been thinking," she muttered again, louder this time, and punctuated with a sharp pinch to his ribcage.

"Ouch!" His eyes popped open and he stared up at her, wide awake and attentive now as he rubbed the spot she'd just abused. "Thinking, huh? When did you have time for that?"

"Ha-ha." She made a face, barely resisting the urge to stick her tongue out at him. "No, seriously. I'm a little worried about Chuck."

He blinked up at her, brows knitting over his chocolate-brown eyes. And just like real chocolate, they made her hungry. She leaned in and pressed a quick kiss to the corner of his mouth.

"Your sister?" he asked, sitting up a couple of inches to take a better-placed peck of his own, right in the center of her lips.

Chloe nodded. "When we switched places, she was going after your brother. Something about a story she's working on for the *Tattler*. But she doesn't know about the vampire thing, and if she finds out that's what Sebastian is . . ."

She took a deep, shuddering breath, trying not to talk herself into a panic.

"That's a good reason to be worried about her," Aidan agreed, pushing himself all the way up and swinging his legs over the side of the bed. "Sebastian would never hurt her. I hope you know that."

She bit the inside of her lip without a response. She actually *didn't* know that, because she didn't know Sebastian Raines at all, other than as owner of the Inferno and catching the occasional glimpse of him wandering around the casino floor.

As much as she loved Aidan, as impulsive and open and laid-back as he was, Sebastian seemed to be the exact opposite. She'd never seen the man smile, even in rare photographs printed in the local newspaper and gossip mags. Never seen him wearing anything other than staid designer business suits—and those only in black, charcoal, or navy blue. And she'd never heard so much as a whisper about him doing anything spontaneous, fun, or the least bit undisciplined.

He might be her brother-in-law now—*yeeps!* what a sobering thought—but that didn't mean she particularly liked him.

"He wouldn't," Aidan reassured her, practically reading her mind. "He might have wiped her memory if she got too close or saw something she shouldn't, but that's it."

That sounded fine, but if he wasn't concerned about his brother being alone with her sister, why was he moving around the room like an ant at a picnic, gathering dropped clothes and dressing in close to record time?

"Is your sister the reactionary type?" he wanted to know. "Or is she pretty calm, cool, and collected in a crisis?"

Slipping out of the bed, she started picking up her earlier discarded clothes, too. "Normally, she's fairly level-headed. She's always been the smart and rational one. But since neither of us have ever come face-to-face with a vampire before tonight—that we're aware of, anyway—I'd have to say she might react . . . badly."

Fully dressed now, Aidan stood with his hands on his hips, watching her. "Let me call him, see if he's even run into your sister. Maybe we're worrying for nothing."

He grabbed his cell phone from the dresser and hit a button, speed dialing his brother's number on his way out of the room. At the door, he paused and turned back to her. "But you might want to get dressed quick, just in case."

"Just in case" turned out to be a lack of answer on Sebastian's end of the line. When Aidan returned to the bedroom, face blank, Chloe was back in her sister's jeans and top. If she didn't get a shower and a fresh change of clothes soon, she swore they'd start walking around on their own.

"I couldn't reach him," he told her. "I think we should go over there." *Just in case.*

He didn't have to say the last; it was floating in the air around them like a noxious odor. Two minutes later, they'd piled into his Ferrari and were tooling down The Strip toward the Inferno. Using a private rear entrance to the hotel, they hurried down the thickly carpeted halls and into the elevator that would take them up to Sebastian's penthouse.

From the moment they got out of the car, Aidan had her hand in his. She squeezed it tightly over and over, unaccountably grateful to have him with her, to have him supporting her, looking out for her, rushing off with her to check on her sister simply because she was concerned about her twin's welfare.

If this was an inkling of what her future held, she might not mind being married, after all. Even to a vampire.

The elevator doors slid open with a soft *whoosh* and Aidan tugged her out, leading her straight to Sebastian's front door. Despite her eagerness to track down Chuck and make sure she was okay, Chloe couldn't help taking a minute to glance around, guppy-mouthed, at her surroundings.

Every inch of the Inferno was high class and decadent. Sebastian Raines hadn't spared a single expense in building the hotel and casino, or in capitalizing on the different aspects of Dante Alighieri's *Divine Comedy* when it came to decorating. He'd nailed the first part of the epic poem, and the casino's main namesake, *Inferno*, as well as *Purgatorio* and *Paradiso*—or Purgatory and Paradise, as those areas were called within the hotel. Not to mention some of the Nine Circles of Hell—Limbo, Lust, Avarice, and Wrath.

All of the Hell-ish locations followed the obvious look of fire, flames, sulfur, and brimstone. Then the colors and themes lightened a little as they moved through the other "levels," all the way to the bright, happy, and for some reason, island-motifed Paradise.

But though she'd seen nearly every room on every floor of the hotel and casino, she had never been in the owner's private elevator or in his private penthouse. Given how much the Raines brothers were worth, she shouldn't be surprised by the luxury here—in the hallway alone—and yet she was. The thick, plush carpeting cushioning her feet like two inches of marshmallow fluff . . . the artwork covering the walls in gilt frames, which were no doubt priceless originals. . . . She didn't know the first thing about art, but she did know names like Monet, Rembrandt, and Renoir, and she would bet creations by all three of them, plus some, were staring down at her right now.

Aidan rapped sharply on the door, and all Chloe could think was, *If this was the* outside *of her brother-in-law's living quarters, what the heck was the inside going to look like?*

Maybe she wasn't going to find out. After several long seconds, Aidan knocked again. And then again. Either his brother wasn't in, or he was ignoring them.

Aidan muttered a curse, and Chloe started to wonder where her sister might be. If Sebastian wasn't home, maybe Chuck's plan to follow and get close to him hadn't worked out. Or maybe Sebastian was at dinner, on the casino floor, or even out and about downtown, with Chloe trailing behind him.

"Cell phone," she blurted out. When Aidan glanced at her, she shook her head and said, "I don't know why I didn't think of it before. I should have called her cell phone."

When they'd parted ways, Chuck certainly hadn't had one on her—there wasn't room to hide a Tic-Tac in those costumes, let alone a cell phone—but Chloe didn't know where her sister went after the show. She might be back in civilian clothes by now and have her phone with her once again.

"We'll check inside first, and if we don't find anything, you can use Sebastian's phone to see if you can reach your sister."

With that, he began tapping out numbers on the security panel on the wall beside the door, but before he could finish, the door swung open and Sebastian Raines stood scowling out at them.

Chloe's eyes went wide. She found the elder Raines

brother intimidating enough when he looked like he'd just stepped off the cover of *GQ*—expensive suit pressed, collar buttoned, hair slicked back. But seeing him in the alto-gether—well, except for a pair of black silk boxer shorts—nearly made her tongue fall out of her mouth and hit the toe of her shoe.

Not because she was sexually attracted to him. Sure, he was a good-looking guy. If by "good-looking" you meant tall, dark, handsome, sexy, hot, debonair, cover-model poten-tial, hubba-hubba, homina-homina-homina.

But since Chloe had her own hot, sexy, hubba-hubba Raines brother to drool over, she honestly *wasn't* goggling at him in that way. Instead, her main physical reaction was plain old shocked stupid. In her wildest imaginings, she never would have pictured her boss, the gazillionaire casino mogul and (now that she knew) vampire, walking around his million-dollar penthouse apartment half-dressed and looking as though he'd just come through a sandstorm.

His black hair was a disaster, flattened in one spot, but sticking up in all directions everywhere else. She'd seen peo-ple stick their fingers in light sockets and walk away with a better coiffure.

His narrowed eyes were storm gray and gritty with sleep. Had they woken him? It was early—early evening, at any rate—but not particularly early for a vampire, according to Aidan. Maybe Sebastian was a late riser. (Har-dee-har-har.)

"What do you want?" Sebastian bit out in a voice as scratchy as his angry expression.

"Hey," Aidan said.

He didn't act the least put off by his brother's snarly de-meanor or less than pristine appearance. Or maybe he just seemed uber-calm because Chloe was shaking so badly in her sister's borrowed tennies.

"Are you, um . . . alone in there?" Aidan asked, going up on the balls of his feet to peer over his brother's broad bare shoulder into the rest of the penthouse.

"What the hell do you care?" Sebastian growled in return.

Still not intimidated, Aidan turned to her and said, "This is Chloe. She's a dancer down at Lust—and my new bride."

Sebastian's dark brows came together in the mother of all scowls. His mouth turned down for a moment, and then he muttered a heartfelt, "Shit."

Running his fingers through his already mussed "my-best-impression-of-a-porcupine" hair, he shook his head. "I forgot. I was going to run out and find you, try to stop you from doing something stupid, but I got . . . let's just say distracted."

He muttered another curse beneath his breath, then took a step back. "You might as well come in. I guess the damage is done."

Wow. Talk about a warm and fuzzy, "Welcome to the family!"

Aidan followed his brother without hesitation, but Chloe hesitated big-time. She stayed in the hallway, rooted to the spot by fear and trepidation. Not only was she still concerned about her sister—if Sebastian Raines was here, where was Chuck?—but also for herself, having to deal up close and personal with her very reluctant brother-in-law, who also happened to be her big bad boss.

Noticing her absence, Aidan turned back, a curious expression on his face. "It's okay," he told her, reaching out to take her hand and tug her bodily past the threshold. "He won't bite, I promise. That's my job," he added in a whisper just above her ear before pressing a reassuring kiss to her cool cheek.

Wandering into the living area of the posh apartment, Sebastian dropped down on the edge of a black, overstuffed leather sofa and buried his face in his hands, scrubbing his eyes roughly before driving his fingers through his hair once more. The nervous gesture wasn't making his hair look any worse, but it wasn't making it look better, either.

"So you're the sister," he murmured, lifting his head to study her more closely. "Chloe the dancer. The real dancer."

The way he said "the real dancer" made Chloe's stomach

drop like a stone. Did that mean he'd come into contact with Chuck, after all, and knew she *wasn't* really a showgirl in the Lust revue?

Oh, no. Was Chuck even now lying lifeless somewhere with a couple of fang marks in her neck, sucked dry by an enraged bloodsucker who would do anything to keep his secret under wraps?

Breathe, Chloe, breathe, she told herself, even though her heart was beating hard enough to crack a rib.

Aidan had assured her his brother wasn't the killing type. If Chuck had run into Sebastian and piqued his ire, she was probably just wandering around downtown Vegas with amnesia, thanks to his vampire brainwashing woo-woo. Which wasn't necessarily better than being dead in an alley somewhere, depending on what kind of Sin City vultures and vermin she ran into, but at least it wasn't *death*.

Screwing up her courage—which took a couple of deep breaths, a few more fistings and unfistings of her hands, and three clearings of her throat before she could push words past her petrified vocal cords—she asked, "Where's my sister?"

Aidan's hand tightened on hers, though she didn't know if it was to offer his support or warn her away from confronting his brother quite so directly.

Sebastian arched a brow. Any other time, that silent gesture would have had her wetting herself like a toy poodle. As it was, she was a bundle of exposed nerves. But her twin's safety was at stake here. And even though Chuck was usually the one to ride to her rescue, it was her turn to suck it up and be the hero.

Clearing *his* throat, Aidan did his best to smooth things over. "It seems Chloe and her *identical twin sister*, Charlotte —whose nickname happens to be Chuck—did a little switcheroo before the show. Chuck put on Chloe's costume and went onstage while Chloe wore Chuck's street clothes and sneaked off to meet me."

His brother didn't respond. He simply sat there looking impervious and amused, waiting for the rest of the story.

"Apparently, Chuck was working on some sort of story about you. She's a writer for the *Sin City Tattler*."

"A writer. For the *Tattler*," Sebastian repeated with what sounded like mild interest.

Though she couldn't begin to decipher it, a look passed between the two brothers.

Aidan nodded. "We thought you might have run into her. Or caught her on camera following you around, maybe trying to sneak up here."

One corner of Sebastian's mouth ticked upward and his gaze skittered off to the left toward the rear of the apartment for just a fraction of a second. Straightening from his hunched position, he leaned back against the sofa and stretched his arms out as far as they would go on either side.

"I saw her," he told them slowly. "She was skulking around, poking her nose where it didn't belong."

Chloe's pulse jumped as terror washed over her. "What did you do to her?" she demanded in a strangled whisper.

"Why, I killed her, of course."

King

"**O**h, he did not!"

Chloe's heart stuttered in her chest as she whipped around to face the voice from the far end of the apartment. A second later, her sister appeared wearing only a man's sapphire-blue dress shirt. It was open at the neck and fell to her thighs, leaving her legs bare the rest of the way down.

Her hair, much like Sebastian's, was a rat's nest of spikes and crooked curls and flattened areas.

"Oh. My. God."

Sailing across the room like a beauty queen, she wrapped her arms around a still open-mouthed Chloe and gave her a quick hug.

"I'm fine. Sebastian has been a perfect gentleman." Cocking her head and tossing a glance over her shoulder to where he sat, she said, "Well, mostly a gentleman, anyway."

Sebastian's only response was a lascivious grin.

"Oh. My. God," Chloe said again. Oxygen was wheezing in and out of her lungs like they'd sprung a leak. She blinked a couple of times, playing Pong with her eyeballs as she looked from Chuck to Sebastian and back again.

"You slept with him," she accused, finding her voice and then some. "And you slept with her!"

Why was she shrieking? Why was she acting so shocked and disapproving? She didn't care whom her sister slept with, as long as she stayed away from the skeevy, disease-riddled segment of society and picked a guy who was half decent to her. Any more than Chuck cared whom she slept with, with the same caveats.

She was just so stunned. She'd thought her twin was working on a story, and had been frantic this last hour or so, worrying about her safety.

Now she discovered that her sister's idea of "research" apparently included getting naked and boffing her research subject. What had happened to "observe and report"?

Chuck gave her a look, and kicked her lightly in the shin with her bare foot. "Don't look so surprised. Just because it's been a while doesn't mean I don't still have all the working parts."

Aidan started to laugh at that. Then he realized his mirth might not be appropriate or appreciated, and tried to swallow it back, making a strangled sound deep in his throat.

"You must be Aidan," Chuck said, shifting toward him and holding out her hand. "I'm Charlotte, but *please* don't call me that."

"It's Chuck, I know," he said with a grin, bringing the back of her hand to his lips for a polite, if old-fashioned, kiss.

"It's nice to meet you. And you," she said, returning her attention to Chloe, "know Sebastian, but I'm not sure you've actually met."

Chloe squeezed her eyes shut, then covered her face with her hands and gave a silent scream until the sound bounced off the inside of her skull. When she felt as though she could look at her sister and the two Raines brothers without screaming for real, she lowered her arms and snapped her eyes open.

"I thought you were dead," she told Chuck in such a calm tone, she surprised even herself. "I've been frantic, thinking you found out he was . . ."

She trailed off, not sure she should drop that particular bomb on her sister, if Chuck didn't already know what Sebastian truly was. Especially since revealing Sebastian's secret identity meant also revealing Aidan's . . . and the fact that she'd married him regardless.

"Or that he caught you following him, and had you arrested or hauled away by his Goon Squad or something equally horrific."

Rather than look repentant, Chuck smiled. The bright, wide, teeth-flashing smile of a woman who'd been enjoying herself to the fullest in the most carnal of ways. Chloe should know; she was pretty sure she'd looked that way quite recently herself, after Aidan had rocked her world for the umpteenth time since their quickie wedding vows.

"Nope," she answered lightly. "And I know all about Sebastian. Aidan, too," she said, tipping her head in his direction. Then she turned down one side of her shirt's collar to reveal the reddish-brown puncture marks, surrounded by a small amount of black-and-blue bruising. That, too, Chloe recognized from her own recent Adventures in Vampire Nuptials.

"I need to sit down," she muttered, teetering her way to the nearest end of the L-shaped sofa and dropping onto the cushioned seat before her legs gave out.

"I know," Chuck said, wandering over to where Sebastian was stretched out, watching the conversation play out in front of him, and climbed onto the sofa beside him. She sat between him and the arm of the sofa, but he curled his arm around her shoulders and tugged her bare legs across his lap so that she was draped half over him and tucked very protectively against his side.

To his credit, Aidan came to stand beside his woman, as well, seating himself on the opposite sofa arm. He took her hand in one of his own, then put the other on her far shoulder.

"It's unbelievable, isn't it?" Chuck continued. "But the funny thing is, I suspected all along. I didn't tell you, because I thought you'd think I was crazy, but that's what my story was going to be about. I came here trying to find proof that Sebastian was an honest-to-goodness vampire."

She looked at him, running her palm along his cheek with affection as she smiled up at him. "And I did. But, of course, I can't write my article now, because that would hurt him and ruin everything, and I definitely don't want to do either of those things. Ever."

Sitting there with the clouds clearing from her brain and all the pieces of the puzzle coming together, Chloe's pulse began to slow. Chuck looked positively blissful, and though normally, Chloe would be giving her all kinds of warnings about sleeping with a near-stranger, falling in with a man who could destroy her on a whim, getting involved with someone she *knew* to be an actual vampire . . .

But then, she didn't have a lot of room to talk, did she? She'd done basically the exact same thing.

And how freaky was that? She knew all about the Twin Thing—how often they shared thoughts; felt each other's pain; even how many married at the same time, gave birth at the same time, and died at the same time.

But though she and Chuck were extremely close, and did often share thoughts and ideas or finish sentences for one another, they'd also been independent enough that she'd never actually believed they'd follow in each other's footsteps. She was a professional dancer, for heaven's sake, while Chuck had gone in a completely different direction and started writing for a living.

So what were the chances that they'd fall in love with a couple of brothers—*vampire* brothers, no less—at exactly the same time? Now *that's* a story just unbelievable enough for Chuck's tabloid magazine. It ranked right up there with grandmothers giving birth to their own grandchildren and being probed by aliens.

"And you," Chuck said, dragging her out of her musings. "You two ran off and got married, didn't you?"

She said it with a secret smile, since she'd known the

whole time that was part of Chloe's plan. What she hadn't known was that Chloe would end up abandoning her plot to land a rich husband and actually tumble head over heels for Aidan.

Chloe nodded and held out her left hand, showing them both the Rock of Gibraltar now residing there. "I took him to meet Jake and Mom."

Chuck's eyes widened slightly at the admission. "And . . . ?"

It was the most prompting she would risk until she knew more about how that visit had gone, and Chloe appreciated her discretion.

"They loved him," Chloe told her. Then added softly, "I love him, too."

"You do?" Chuck asked with just a hint of caution to her voice.

Chloe nodded again. "I really do."

A beat passed, and then Chuck dropped her head onto Sebastian's bare shoulder. His very broad shoulder, which led down to a very impressive chest and abdomen.

Not that Chloe noticed such things. She had her own handsome Raines brother to drool over, and though Sebastian had quite a nice physique, he wasn't nearly as well-built as her Aidan. In her humble opinion, anyway.

Beside him, her sister's mouth slid into a wide grin, her eyes glittering with delighted excitement. "Me, too."

"So is there a chance the two of you will be tying the knot soon, too?" Aidan asked, oblivious to the undercurrents passing between the two sisters.

Sebastian's deep voice filled the room. "Not so long ago, I would have said absolutely not. I didn't think it would be possible for us to carry on normal relationships with human women. But it looks like we're about to prove that theory wrong." His arm tightened around Chuck, and he pressed his lips to the crown of her head. "At the very least, I'm willing to give it a shot."

"Wow," Aidan breathed, leaning back a few inches in feigned shock. "I never thought I'd see the day."